"THEY CALL THEM FREE FIRE ZONES . . .

they're areas designated as belonging to the enemy. The rule is, anything in the area is enemy. Should be killed,'' Chick said.

"Body counts," whispered Masters.

"Direct hit, sir. I have no idea who determines the Free Fire Zones, or how. For all I know, villages bribe people to *not* declare theirs a Free Fire Zone.''

"Are you serious?''

"Absolutely sir. I've got no proof. But I have yet to figure out what the hell makes a Free Fire Zone and what doesn't. Except that you need enough warm bodies to drive up a lance's count. We just kill people, and Blake and the Loyalists assure us we're doing the right thing." Chick raised his fingers to his eyes, giving a sharp sigh before continuing. "I keep shooting, but you know, you kill enough ten year olds. . . .''

IDEAL WAR

BATTLETECH®

IDEAL WAR

Christopher Kubasik

A ROC BOOK

ROC
Published by the Penguin Group
Penguin Books USA Inc., 375 Hudson Street,
New York, New York 10014, U.S.A.
Penguin Books Ltd. 27 Wrights Lane,
London W8 5TZ, England
Penguin Books Australia Ltd, Ringwood,
Victoria, Australia
Penguin Books Canada Ltd, 10 Alcorn Avenue,
Toronto, Ontario, Canada M4V 3B2
Penguin Books (N.Z.) Ltd, 182–190 Wairau Road,
Auckland 10, New Zealand

Penguin Books Ltd, Registered Offices:
Harmondsworth, Middlesex, England

First published by Roc, an imprint of New American Library,
a division of Penguin Books USA Inc.

First Printing, March, 1993
10 9 8 7 6 5 4 3 2 1

Series Editor: Donna Ippolito
Cover: Boris Vallejo
Interior illustrations: Laubenstein
Mechanical drawings: FASA art staff

For Joy, who, during a phone conversation on the subject of corpses, kept me on track about the matter of war.

A belated thanks to Jordan Weisman, L. Ross Babcock III, Sam Lewis, Donna Ippolito, and Tom Dowd for their faith and support. You helped my dreams become reality. What an extraordinary gift!

And big kudos to all the folks who provided inspiration for the farcical elements and obscene tragedies sprinkled throughout the book: the Viet Cong, the ARVN, the wacky Diem clan, a group of U.S. presidents with more hubris than historical perspective (the French *warned* us), and finally, Robert McNamara, William Westmoreland, and the ladder climbers at the Pentagon (c. 1960s) who somehow got the notion you could fight a war like taking a final for an M.B.A degree. Thanks guys, I couldn't have written the book without you.

Part 1

POLITICS

= 1 =

Marik Palace, Atreus
Marik Commonwealth, Free Worlds League
19 May 3054

A dozen candles lit the study, their flames painting broad, flickering swaths of golden light all around them. The rest of the room remained hidden in inky darkness—like space, Paul Masters thought. His dinner companion and host, Captain-General Thomas Marik, head of House Marik, ruler of the Marik Commonwealth, and military commander of the Free Worlds League, must have chosen the Gothic lighting to match his brooding temperament. His friend's odd ways both charmed and unnerved Paul, just as they did everyone Thomas had encountered since assuming the reins of the Marik Commonwealth years earlier.

Some patches of candlelight illuminated shelves holding worn and ancient books. Among the eerie shadows were several unique items . . . small statues of the human body, design models of BattleMechs and JumpShips, and one especially fascinating piece of ancient technology—an early artificial heart.

The light partially illuminated several glass-framed items hanging on the walls—swirling oil paintings, clever holographs, and ancient blueprints, including

Thomas' prized possession: a replica of the Kitty Hawk flight plans from almost a dozen centuries earlier. Masters had never given thought to the first airplane flight until the day Thomas recounted the story of those first few seconds of man's journey away from solid ground, his eyes shining like a boy's.

The hour had grown late, and they could no longer hear the steps of servants beyond the door nor the forced laughter of courtiers wandering through the palace corridors. The room's heavy curtains were open just enough to reveal the night sky and its thick blanket of stars. In the near obscurity Masters precariously cut into his roast meat and tried to spear buttered chunks of boiled potato while hearing Thomas' silverware also ringing softly against the china plates.

"Must we eat in the dark?" Masters asked.

"Dark rooms for dark thoughts," Thomas said, like a ham actor playing a ham ruler.

Masters laughed. "Dark rooms for dark deeds," he countered.

"Dark rooms to better show a flicker of illumination, to reveal the slight flame that might otherwise be missed in the bright and busy light of day."

"As ever, Thomas, you're the only man of imagination I know."

"Not a particularly valuable commodity these days."

"No. The lemmings are caught up in what they believe to be the sweep of history. They have no idea that we *make* it."

"Exactly," Thomas said emphatically, then he paused, as though reflecting on a new thought. "What *is* a lemming, Paul? Have you any idea? I've heard and used the expression all my life, but I just realized I haven't a clue what one actually is."

"A lemming is . . . ," Masters began, then was startled to realize he didn't know either. "No idea. A mythical animal maybe. Aren't they creatures who throw themselves off cliffs because everyone else is doing it? I don't know. Maybe they came from some joke the Romans made about Christians hell-bent for martyrdom in the Colosseum.''

"Ah! Bread and circuses," Thomas said, as if struck by a sudden inspiration. "Maybe that's what would sate the blood-lust of my people.''

"Not your style, my friend. You'd end up sitting on your throne weeping for anyone dumped into the arena. Spoil the whole effect.''

"True.''

"Besides, you don't need bread and circuses. Your people are content. The last major interstellar war was fought on the other side of the Inner Sphere, and the Fourth Succession War barely touched us either. Even the Andurien revolt wasn't so bad. It dragged out too long, but it wasn't a major conflict.''

"Exactly. My people, sir, are bored. They have forgotten. They want blood back in their lives. Happens every generation or so, from what I've been able to deduce.''

"Just like lemmings?''

"A leit motif? So soon into the meal? Delightful!''

"But nothing to brag about. Our minds are caught in loops. You and I fret about the same ideas every day, no matter what form the day takes.''

Thomas paused, reflecting again. "But are our concerns valid?''

In the darkness Masters shrugged and cut more meat. "As long as they remain merely our concerns, what does it matter?''

"But if we bring them to others?''

"Ah.''

"Ah, what?'' Thomas put his utensils down. "Paul, things are very bad. It's true that we haven't had a *horrible* war for some time. But . . .'' Thomas broke off, and remained silent while one of his ancient face-clocks ticked away loudly somewhere in the room. Masters looked at his friend, even in the dim light perceiving the burn marks, scars from the assassin's bomb that had killed Thomas' father and older brother almost 20 years ago. Thomas had never tried to have the scars removed.

In all the years Masters had never asked why, assuming it was something very private that could not be spoken. Thomas' version of a hair shirt, Masters guessed, a constant reminder of his awful imperfection to keep him humble. No matter that his friend reigned over hundreds of worlds, he would never let it go to his head.

"I believe we are at a crossroads," Thomas said finally. "Everything is at stake now. Or, at least, once again. I've been going over reports of the Clan invasion. . . ."

"Whose?"

"Word of Blake's. When they settled on Gibson, I asked to see the war reports they'd compiled. They hesitated. I asked again. They waffled. I asked once more. They lost them in a bureaucratic shuffle. I told them I'd throw them out of the Free Worlds League to wander the stars forever if they didn't damn well please me. They relented."

"And?"

"Complete nonsense."

"What?"

"Well, perhaps I should say I don't understand the documents. I've read all the damn books. I've led battles, drilled with you in BattleMechs. And I've never seen anything like what they sent me. Numbers. Nothing but numbers. Pages and pages of numbers. Tables and tabulations and hundreds of ratios."

"Lists of the dead?"

"Nothing so romantic. Not a proper name to be

found. But a victory might be explained in terms such as, 'The above data shows that combat profit was inevitable, given the attrition ratios possible and so on and so on.' "

"Losses?"

" 'As the above data shows, a combat debit was inevitable. . . .' "

"Combat debit? Combat profit? What does that . . . ?"

"A win and a loss, I believe. But Word of Blake depended on these numbers to justify the conclusions, and I swear I have no idea how they supported them."

"Thomas, no offense, but your combat experience is limited and you did start late in life."

"Humor me for a moment, Paul. I should be able to handle some post-action reports. Einstein said if you can't explain what you're doing, it isn't worth doing. Well, I've given tens of thousands of religious zealots refuge with the borders, promising them refuge and a new home, and they can't explain to me how they fought a war. That worries me. And this is the strange part. The document is written almost as a scientific report. I'm from their tradition. I *should* understand it."

"Well, there's your problem. War isn't a science. It's an art."

"So you and that Prussian of yours keep insisting. I much prefer science. Clean. Simple."

"And part of your past. You're with us messy soldiers and ugly politicians now."

"God, yes. How did I end up here?"

"I know it was never proved," Paul said, "but might it have something to do with a cousin killing your father and brother?"

Thomas picked up his wine glass. "Oh, that's right. Thank you for reminding me, Captain Masters. Successor House family gatherings. God, how I hate what I'm a part of."

"And you may well be one of the most miserable of the Successor Lords."

"Thank you again."

"Well, it's clear the Davions, Kuritas, Liaos, and Steiners all revel in being wealthy megalomaniacs. It makes me wonder what your problem is. But if we might leave your misery for a moment and return to war. I've always considered ComStar, and now Word of Blake, rather odd. I probably wouldn't understand a report they wrote either, and I'd wager neither would most people in the Inner Sphere. And most of us would accept that as normal. The True Believers are secretive and strange."

"Yes. But again, I studied with these people until my father's death. They were my family. More important, I believe the report reflects changes coming to war across the Inner Sphere. This isn't just about ComStar and Word of Blake. I can't put my finger on it."

Masters took a sip of wine. "I'm not sure this ties in, but the reports I've been reading show that the intensity and pace of combat have increased rapidly over the last thirty years. The Fourth Succession War was especially fierce."

"Exactly. War is changing. It's not anything we haven't seen before in the history of the human race, but we're building back up to levels that were lost to us for generations. Humanity has almost destroyed itself several times over, and if I have anything to say about it, it's not going to happen this time around. But to do that I need to gather more power. Not economic power. My God, we must already look like a fat, succulent pig to the rest of the Inner Sphere. No, we need political power. The Free Worlds League is the only balkanized Successor State. That must change."

"Yes, your counterparts are definitely more opportunistic than you."

"Which is why I've got to make us look less like an opportunity. I don't feel any need to go conquer the seedy little maggots. I just want them to leave the Free Worlds League alone so we can get our affairs in order. And I think your plan to create an elite class of MechWarriors will help."

Masters froze, his fork poised just short of his mouth. He'd proposed the plan a year earlier, but had never thought Thomas would accept it. The political tradition of the Free Worlds League was a parliamentary republic. The creation of a military ruling class would not sit well with most of the League's memberworlds. "You're serious?"

"I've never been more serious. I see no other way. We're beginning to recover technology lost after the collapse of the Star League. People will want to grab the new kinds of weapons now possible and shove them down the throats of their enemies. 'Do what has to be done to win,' and so forth. And even without that, you're right about the tempo and intensity of warfare increasing. It's been happening for decades, and with the release of ComStar's ancient technology files and the discovery of the weapons cache by the Gray Death Legion, it's only going to increase more. We could all be in great trouble very soon. The Ares Conventions are now only a battlefield for lawyers. The code of honor among MechWarriors is disintegrating. Tactical nukes might well return."

The thought of nuclear weapons brought Thomas to a sudden dead stop. When he began to speak again, his voice was very quiet. "I don't think I will ever forgive ComStar for releasing the technical files. They broke their oath. The files should have remained secret forever."

"Well, the weapons were already around. It isn't just access to the files."

Thomas seemed not to hear. "Heresy. Pure heresy."

Masters didn't know what to say. Thomas, like all those trained within the mystical ranks of ComStar, seldom mentioned the religion to non-believers. "Thomas? What do you want me to do?"

"I received word from New Avalon today. . . ."

Masters' right hand tightened. "Joshua?"

"He still lives," Thomas said softly. "They tell me the leukemia is in remission." He laughed. "We travel the stars, and yet my son is dying from a disease our species has been trying to defeat for more than a thousand years. A thousand years." He paused, collecting his thoughts. "I thought about him today, before you arrived, as I thought about moving forward with this plan. I remembered when I first held Joshua in my arms eight years ago, when he was first born. And since that time I have seen so little of him."

Thomas drew in a sharp breath. "He seemed so perfect at that moment. Flawless. He had no sins upon his soul, no evil intent in his mind. No one had done him harm, and nothing had tempted him. I thought that if I were a good father, I would be able to keep him safe from everything. I thought, 'This boy will grow up well-protected. I will teach him properly. I will teach him how to love, how to fight for the good of humanity, how to protect himself. He will be amazing. I will keep him safe from all the pain and disease and scars that have plagued me.' But of course . . . we all have visions of possible good, but so little ever works out."

He stopped and pushed his plate out of the way as he leaned across the table. His voice became conspiratorial. "What I am suggesting, Paul, is for a good reason. It is also very dangerous. A military ruling class is something I would have vehemently opposed just ten years ago. Can you promise me it will not become tainted? That our good intentions will not be perverted into something to bring us sorrow in years to come?''

"I can't promise you that. You know that the Free Worlds League has always been balanced between a parliamentary democracy and military feudalism.'' Masters weighed his next words carefully. "But I truly believe the only way we can stop war's technology from escalating is to put power solely in the hands of the MechWarriors. Not soldiers, and definitely not technocrats. MechWarriors alone. Because Mech-Warriors have a very palpable reason for wanting to prevent military technology from increasing in scope: it would make us warriors obsolete. Atomics would certainly spell the end of 'Mech warfare. To avert disaster, we need to gather strength under your rule. We need to re-establish the conventions of war. Such a concentration of power in the hands of MechWarriors would accomplish these goals.''

"No guarantees?''

"No, sir.''

"I suspected. I knew.'' Thomas sighed. "ComStar was so much more peaceful.''

"The old days.''

"How I miss my youth.''

It worried Masters to hear Thomas wander on. It was so unlike him. "Sir?''

"I'm all right, Paul. I'm simply avoiding the necessity of raising something unpleasant with you. Rather, I think it's glorious, but you might find it so ludicrous that this conversation might become unpleasant.''

"I doubt that.''

"You forget how pragmatic you are and how much of an idealist I am. The fact that we are such good friends must be based in part on the fact that we don't see each other very often.''

"We're friends and we always will be,'' Masters

said quietly. "But tell me, what is this horrible matter you want to bring up?"

"Essentially we are talking about a military coup."

"Exactly. If the plan is presented correctly, I'm sure I can find enough MechWarriors to support us. Once we make it clear that the MechWarrior profession is threatened by the advance of war technology . . ."

"Yes. And the MechWarriors seize control, and make everyone who is not a MechWarrior live as second-class citizens." Thomas' voice tightened. "That is the way of the Clans."

Masters hesitated. "We don't know that. The invasion took place on the other side of the Inner Sphere, more than three hundred light years from our borders. No one in the Inner Sphere had any idea that the descendants of Kerensky and his followers still lived. It's been centuries since General Kerensky and his people exiled themselves from the Inner Sphere. Whatever they became in the intervening years is still a mystery. Even the people the Clans have conquered still don't know exactly how the Clanners live, and certainly, we, on the other side of the Sphere, have heard only half-truths. It will take years for all the information to be sorted out, years before we know who these Clanspeople really are."

"You defend them? They fought in cities. They attacked civilian populations with nuclear weapons. No one has used such devices for—"

"Sir, we will not become the Clans. That I can promise. All I want is for the military elite to unite the Free Worlds League under your rule."

"No, no, even if we put aside the Clans for the moment, that isn't good enough."

Masters paused, uncertain of what to say. "I'm not sure I understand."

"If we blunder out and declare that I'm finally making a bid for House Marik's absolute rule of the Free

Worlds League, and that we're going to do it through a coup conducted by a group of MechWarriors, the other states of the Free Worlds League will turn against us.''

"There will be resistance, of course."

"And too much of it. We need the people *with* us. I will not attempt a complete unification at the expense of alienating my people. It wouldn't be worth it. We'd spend all our time putting down one revolt after another. They'd see us as invaders in our own state. No, I need the majority of the people—the vast majority—with us. Only this way will the plan produce the desired effect of building our strength against the other Successor States."

"But if the MechWarriors are to have control—"

"Paul. We will get there. But we must be careful, cautious, and clever. We will begin slowly, prepare the moment to create the right story."

Masters rubbed his fingertips against the tablecloth, a bit agitated. "What do you mean by 'story'?"

"What if, instead of staging a coup throughout the Free Worlds League, we create, first, a knightly order of MechWarriors. Create something romantic."

"Romantic?"

"Yes. We not only create a ruling warrior class, but we re-trench our feudalism. We make it clear that something *extraordinary* is happening."

"I don't . . ."

"We create something that people want, rather than something we impose on them. We get them to invite the idea rather than defend themselves against it."

This did little to alleviate Masters' concern. "How do we do this?"

"We begin slowly. We start with a new knightly order, created from whole cloth. A special order of MechWarriors loyal to me. Unlike the current custom, these knights will be called 'sir.' They will be the elite.

We will invite them from all over the Free Worlds League, regardless of previous loyalties. That will be the difficult part. We must find those MechWarriors who share your concern for the fate of the Mech-Warrior, and more important, who have a bit of the noble streak in them. Others like you.''

"How do we . . . ?''

"Intuition,'' Thomas said, tossing the question aside. "We find them through intuition. Now, we don't do anything with the knights right away. We just let the Free Worlds League and the Inner Sphere know that such an order exists.''

"But the enemies of the Marik Commonwealth in the Parliament will be quick to jump on this. It's tantamount to announcing plans to unify the Free Worlds League under House Marik. That's as good as a coup.''

"Except that we won't have done anything yet.''

"No, only invited some of their best MechWarriors to desert them. The Principality of Regulus, in particular, will be suspicious and threatened. And you're saying we won't be prepared for the coup.''

"There will be no coup, Paul.'' Thomas paused, letting the statement sink in.

"What?''

"My rule will come by invitation or not at all. It is that simple. I will build what I think people want, and they will tell me whether I am right.''

"But . . .''

"Paul, your concern is for the MechWarriors. Mine is with all the people of the Free Worlds League. I will not seize control of the League. That is a tactic for other rulers in other Successor States.''

"Then will you please tell me what you mean by a good story?''

"Simply put, everyone sees life in terms of a narrative. We just do that. It is humanity's way. And if people see themselves as the oppressed, they will fight

back, because that is the intriguing role of the oppressed. If people see themselves as participants in
something glorious, they will support the game whole-
heartedly.''

"Game?''

"Game. I am my father's son, after all.''

"I don't think most people see their lives as a game,
Thomas.''

"Of course they don't. Which is why they can be
manipulated by people who do.''

Masters became unnerved. "I don't understand.
First you say that you want the people to choose freely,
and now you speak of manipulating them.''

"Well, if we carry off a coup, we're manipulating
them. If I give them a choice, I'm not manipulating
them. But because I know it's a game, I can shape the
choice so they choose what I want them to choose.''

"I don't understand.''

"I know. It will take time. Here.'' Thomas went
over to a table set against the wall. Masters saw him
lift something from the table and carry it back. A
book. "This is for you. A present.''

Masters took the book, a cloth-covered tome with
worn edges. The title had faded, and he could not read
it in the dim light. "What is it?''

"*Le Morte d'Arthur*,'' Thomas told him, "by Thomas
Malory.''

2

"Thomas Malory?"

"An English knight who lived fifteen hundred years ago. He wrote the book while in prison for the crime of rape."

"Rape? Is this the story of the rape?" Masters put the book down on the table, as if it might contaminate him.

"Not at all. It's the story of a legendary king and the adventures of his knights. Almost all the characters are imperfect—some decidedly so—but all strive hard to do right. The book is Malory's plea to God for forgiveness. The characters strive for an ideal even though they cannot reach it."

"What has this . . . ?"

"Just read it. Please."

Almost anyone else would have run from the room, perhaps to fetch a doctor. But Masters had known Thomas for too long. It was far more probable, Masters knew, that Thomas' brain had simply come up with a new way of looking at things, a valuable bit of illumination to make the world a bit clearer. "Yes. Of course I'll read it. I'll read it on the way back to the base.''

''No. Stay. I want you to read it here. I want your reaction. We have many things to discuss.''

''But I'm due back—''

''Paul, I'm the Captain-General. It can be arranged.''

Masters opened the book later that night after returning to his quarters. Comfortably propped against the pillows he read about the lives of Arthur, Merlin, Lancelot, and others. The style was difficult, and it took a while to become accustomed to the rhythm. He was used to the simple, straightforward style of a dry and mechanical age, while Malory crammed many complex, bold ideas into single, long sentences. Lists of names sometimes appeared, running half a page, and Masters had little idea who each person was.

But the story was magical. He had never read anything like it. He identified immediately with the warriors, their desire to be recognized for their martial skills, their desire to succeed despite their shortcomings. Arthur's knights encountered mysterious women and fought giants and one another. Masters read and read through the night and until noon of the next day, when exhaustion finally sent him to sleep. Within a few hours he was awake again, reading once more, until delirium took hold of him and he collapsed into sleep once more.

For three days he did not leave his room, eating only when a servant carried in a tray of food. For three days he read.

Masters finished the story one night at about four in the morning. The tale, and the way he had devoured it, left him dazed. He got up from his bed and put on a robe, then went out to wander the corridors of the palace. Being in the guest wing, he did not expect to run into anyone at this late hour.

His path led him to the double doors leading to the palace's BattleMech holding area. Stepping out into the warm night air, he was greeted by a sky shimmering with stars. Ahead of him was a large area surrounded by a high fence, guard towers, and security lamps. Five BattleMechs stood in the holding area, including his own *Phoenix Hawk*.

From where he stood the 'Mech looked like a huge, stoutly built man carrying a large pistol in his right hand. The pistol was actually an extended-range large laser built into the 'Mech's arm. Its design enhanced the anthropomorphic air of the machine. The war machine also had a medium pulse laser built into the right wrist, anti-missile defense systems in the right arm, a frightening anti-infantry machine gun system in the left arm, and a heavy supply of ammo built into the torso. The *Phoenix Hawk* had originally come with a second large laser, but Masters had replaced it several years ago with short-range missile four-packs. Sitting atop the torso was a cockpit shaped like a head. Masters controlled the behemoth from inside there.

A guard patroling the area spotted Masters. "Good evening, Captain," he called.

"Good evening."

"Checking up on him?"

"Yes," Masters said absently, "checking up on him." But he was not looking at his *Phoenix Hawk* the way he normally did. He usually saw the 'Mech as a mountain of metal, forty-five tons of battle platform. Not this time. As he walked toward it across the field, a new image grafted itself to his vision, the same way Malory had taken elements from his own time and mixed them with an ideal to create a new, romantic insight.

His BattleMech, he realized, was like a suit of armor worn by Arthur's knights. Both armor and a BattleMech provided practical protection, but they also made the warrior wearing them larger than life—a BattleMech decidedly so. They lifted a living warrior out of the ordinary into a realm where more could be expected from him.

Masters reached the foot of his 'Mech, which towered ten meters above him. Without even thinking about it he began to climb up the ladder that hung down the 'Mech's left side. The metal rungs felt strange against his bare feet, unexpectedly cool and smooth.

His thoughts turned to his mother, Jean Masters, one of the Marik Militia's most famous MechWarriors. Renowned for her battlefield cunning and peacetime grace, she had also argued frequently with her superiors, fighting to keep the battle etiquette of Mech-Warriors intact, while those around her surrendered to the march of "progress." "Times are changing, Jean," he had overheard countless officers and MechWarriors tell her. "They'll pass you by if you don't come along."

She didn't, and the times did. Her superiors passed her over one promotion after another, for she was, in the end, a troublemaker. She always told her son that the lack of promotion didn't matter, but he always saw in her eyes that it did. Yet he'd never believed the sadness was just for herself. When she argued, she argued for the forgotten spirit of the MechWarrior, for the fate of humans across the Inner Sphere who, caught up in the concerns of the moment, did not see where their actions might lead.

Paul Masters had sworn he would never betray his mother's ideals, and had tried to remain true to her principles all his life. But he had always lacked the language to fully understand what she meant.

Reaching the head of the *Phoenix Hawk*, he popped

the cockpit hatch and dropped inside. Settling into the command couch, he hit a button that reeled in the ladder and slowly closed the 'Mech's polarized canopy. Before him the unlit control switches and status lights framed the faceplate that looked out over the palace grounds. The 'Mech would not come alive until he'd put on the neurohelmet that allowed him to pilot the machine and to enter his secret authorization code and voiceprint.

Taking the joystick and the throttle, respectively, in his hands, an odd sensation came over him. In the darkness, dressed only in a robe, his thoughts full of Malory's knights, Masters felt himself become larger than life. He felt his flesh extend to the edges of the metal cockpit, and then beyond, stretching to the surface of the *Phoenix Hawk* itself. He was ready for something *extraordinary*. The pace of his breathing increased. His thoughts tumbled in and out of the military texts he had read throughout his life. He found himself hungering for the ideals so often proclaimed by the military, but so rarely found. The Grail, he realized, or at least his Grail, was a conduct that allowed him his profession. Killing was never good, but he was good at it. He needed forgiveness for that, and he needed a compass to help him find that forgiveness.

His mother had taught him that a BattleMech was an extension of the man or woman who piloted it. He understood now. That was the beauty of a 'Mech being shaped like a human. It was powerful, larger than life. A giant. She told him that no matter how well a warrior knew how to use a 'Mech's weapons, he was no more than a servant to the 'Mech if that was all he could do. A MechWarrior must have a spirit so large that it filled the machine, as Arthur's knights were larger than life, greater even than the thick plate mail in which they were swathed while astride their huge war-horses.

But a BattleMech is so huge, Masters thought. How can we possibly fill such roles? And then it occurred to him. As technology grew bigger and bigger, nearly dwarfing the people who used it, the human spirit would also have to expand to match the advance of machines. He couldn't be sure, but he thought that might be why wars were spinning out of control. People had given up, had handed over their souls to the machinery, letting the weapons become mythical rather than the people who used them.

If MechWarriors were to survive in the face of competing technologies, something extraordinary must happen. Something extraordinary like a new knightly order based on ideals rather than mercenary contracts.

He understood Thomas' plan now, and embraced it. It was an outlandish idea, sure to inspire ridicule. But hadn't the barons and lords mocked Arthur when the boy-king drew the sword from the stone and claimed Britain as his own? So, too, would others mock Thomas as an idealist-king, but no matter. Standing at his side he would always have Paul Masters.

The MechWarriors gathered in the courtyard of Thomas Marik's palace, one hundred fifty of them. In the previous six months Thomas had been inviting them from all corners of the Free Worlds League, and not one had declined to come. Thomas and Masters had chosen well, men and women who leaped at the opportunity offered, who instinctively appreciated what was at stake. Not that it had been an easy choice for the warriors to make. For many of them, accepting the invitation meant cutting ties with fellow warriors, with local governments, sometimes with families. At stake was the matter of loyalty, and none of these Mech-Warriors took loyalty lightly.

The warriors stood in a large circle, in the center of which was a massive holomap, ten meters across. The map floated in the air, showing the stars of the Inner Sphere, thousands of small, colored orbs the size of fists. The colors formed wedges representing the various political boundaries into which human-occupied space was divided.

The Free Worlds League showed up as stars with golden halos. Within the halos were smaller orbs of many colors, the sub-clusters representing the many governments and factions composing the League. Some of these were very powerful and included several star systems: the Marik Commonwealth, the Duchy of Andurien, the Principality of Regulus, the Principality of Gibson, and a dozen others.

Outside the League, filling out the sphere, floated thick wedges of color representing the other Successor States: red and green for the Federated Commonwealth, orange for the Draconis Combine, blue for the Capellan Confederation. These star empires had been at war on and off for centuries, and another was brewing. The MechWarriors knew it too. War always seemed to be percolating in the Inner Sphere. At the opposite side of the Sphere from the Free Worlds League were the white stars of the Clan Wedge, all the worlds stolen by the invaders from beyond the far-flung borders of the Inner Sphere.

Just as the MechWarriors formed a ring around the holomap, so their 'Mechs formed a giant circle around them. Like their human counterparts, the massive metal doppelgangers stood at crisp attention.

Surrounding the ring of 'Mechs were spectators crammed into bleachers set up around the courtyard. The guests included heads of state, other MechWarriors, diplomats, and family members.

According to Thomas, however, the most important group were the randomly selected citizens from across the Free Worlds League who had no direct contact with the wheels of power. These folk stood down front, with a clear view of the spectacle, and they would eventually carry the story of the ceremony back to their families and friends on worlds dozens of light years away.

Of course, the ceremony was being broadcast live, via hyperpulse generator, the marvel of technology controlled by Word of Blake. Within weeks everyone in the Free Worlds League would know what had happened at the Marik Palace on Atreus.

Thomas Marik climbed a staircase attached to a tall, wide pillar set at the center of the holomap. The glowing stars of the holomap moved about like will-o'-the-wisps against the purple robe and long scarred face of this sixty-five-year-old man.

The sunlight had begun to fade, and the night's actual stars began to appear in the darkening sky, shining through the holomap. Masters smiled at the beauty of it; the ideal against the real. Malory's romantic vision had put a new spin on the way he saw the universe. He knew it wasn't real, but he knew that was the key. Malory's tale might not be accurate, but it bent just slightly what Masters had thought possible, like light curved by the pull of a sun.

"MechWarriors!" Thomas said, standing even taller as he gripped the railing set around the pillar. The crowd settled into silence. "We are at a crossroads. Six hundred years ago, after interstellar wars threatened the extinction of our race, the leaders of the Inner Sphere created the rules of warfare known as the Ares Conventions. And entrusted with the responsibility of conducting battle according to these rules were the warriors of the Inner Sphere. When wars were fought, it was you, the MechWarriors, who monitored the level of destruction, who were careful to engage only other warriors, not civilians.

"Although the first BattleMech was not built until several decades after the creation of the Ares Conventions, they were the perfect tools to implement the ideals of the Conventions. A 'Mech empowered the noble man or woman to settle the disputes of parties at war as they should be settled: through the skills of the warrior, not through an indiscriminate rain of bullets and shrapnel.''

The circle of one hundred and fifty MechWarriors raised their voices in a shout of approval. Applause drifted down from the bleachers.

Masters looked around. The faces were both young and old, dark and light, and of all races. Some had been poor as children, some rich. But this they all shared in common: they knew what a BattleMech represented, even if they had no way to express the idea in words, for the language of honor and imagination had eroded slowly over the years. Now, each face was raised toward Thomas Marik, some approvingly, some still with skepticism. Each one knew what Thomas would propose, but the moment of decision had not yet arrived. Until that time, Marik had to make his case clear, to make them choose to leave behind their previous loyalties and to swear their fealty to him. The real concern, which pricked Masters' thoughts like a splinter, was that despite the careful background checks and conversations with all the candidates, one or more of them might have accepted the invitation as an opportunity to discredit Thomas at the moment of the oath-taking. As things stood, the ceremony was an impressive event being beamed throughout the stars. If, however, some MechWarrior were to denounce Thomas in the midst of the ceremony, the whole thing would become a horrible blunder instead of a great triumph.

''The spirit of the Ares Conventions did not truly take hold for hundreds of years, not until the treasure of humanity's knowledge was nearly wiped out during the first three Succession Wars. Lacking so much of the science that catapulted humanity on our voyage among the stars, we had to fight wars much more cautiously. Through sheer necessity we limited the conduct of war. We respected our warrior class, allowing the enemy to retrieve wounded soldiers. We kept the fury of battle low in order to salvage parts of 'Mechs for future battles.

"But now these chivalrous practices are in jeopardy. Times have changed. Our scientific progress has retrieved knowledge that had been lost through the devastation of war. Wars like those in the days of old are becoming possible once more. Fear now grips people across the Inner Sphere. They no longer trust the warrior class, but want victories at any cost. Cities are now battlefields, civilians killed at a terrible rate, production facilities becoming targets once again. I fear that we are headed down the same dark path that nearly destroyed us centuries ago. This time we may not escape hurtling over the precipice. This time we may simply fall."

Again Masters looked around the giant ring of MechWarriors. The faces were somber now. Some of the warriors looked down, their minds full of thought. Would they accept Thomas' offer?

"Across the Inner Sphere, hundreds of light years away, we know of the invasion of the Clans into the Inner Sphere. We have heard the tales. We know that though the Clanspeople are descended from our stock, they are not *human*. They have no respect for life, but worship only *war*.

"Some say we must be ready to fight as they do, to descend to their barbaric level. I say no, we must not. If you become the enemy, the enemy wins, no matter the outcome of the battle. We must be ready to fight the Clans, and we must be ready to fight the other desperate Successor States that surround us, but we must fight them our way."

Marik paused and turned slowly around the dais, gazing into the eyes of the surrounding MechWarriors. "We must remain true to what we know is right. In the last few centuries we have taken steps toward saving our race from total destruction. Now we find ourselves at an old crossroads. Will we continue to work toward the goals established in the Ares Conventions, or will the proliferation of combat technology return us to the days of indiscriminate total war?"

"And what would you have us do?" shouted a big bear of a man named Gainard.

Masters looked up at Thomas Marik. He seemed ruffled momentarily, but only someone like Masters, who knew him well, would perceive it. To everyone else Thomas would appear in firm control.

"I have gathered you here to make you an offer. You are aware, no doubt, that the face of the military caste is changing quickly. The day of the MechWarrior families is quickly coming to a close. Soon the noble title of MechWarrior will no longer be passed down through generations, but won by anyone who can apply to the appropriate academy. MechWarriors have become sucked into the same organizational structures as the dry military units of the past."

Many of the gathered MechWarriors began to shift uncomfortably, and Thomas raised a hand to still them. "I do not speak of anarchy. We need units of organization, of course. But MechWarriors are not merely soldiers, and that is what the worlds of the Inner Sphere would have you be. Where once a 'Mech was a prized and valuable object, making its pilot an exceptional person throughout the Inner Sphere, technology is making BattleMechs cheap and common, and thus, by extension, also the warriors who pilot them." Again a shifting in the crowd, this one not of protest, but acknowledgment of an uncomfortable truth.

"Think of Solaris Seven, a world devoted to turning the art of 'Mech warfare into a cheap sport. This is not what we want to see happen." Here the Mech-Warriors nodded their agreement, and some spoke softly to each other, affirming Thomas' concerns.

"I offer you this. I offer you a place in my new order of knights, the Knights of the Inner Sphere." This time a loud murmur passed through the ring of warriors, and Masters smiled. So did Thomas. They had kept the name a secret until this moment.

"I know," Thomas said. "It is a presumptuous title, for I can speak only for the Free Worlds League. But I have chosen the name because my knights will represent all MechWarriors who believe that a warrior should be free of the petty politics of transitory warlords, bound only by the ideals of his *profession*. These ideals extend far beyond the borders of the Free Worlds League. And far beyond the borders of the Inner Sphere. And, in fact, far beyond the flesh that binds each of our souls. For these ideals existed before our time, and will endure forever. They are the ideals mirrored in our religions, our philosophies, and in our stories. We can only try to represent them in our lives, as you, all of you, attempt to mirror them in your conduct as MechWarriors."

Thomas paused, and let his gaze travel the assembled warriors once more. Then he began to speak again in a deep and resonant voice. "If you would live to be more than common men and common women, join my cause. I ask you now, who stands with me?"

3

As Thomas spoke his question, silence fell over the proceedings. To Masters, the stillness seemed interminable. He wanted to raise his sword and utter a cry of loyalty, but too many knew of his friendship with Thomas. The gesture would seem hollow, no more than a stunt.

But then he heard the sliding of steel to his left. And then to his right. He looked and saw MechWarrior after MechWarrior drawing his or her ceremonial sword. The swords were from countless worlds and cultures, some curved, some straight. And yet, after all the centuries of autocannon and missiles and lasers, the sword was still the symbol of the warrior's profession.

"I am with you Captain-General Thomas Marik," called Gainard, his voice full of feeling.

"I am with you!" called out another. "I am with you!" shouted yet another. One after another the warriors raised their swords and declared their fealty to Thomas and the order of the Knights of the Inner Sphere. Masters' relief brought tears to his eyes.

Thomas' impulse had obviously been correct. There was something loose in the Free Worlds League, a fear of a possible future in which the chaos of war would engulf the stars.

Soon it was complete, all swords raised but Masters'. It was then that he finally lifted his blade and said proudly, "I am with you, Thomas Marik."

Thomas, his body surrounded by the holomap's mass of colored stars, looked down at Masters and nodded. Then he turned slowly, addressing each knight. "I am honored, warriors. I am most honored. And I will not disappoint your trust. Let us seal this oath with an ancient ceremony from the days of Terra's past, a ceremony that has not seen use for more than a thousand years."

Masters watched as Thomas changed from a man who spoke of communal interests into a leader who rose above them all. He seemed to become taller, his face grimmer, and when he spoke again, his voice was deeper. "If you would swear loyalty to me, kneel now."

Almost as one, the assembled MechWarriors dropped to one knee.

"Do you swear and acknowledge me as your true and lawful liege?"

"Yes!" went the cry, true and clear.

"Do you swear fealty to me, and swear your services to me, to be forever in my service, until death shall take you?"

"Yes."

"For my part, I do swear to defend and honor each of you as befits a true knight. From this day hence you shall no longer serve in the military bureaucracies of your past, but exist outside all structures but one: the Knights of the Inner Sphere."

A shiver passed through Masters. He looked around him. Finally he had found a family, a group one hundred and fifty strong, who cared as he did about the fate of warfare, a group unwilling to let events simply roll over them, but who would shape history according to their desires. "Wear the title proudly, for you are now more than you were before, and the worlds of the Inner Sphere will recognize you as such. Wield your weapons and your skills to serve and defend me well."

As they had kneeled, now the group of men and women rose again as one. Infected by the fervor of becoming forged as a group, they shouted, "All hail Thomas Marik!" A tremendous roar of approval swept over the audience, the clamor deafening. Masters felt his breathing quicken. There. It was done. They had begun the process of cutting across the balkanized powers of the Free Worlds League. One hundred and fifty MechWarriors had broken their former ties and sworn allegiance not to a state, but personally to Thomas Marik.

Now all they had to do was survive the backlash.

The knights celebrated wildly in the palace's great hall, along with the hundreds of guests. Servants carried bread and cheese and roast meats and broiled fowl and fish and wine and ale and beer; dancers and jugglers cut their way through the crowd; musicians played and the knights and guests danced and danced.

Sir Paul Masters had not been so happy since his first days of warrior training more than twenty years ago. Everything seemed in place now. Being a MechWarrior was no longer just a job. He'd embarked upon a vocation.

He stared down into his wine glass and smiled. It was all coming together. It was going to work.

Masters looked around and saw some guests scurrying over to one another, open shock on their faces. They really had no idea that the MechWarriors would swear fealty to Thomas, and now clutched at one another as their long-held social structures began to slip away.

It wasn't just that there were knights now. MechWarriors had always been knights. Nor was it that Thomas was encouraging feudalism. Feudalism had ruled interstellar governments for nearly as long as humanity had settled the stars. Throughout the Free Worlds League—and the Inner Sphere, for that matter—were counts and barons and duchesses. They were in granted continents, or asteroid belts, or worlds, responsible for overseeing the safety of the population and acting as their lord's eyes, ears, and military arm, for communication was slow between all but the most important of worlds, and travel through space even slower. Often the royalty had little to do with the planet they watched over; it was an interstellar superstructure that existed beyond the local governments of star systems. A man might be baron of a world with a constitutional republic and never interfere with local politics as long as things ran smoothly. Or he might become quite involved. As long as the liege's wishes were being carried out, it was the vassal's business how he behaved.

No, what startled some of the guests was that Thomas *meant* it. For at least a century, the bond of loyalty that should exist between liege and vassal had been evaporating like sea water from a rock. It was clear that Thomas the idealist, Thomas the upstart—who had no business even being a Successor State ruler—was letting the romantic images of feudalism go to his head.

A woman whose name he remembered as Boyer came up to him. ''Dance?''

She was small, her brown hair short, her skin dark from days spent in the sun. He was drawn to her, seeing the evening's giddiness lighting even more her bright, intelligent eyes. He could sense that she also wanted to toast the festivities with intimacy.

"Dame Boyer," Masters said, adding her new title. He placed his glass on the table beside him.

"*Sir* Masters," she said adding his, and smiled. He took her hand and put an arm around her waist as he led her out to the dance floor.

Both had already consumed a great deal of liquor, making them sway awkwardly and out of time with the music as they moved across the floor. She laughed, and let her cheek rest against his chest. Her laugh quickly became a snorting sound, which only made her laugh harder. Masters joined in, letting loose his own deep guffaw. "I'm sorry," she said, tears appearing at the corners of her eyes.

"No, no. It's fine. Everything's fine."

As their laughter subsided, he pulled her close. They slowed their dancing, trying to keep their momentum under control. She kept her head against his chest, and when she spoke, the words seemed to vibrate near his heart. "Can this really be happening?" Her voice was serious, and he realized that she was cataloguing the same doubts that had plagued Masters when he and Thomas had discussed the plan for the knightly order months and months ago.

"Yes. It's really happening. Whether it will work, whether it will bring us good fortune or ill, I do not know. But it is happening."

They moved even more slowly now, out of time with the spirited music being pounded out by the musicians. Couples swirled around them, a blur of colors and laughter. Boyer raised her head, which put her lips near his neck. He felt her breath warm against his flesh, letting his own float down to her ear. "Oh," she said, and laughed.

A voice cut through their intimacy. "Sir Masters?"

Without turning, Masters snapped, "What?" in a

tone he hoped would communicate his desire not to be disturbed.

"The Captain-General, sir. He'd like to see you now."

Masters turned and saw a seventeen-year-old page standing behind him. He looked back to Dame Boyer. She arched her eyebrows and stepped away. "There it is," she said, and smiled.

"Exactly," said Masters. "Wait for me?"

"Maybe." She swayed her hips a bit.

"Exactly." He smiled and turned toward the large doors at the end of the hall. The page rushed to get ahead of him so he could lead, but Masters said, "Lad, the study, correct?"

"Yes."

"I know the way. Go get yourself something to eat."

The woman walked directly up to him, and even before he could greet her, she was taking his hand and saying, "I hear you're the one who arranged all this."

"I . . . ," he said, and tried to extract his hand from her grasp, more from surprise than from embarrassment. She responded by sliding her fingertips against his, like a cat rubbing its head against a hand, and then running her fingernails up his arm. Then she lightly raked the nails back down his forearm and again took his hand in hers.

"I didn't exactly arrange it," Masters said. "I helped the Captain-General." He wondered if she was royalty or merely someone hoping to have a liaison with a now-famous MechWarrior. "Have we met?"

"Countess Dystar of Gibson."

Now he remembered having seen her picture. "Sir Paul Masters," he said, and stepped back to lift her hand to his lips. "A pleasure. Now, if you'll excuse me, I must attend to my liege."

She stepped closer again. "Can you attend to me later?"

He smiled. "You are direct, aren't you, Countess?"

She smiled back. "Do you think so? I'm restraining myself actually, considering the fact that we're surrounded by hundreds of people."

"Well, I really must be going. And I promised a dance to someone else. But maybe we'll meet some other time. A pleasure meeting you."

"Is Thomas Marik really so much more interesting than me?"

"You wouldn't try to delay me in attending my liege, would you?"

"Oh, no. I just want to make sure you've thought through what you're missing."

"Countess, if I were to think it through, I would never get to my meeting." She gave a laugh both delicate and mirthful, champagne pouring into a glass. "Good evening."

He moved past her, then felt a slap against his bottom as he did. Walking on, he couldn't help but think, What a crude and endearing woman.

Master moved through the corridors of the palace, which were alive with couples flirting, groups conducting politics, and others sometimes combining romance with affairs of state. His journey took him down a great hall filled with statues of previous Marik family members. The line stretched all the way back to Johan Marik, a German prince of the thirteenth century. The Marik family had ruled a portion of Europe near Switzerland until Terra's first world war, when the ravages of battle destroyed their homeland.

After passing the last of the statues, he saw ahead of him a man in Regulan military dress uniform seated on a marble bench set against the wall. The man's head was lowered, as if sad or drunk. As Masters approached, the man lifted his gaze, becoming recognizable as Colonel Roush of the Regulan Hussars. "Nathen, good to see you," Masters said. "I didn't know you'd be here." He'd met Roush several times before, having found him to be a good enough fellow. Though Regulus and the Marik Commonwealth were rivals, Masters saw no need to bring that tension to bear here and now.

Roush looked up at Masters like a gunner gauging a shot, then dropped his glass, which shattered against the marble floor. The sound of the glass splintering seemed beyond his range of hearing. "Wouldn't have missed it for the world, Masters," he said, standing up with a bit of a sway. "You and your liege. Pretty fancy. I wanted to be here to see the ruin of the Free Worlds League."

A flash of red went off in Masters' mind. Roush was angry, and they had both been drinking. He had to be careful. Was the man jealous? Though Masters knew that the knighthood offered by Thomas would not interest Roush, perhaps he still felt slighted at not being invited to join the Knights. The colonel was a fierce Regulan nationalist, who had long been pressuring the rulers of the Principality of Regulus to invest in new weapon systems to keep them from "being left behind" in the war of technology.

There it was, pure and simple. Roush hated the idea of the Knights and what they stood for.

"I know what you're up to. You and Marik. You're pushing his bid to rule the Free Worlds. It won't work. Do you think that Marik can pull together a private army and no one take notice?"

"We didn't try to hide it."

"No, but you're hiding what you plan to do with it."

Roush continued to sway as he spoke, and Masters

thought it prudent to leave before things got even hotter.

"Where're you going?"

"I have a meeting with the Captain-General."

Roush seemed surprised, as if thrown off track without knowing exactly how it came about. "Oh." Then he grabbed his resolve and said, "What do you think is going to happen when the other Successor States find out that we're moving backward in our war efforts?"

"We're not moving—"

"Of course we are, you idiot." Roush stepped forward and jabbed Masters in the chest. "We're going to be weak."

Masters stepped back, not wanting to unleash the flush of anger rising in him. "The Free Worlds League will be stronger because . . ."

"I know," Roush said mockingly. " 'Stronger in spirit.' I read the press release. Do you think that matters? When it comes to war, you must do anything to win. 'War is an act of force, and there is no logical limit to the application of that force.' "

"Von Clausewitz lived in a different age, Colonel. He didn't have weapons that could ravage an entire planet within moments."

"That doesn't change the reality of war: the side that can destroy the enemy first wins."

"No. Clausewitz said that the job was to disarm the enemy. He also said that societies can use intelligence in order not to destroy cities. The Captain-General is attempting to strengthen the MechWarrior tradition, a product of intelligence and choice, in hopes it will help prevent humanity from destroying itself in all-out war."

"Von Clausewitz would have called you a fool."

"I would have called him an infant in the history of humanity. I also point out that we are preserving the profession of the MechWarrior. Too many improvements in war technology will weaken the role of BattleMechs. Right now they cannot be harmed by any mobile weapons. But it is quite possible that if we pursue certain lines of technology, MechWarriors like us could find ourselves obsolete. BattleMechs are too expensive to justify if they are not the kings of the battlefield.''

"Is that all you are concerned with? Your job?''

Masters laughed. "Yes, in part. I'm surprised you're surprised. Why shouldn't I fight for my job? I'm a soldier. I like fighting. I want to keep fighting. Before the collapse of the Star League there existed a great deal of war technology, weapons not so much for use by soldiers as to be unleashed. Gases, tactical nukes, laser beams that shot across the field in random directions and blinded soldiers. What work is there for a soldier with weapons like that? We become just corpses waiting to happen; body counts for the home front. No, Colonel, I'd rather have a primitive war in which I have a real part to play.''

"The weapons will always grow. It is the way of it.''

"Not so. At the end of the sixteenth century the Japanese were making the best firearms in the world. But when the samurai realized the weapons would make their skills obsolete, they stopped using them. A peasant with five minutes of training could cut down a sword master with forty years' experience. Within a hundred years, firearms had disappeared from Japan.''

"A fairy tale—''

"What would I gain by lying?''

"And what do you think the other rulers of the Inner Sphere will think when they realize the implications of your Knights? You think they'll simply come charging in?''

"There are no guarantees they will not. But there

are two things to consider. First, since the object of war is to disarm the enemy, if we are not a threat, we might not be a prime target.''

"No! That will make us all the more likely to be attacked.''

"And second, remember that von Clausewitz makes it clear that a nation's strength consists of two complementary components: the total means at its disposal *and* the strength of its will. Now, for convenience and ease, we have spent countless decades increasing our means in war, but paid little attention to our will. Why? Because will isn't measurable or quantifiable. It makes technocrats nervous because it doesn't help them work up government contracts to fund projects when there is no war. It makes politicians nervous because the will of the people can't be manipulated. What happens, they always have to wonder, if the people suddenly don't want to fight a war anymore? Better for both parties to depend on technology alone. If it is possible to build a weapon that any button-pusher can use easily and quickly, then governments don't have to depend on their citizens to back their policies. A war can be fought and won or lost even before the people know what's happened.''

"And . . . ?''

"Thomas and I believe that the Knights of the Inner Sphere will make the will of the people in the Free Worlds League stronger here than anywhere else in the Inner Sphere. We are giving the people a chance to participate in something glorious. Elsewhere people are simply chess pieces in insane politics. People will look to the Knights for inspiration. We will have the best-motivated population, and knowing this, the leaders of the other Successor States will hesitate to attack.''

"A dream.''

"Exactly. Now, if you'll excuse me.''

"No," Roush said, grabbing Masters by the shoulder and swinging him around. Swaying, unbalanced, Masters couldn't do much more at that moment than watch Roush's fist come rushing toward his face.

4

Catching Masters full in the nose, the punch sent him sprawling across the corridor like a BattleMech with ruined gyroscopes, then crashing against the wall. So dazed was he that it took a moment to remember where he was and what was happening.

He grabbed the edges of the marble bench, shaking his head to clear it. When he could see again, he fixed his gaze on Roush. "Colonel. You're drunk. Let's say we just—"

But Roush was already rushing him and shouting, "You will not destroy my home!" Taking Masters by the throat, he slammed his head into the wall. Sharp pain lanced through the base of Masters' skull.

The hell with it, he thought, bringing his hands up between Roush's outstretched arms and snapping them apart with all his might. As Roush's hands flew wide, it left his middle open. Bringing up one foot, Masters slammed it into Roush's gut. The other man let out a cry and staggered back. As he did, Masters rose and took two quick steps forward. With a clean, precise motion, he swept kicked Roush's legs out from under him, sending the man to the floor.

Part of Masters wanted to simply leave and let the matter rest, but Roush's arrogance in attacking him in Thomas' home was too much to bear. As Roush struggled to get up, Masters dropped down onto the man's stomach and forced him to exhale with a horrible gasp. Then he jabbed one hand against Roush's neck and said, "If this is how your people reward hospitality, Colonel, it will be my pleasure to dismantle the Principality of Regulus."

Hearing the clatter of boots approaching, Masters looked up and saw two palace guards rushing toward them. He got up off Roush, who remained on the ground, still gasping for air and looking quite surprised. When the guards came up, one asked, "Sir Masters, are you all right?"

"Yes, I'm fine," he said, gingerly touching his nose to assess the damage. His hand slid against a thick layer of warm blood that covered his upper lip and dripped into his mouth and down his chin. He cursed, and pulled a handkerchief out of his pocket.

"Get him out of here," he told the guards.

"Blake's word! What happened to you?" Thomas exclaimed, astonished, as Masters entered the study.

"I had a discussion about the Knights with Colonel Roush of the Regulan Hussars. We didn't see things eye to eye." His vision slowly adjusted to the soft, dim light.

Thomas got up from behind his large desk and crossed the room to Masters. "That handkerchief's soaked with blood. Are you all right?"

"I'm fine. The palace doctor tells me nothing's broken. It's just a lot of blood."

"Are you unsteady on your feet, Sir Masters?"

"Fine, sir."

"Well, sit down before you fall down. It's always better to surrender to gravity than to succumb to it."

"Sir." Masters took the first well-upholstered chair and sank into it, deciding he wouldn't move again for some time. Maybe for a day or two. "Is there a reason I'm here? A fellow knight and I were exchanging caresses of warm breath before your call brought me into close quarters with that boor."

"My apologies, but there's someone I want you to meet."

A knock came at the door. "Captain-General Marik."

"Yes," Thomas said, his voice suddenly strong and certain.

"Word of Blake Precentor Gibson here to see you."

Thomas took several long-legged strides to the door and opened it himself. Standing in the corridor was a page, and behind him a plump, dark man with a leonine mane of gray hair and an enormous handlebar mustache to match. He looked to be about Thomas' age, and when they saw each other, the two men laughed and embraced. "Thomas!" Blane said, and Thomas returned with "William!"

"It's been far too long, Thomas."

"Affairs of state, and so on."

They broke their embrace and Thomas gestured for Blane to enter the room, then shut the door.

"Sir Masters, I'd like to introduce an old friend from my days in ComStar, William Blane, Word of Blake Precentor on the planet Gibson. William, this is the most beloved of my Knights of the Inner Sphere, Sir Paul Masters."

Precentor Blane looked visibly shocked at the sight of Masters' bloated and bloodied nose. "Are you all right?"

"A fight. I'm a soldier. Just doing my job."

Precentor Blane stepped forward and shook Masters' hand. "Well, as long as you won. Congratulations, sir. You two should know what a stir you've created with the announcement of the Knights. I was in the tavern of my hotel earlier and all the news channels were covering it. Discussion among the patrons was most animated." Blane's cheeks filled out and turned red as he spoke. He seemed a very happy man.

"Good or bad discussion, Precentor?" asked Masters.

Thomas headed toward the bar. "Will you have something to drink, Bill?"

"Yes on that drink. Whiskey. Straight. And you, Sir Masters—call me Bill, please. Precentor is a title I hold dearly and in all respect, but there are times . . . Anyway, the patrons. Yes, you've created quite a rumble. It'll take a few weeks for the news to spread across the Free Worlds League, of course, but soon it will be the talk of the stars. Mark my words."

Despite his words, Blane's joviality faltered and Masters realized the pleasant mood was a pumped-up facade. The Precentor's good-natured smile fell away, and when next he spoke, his tone was deadly serious. He rubbed his forehead. "Do you two have any idea what you're doing?"

Thomas turned and gave Masters a faint smile. "We were just discussing that when you arrived." He handed Blane a whiskey.

"Tom, people are already beginning to wonder if you're plotting a coup. This whole thing has caught everyone off guard. People nearly came to blows in the tavern. Blake knows what will happen when word of it reaches the other principalities. The minute Regulus gets word, they'll surely begin polishing up their atomics."

Both Masters and Thomas looked at him, their faces suddenly white.

"Just an exaggeration," the Precentor said, trying

to restore calm. "That's all. I haven't heard that they've actually dug something out of their basement. But you know what I mean. They won't go to war over this, but Cameron-Jones isn't going to sit still. You've grabbed three of his best MechWarriors."

"He should have treated them better," Thomas said, walking back to take a seat at his desk. At his signal Masters also returned to his well-padded chair.

Blane remained standing, too agitated to light anywhere. He laughed nervously. "Well, yes. That's easy for you to say. But you've encouraged treason."

"Yes, Bill. I have. I broke the rules. I've encouraged treason. I've rewarded those who practiced it. But when the rules are fallow, when they can no longer support the human spirit, they must be disregarded. If I lose in the long run, I'll be labeled a traitorous bastard. If I win, I'm a legendary revolutionary."

"We're a bit old to lead revolutions, Tom." Blane waddled over to a chair and finally sat.

"Nonsense. Age gives perspective. And besides, Bill, you've left ComStar to join the Word of Blake reformation. How can you point a finger at me for breaking the rules?"

Blane knocked back half his glass. "That's a completely different matter. The split between ComStar and Word of Blake is a religious issue. It's private. What you've done has thrown the entire Free Worlds League into confusion. Or it's about to."

"Well, I certainly hope so. It's one of my goals."

Blane looked down at the floor and began to rock slightly in his seat. "What right have you to play such games when there are so many other matters of military importance in the Free Worlds League?" he said plaintively. "This is absurd, Tom. A knightly order? We use feudalism to control the interstellar governments between stars because it's the only way to do it.

No one wants to become even deeper entrenched in its mire. More than one man has suggested that you've lost your mind. I chalked it up to your romanticism. But it's one thing when you wax eloquent about the need for ideals while strolling along the seashore on a moonlit night. It's quite another when, by a series of odd chances, you actually end up with enough power to implement the madness.''

Masters stood up, a desire to wring the Precentor's neck swelling within him. His hands had clenched into fists, but when he looked to Thomas for a nod, Marik waved his hand, a silent command to wait. Unsure what to do, Masters walked to the far side of the room, where he stood with one elbow resting on a bookshelf. He thought that assuming nonchalance might be a way to trick himself into calming down, but it didn't work. The fight with Roush mixed with drink made him even more edgy.

''Bill,'' said Thomas, ''I think that the military situation of the Free Worlds League, of the entire Inner Sphere, must be addressed, and addressed now. The concern about another Clan invasion, the increasing probability of another Succession War, the disputes within the Free Worlds League, and, of course, the war on your own planet, all are issues of military concern. The question I am trying to address is how will we answer these military concerns? The solution that everyone, including your own people, is throwing at me, is to use more firepower and to make harsher assaults. But I do not agree. My plan for restructuring the armed forces of the Free Worlds League has everything to do with threats that already exist within the Free Worlds, and with threats still to come. I want to deal with these matters before we are forced, out of desperation, to take actions that could make us despise ourselves.''

Precentor Blane leaned back in his chair and rubbed

his hands over his face. "Thomas, you know the power of technology. You studied with ComStar for many years. Technology has its own inner life. Our role is to pursue that technology, to try, in our own feeble way, to keep up with it. To respect it and shape it to save the Inner Sphere."

"Yes." Thomas stood and walked around the desk. "Exactly. But I think that some technology seduces us. It calls us to pursue it, yet it is actually no more than a false lead, or worse, a possible danger to our race."

Precentor Blane looked up from behind his hands, his face wary, almost afraid. Masters wondered if Thomas had stirred up a ComStar theological land mine. The organization was so shrouded in secrecy that it often didn't make much sense to Masters. When two True Believers started going at it, they could leave outsiders behind in a cloud of veiled allusions and half-spoken assumptions.

The two men stared at each other for a long moment, then both began to slowly turn their heads toward Masters. "Perhaps this is not the time," Precentor Blane said slowly .

"I agree," said Thomas.

A pang of jealousy reverberated through Masters. Though he felt closer to Thomas Marik than to any other man, he knew that his friend's days in ComStar would always be closed to him, and Thomas' continuing connection with Word of Blake would always remain outside his understanding.

"Then what of Gibson?" asked Blane.

"You tell me. You have come here seeking help?"

"Not so much help as time. The war is going well, but we need more time to win it."

"So it is a war," Thomas said. "When I called it that before, you didn't contradict me. And now you use the same word. Yet the last report that crossed my

desk called the conflict on Gibson a small uprising that
would be put down within a month. That was over a
year ago. I don't suppose you could explain this little
discrepancy, eh, Bill?''

5

Marik Palace, Atreus
Marik Commonwealth, Free Worlds League
1 January 3055

Precentor Blane moved his hands in the air as if they were scales measuring the weight of different words. "A war, a rebellion. I don't claim to understand such terms. But I'm here now to tell you what is happening. Both Word of Blake and Countess Dystar are providing funds to prepare troops."

"The Countess?"

"She's hiring mercenaries."

" 'Mech units?" asked Masters.

"Infantry. It's mostly infantry, with 'Mech support. The Gibson Freedom League only has two 'Mechs, the two who turned on the Countess when the rebellion broke out. We're trying to find them, but so far . . ."

Masters shook his head. Thomas' words from the knighting ceremony rang in his ears. During the Fourth Succession War he had fought against massive infantry resistance on Procyon, but it had been a last-ditch attempt on the part of the Procyons, not the basis for the war. Now, instead of being at the forefront, 'Mechs were being relegated to the back of the war, performing as infantry support.

Thomas shook his head. "I need the matter on Gibson settled quickly. As it stands, the fact that I have given sanctuary to the True Believers is beginning to have unfortunate ramifications. Most people have never understood ComStar, and so this schism that has divided the organization in two doesn't draw much sympathy from the citizens of the Free Worlds League."

"You wouldn't turn your back on us?"

"No. But I could have handled matters in a way to make my life easier. If the True Believers could have been dispersed among the Free Worlds as I suggested, it would have—"

"We had to keep them together. We need to build a new community, a new home. We're very clannish."

"No matter. Dropping tens of thousands of True Believers down on any world is going to cause problems. And then you said you wanted them with you on Gibson."

"ComStar has always had a strong presence on Gibson. We had a 'Mech garrison there. I had assurances from Principal Hsiang and Countess Dystar that everything would run smoothly."

"And now it seems that they were wrong. What are we going to do about it?"

"The war is going well. I've looked over the reports. We're anticipating GFL casualty dividends exceeding troop investments by more than ten percent this quarter."

"What?" said Masters.

Blane glanced at Masters as if he were a bug that had only been allowed to live this long because it had been, up until now, quiet. "We're winning," he said quietly. Masters decided to let it go.

"But you need more time."

"The Countess mentioned that you might want to negotiate a settlement with the guerrillas. But we *need* to win this war, Tom. I'm talking about the government of Gibson—those in power. We need to show the people that the True Believers have a home, a home honored by you, by Principal Hsiang, and Countess Dystar. Removing my own interests from the discussion for a moment, you should not settle with these rebels. They are directly contradicting your will.''

Thomas raised his hands in front of his chest and placed them together as if in prayer. ''Very well. You are correct. I do not *want* to settle with the GFL. They should respect my will. They were told that they would host the True Believers from ComStar, and that is what they will do. But the conflict must *end*. Each day it goes on makes it look as though I made a mistake inviting the True Believers here, and that people loyal to me are incapable of putting down the insurrection.''

''It will end. It will end soon. I have word from Precentor Martial Arian that the war is going well and will soon be over.''

''From who?'' Masters asked.

''Precentor Martial Arian,'' Blane said wearily. ''He's not from the Free Worlds League. He's a ComStar commander lately stationed in the Free Rasalhague Republic, now a member of Word of Blake on Gibson.'' He took another swallow of his whiskey. ''The Clans didn't leave much untouched in Rasalhague, from what I hear. He lost everything.''

''Well,'' said Thomas, ''I will be sending you some help. My best knight, Sir Masters, will accompany you back to Gibson. I'll draw up orders attaching him to the Gibson Loyalist forces.''

Blane's mouth opened slightly in surprise. ''The Gibson forces are currently under the command of Precentor Martial Arian. You'll have to check with him.''

''What?'' said Masters and Thomas together. ''The Gibson forces are under the command of Word of Blake?'' Masters asked.

Blane sighed. "A joint effort, I think. It's all very muddled actually. I don't claim to understand it completely. Arian pressed for the True Believer forces to work in tandem with the Loyalist forces. Eventually Principal Hsiang became so impressed with the progress of the True Believer forces that he handed virtual control of the planet's military over to Arian."

"And the Countess?" asked Thomas.

"She's buying mercs and handing them over to Arian to spend as he wishes."

Spend? thought Masters.

"Why wasn't I told about this?" asked Thomas.

"As I said, it's very muddled. Frankly, I'm having trouble sorting through the command structure."

"Fine. Why wasn't I told about the muddled command structure?"

"Actually, I thought you knew. I just realized you didn't when you said you wanted to attach Captain Masters . . . my apologies, *Sir* Masters . . . to the Loyalist forces."

"Why did you think I knew?"

"I thought for certain that Hsiang or the Countess would have told you. Maybe the communiqué was never sent." Precentor Blane looked visibly disturbed. "You really didn't hear about this?"

"No, not at all. But I'll check our records to see what might have happened."

"The Countess is here, Captain-General," Masters said. "For the ceremony. We could bring her to you."

"Excellent." Thomas stepped to the door and alerted a page to bring Countess Dystar to the study. Returning his attention to the room, he said, "Sir Masters will accompany you to Gibson. He will study the war situation closely, and send back a full report."

Blane looked at Masters somewhat distastefully, then

a smile spread across his dark face. "Thank goodness. Someone on the field who can understand the war and who can explain it to me. I must confess that though I've lived on Gibson for fifteen years as its Precentor, I've never engaged much in its politics."

"Which is as it should be," said Thomas. "Your concern was with ComStar, the ComStar members on the planet, and the operation of the hyperpulse generator."

"Yes. Until now. Tens of thousands of my people have landed on Gibson and want to become part of its culture." His shoulders drooped. "Sometimes I find myself unable to deal with Principal Hsiang and Countess Dystar. It will take time for the True Believers to become part of Gibson society."

"Why is that?" asked Masters.

"I don't exactly know how to put it. Dystar and Hsiang always seem to have something else in their eyes when they speak. I'm sorry. I haven't been able to sort it out completely." He laughed. "I suppose that I'd be able to deal with them if I could. Luckily, my principal aide, Precentor Starling, seems to have established a good rapport with them. And with the people of Gibson. Starling and I have our theological differences, of course. But in most other matters we see eye to eye. He's a True Believer emigré, came in with Precentor Martial Arian. I knew I couldn't be the one to establish the connections with the Gibson government and people that these new circumstances required. It needed someone younger, someone who would be living on the planet a long time."

"It is settled then. Sir Masters will serve us both as our eyes and ears on Gibson. Paul, when do you think you'll be ready to go?"

Masters stood up straight, dropping his feigned casualness. "Whenever you command, sir."

* * *

Precentor Blane left soon after. "I can't say I much like the man," said Masters.

"You're drunk and he's a cranky old True Believer. He's not going to trust you, no matter what, and you're inebriated enough to let it bother you. Now, let's talk about what you must do on Gibson."

Masters dropped down into a chair once more. "Scout and report back, I thought. Help them quell the uprising."

"Yes, that, and more."

"More?"

"Yes, more. I'm sending fifty of you, fifty Knights of the Inner Sphere, out into the Free Worlds League to search out trouble. We need to find places where the Knights can 'do good.' You must see if the situation on Gibson will make a good story."

"Ah, a good story. Like Malory? I understand."

Thomas laughed. "I doubt it. Not yet. Not in your state. But I think you will, over time."

A knock came at the door. "Come in."

A page opened the door. "Captain-General, we can't seem to find Countess Dystar anywhere," he said. "She may have left."

"Check behind all closed doors," Masters said dryly.

"Keep looking," Thomas said. "As long as we can't be sure she's left, keep looking."

Masters' thoughts tumbled down dark holes as Thomas spoke with the page. He was going to Gibson to look for a good story? What was he: a journalist? He'd almost been able to follow the notion of *making* good stories, but the idea of searching for one . . . The more he thought about it, the more confused he became.

"Paul," Thomas said, pulling him out of his reverie, "you look absolutely morbid. Go find that woman you told me about. Go celebrate."

Masters' thoughts immediately lightened, and he stood. "Of course, my liege."

He walked toward the door, then turned back. "What if we don't find the countess this evening?"

"You'll get a chance to speak with her when you get to Gibson."

"Of course. Good night, Thomas."

Masters went from the room, closing the door behind him.

As he passed down a corridor taking him back to the party, Masters saw Countess Dystar approaching, her arm around the waist of a diplomat from the Duchy of Oriente. Spotting Masters, she removed her hand, said a few words, and sent the diplomat back the way they'd just come. She walked quickly over to Masters, her dress rustling like dry leaves as she moved.

"Are you all right, dear?" she asked, stepping up to him, her hand hovering for just a moment near his nose, which he hid behind the bloodied handkerchief. "I heard what happened." He pulled back the handkerchief and showed her. "Oh, dear. Well. I'm sure it will heal," she said.

"It will."

"Most Regulans are boorish, but that Colonel Roush is the worst of the lot."

"He might well be," Masters said, agreeing politely.

"I wouldn't be surprised if they were the ones supplying the Goffels on my world with weapons."

"The what?"

"Goffels. The Gibson Freedom League. The guerrillas call themselves the GFL. In the city of Portent—the bastion of civilization on Gibson, let me assure you—we call them Goffels."

"And you think the Regulans are supplying the GFL? That would be . . ."

She laughed. "My, you can be serious. I was only joking, Sir Masters. No. I have no idea. Precentor Martial Arian is convinced someone is supplying them from off-world. . . . But, I'm sorry. I don't even know if you're familiar with the situation on my little planet."

"I have only recently become acquainted with the situation. In fact I'll be traveling back to Gibson with Precentor Blane, and he explained . . ." Her face fell into a pout at the mention of Blane's name. "What is it?"

"Blane is a horrid little man. Now you listen to me, you handsome Knight-aside-from-that-horrible-red-nose-you've-got, that man is trouble. Mind you, I have no proof. But whereas before I was jesting about Regulus, now I am quite serious. There's something about him I don't like. He's quite clever. Comes off as somewhat removed, interested only in Word of Blake." Masters nodded. "But he's got more up his sleeve than all of us."

She placed her hand on his arm and steered him into an alcove set into a wall. She placed her fingers on his inner thigh. "Enough politics. Let's get better acquainted. If you're going to be a guest on my world, I'll need to know more about what you like."

"Actually, the Captain-General is looking for you. He wants your summation of the war on Gibson. I'm sure these details would interest him."

Creases appeared on the countess' forehead as she frowned. "I sent him details months ago. What does he want to talk about?"

"The fact that the Gibson Loyalist forces are under the command of Precentor Martial Arian. He never heard anything about that."

"I wrote him about it months ago. I distinctly remember writing the report."

"He never received it."

"Hmmm. Odd. Must have been a mix-up here at the palace. I can't imagine ComStar—I mean Word of Blake—not passing a message as requested through the hyperpulse generator."

"He's looking into his files as well. Come, I'll walk you back to his study and we'll go over everything there."

He started to leave the alcove, but she pulled him back. "What is it with you soldiers and war? Don't you ever stop?"

"Well, my lady, you seem to have your own obsession."

"Yes, but mine doesn't . . . It's just more fun."

"The two are different, but equally engaging."

"Well, I suppose we all have to find relief from the boredom somehow."

She placed a finger in her mouth and ran it over her teeth, suddenly thoughtful. The change in her attitude piqued Masters' interest. "What do you mean *boredom*?"

"What? You haven't heard? My God, man! Everyone's bored. That's why I'm so busy pursuing bedmates, and why our race goes off and fights. We don't belong here anymore, you know." Her tone had shifted. It hadn't become serious, exactly, but she was obviously expressing something she thought to be true. "We've got models for everything—how stars glow, how to communicate instantly across light years, how atoms do whatever atoms do. We know it all. The only thing we don't understand is people. We're outside of it all. A biologist or a doctor knows everything about a human body except why he is a biologist or a doctor. We don't fit into the universe, not in any way we can understand, so we don't know what to do with ourselves."

Masters was truly confused. "But we are here."

"Exactly. But we're rather embarrassed about the whole thing. If only we could fit some model cleanly. But we don't. We're strange ghosts in the universe, the only objects in all of space that wonder what we should be doing when we wake up in the morning. I don't know what to do with myself, so I jump into beds. You shoot missiles. We get our respective thrills, and for the moment we feel better. But even I use up sex— the excitement wanes after a while, so I hunt for new partners, combinations, positions. What do you think: do we as a race never get bored with how we kill people? Is that why we keep coming up with new ways of doing it?"

"It's not the same thing."

"Oh, no. You see it as some sort of inevitable progress. . . ."

"No. . . ."

She smiled "It *is* all the same thing. We all get bored. We need the next thrill, something to jolt us enough to make us feel like more than ghosts. BattleMechs have provided fun and games for centuries, dear. But the people will want their new stimulation, their new experience. Bigger explosions, higher death tolls. People used to travel to relieve their boredom. But we've traveled to thousands of stars and realized we're all pretty much the same people. And we've always got sex, and I love it. But I've got a special appetite, and even for me sex is beginning to lose its edge. But you know what we can always make better than the last time? A bomb."

Masters felt himself threatened, but not in any way he understood. She was onto something, and he couldn't completely fathom it. He might, he knew, end up with a similar conclusion about these ideas if he pursued them, but right now they gave him vertigo.

"Let's go see the Captain-General," he said, turning away from her and beginning to walk back to Thomas' study. She followed alongside.

"This will be delightful," she said. "If you're coming to Gibson, I must arrange a tremendous party to welcome you."

6

Buried in his chair, Masters watched the Countess Dystar and Thomas discuss the situation on Gibson. He did not listen too carefully, for she was telling Thomas everything Precentor Blane had just told them. So he watched her, and was amazed to discover that she had turned her sexuality off. Somehow, the alluring redhead whom he could only imagine as busily groping for someone's thigh had become a model member of royalty: poised, business-like, and with all the facts at her fingertips. She outlined the situation clearly. But, still, he had just heard it all a short time earlier.

Soon the meeting was over, and the countess left.

"She's . . . ," Thomas began, but his words faltered. He tried again. "She's lying. I think. I don't know."

"She said exactly what Precentor Blane said."

"I know. I can't figure it out. Keep an eye on her."

"I'm sure that will be easy enough."

"What?"

Once more, a knock at the door. "Yes!" said

Thomas, his voice revealing more than a little frustration.

A page timidly opened the door. "Excuse me, Captain-General. I have a message for Sir Masters. I knew he was here."

"Go ahead, boy," said Masters.

"It's from Dame Boyer."

Masters stood. Was he going to see her after all?

"She wanted you to know she waited, but could wait no longer. She hopes to see you again soon."

He fell back in his chair. "Thank you for bringing word to me."

"You're welcome, Sir Masters." The boy left.

"A missed opportunity," Thomas mused. "All the more terrible because you can imagine how perfect it would have been."

"Oh, shut up and pour me a glass."

Thomas laughed and did just that.

Masters and Precentor Blane sat silently in the DropShip's cabin, looking out the viewport into the vast stillness of space. They were days out from the Atreus system now, and stars filled the port on their side of the ship. Without the hindrance of atmosphere, the stars shone sharp and clear, like brilliant grains of sand scattered against an infinite black beach.

"It's beautiful," Precentor Blane said.

Masters nodded agreement.

"It's the only place in the universe that's really quiet."

"I've thought the same thing."

"If only life could be like this. Clear, clean, precise. If only we could set up equipment and know everything there was to know about our lives, the same way I can determine each star's spectral class, the speed at which it's moving, and so on."

Masters remembered the countess' strange discourse. "I'm ambivalent about the quiet, actually. It's nice to come to—to think, relax. But I much prefer the mess of life."

Precentor Blane turned to Masters and gave him the bug-in-the-room look once more, and then his face softened. "Yes. Of course. We all view the universe from different perspectives." He turned once more to the stars.

Masters decided to try to build a better relation with Precentor Blane. If he was going to Gibson, he'd need as many allies in high places as he could get. "I'⸱ sorry about the troubles ComStar is having these day⸱ Precentor," he said.

"Yes, the schism. ComStar has existed for several centuries, growing stronger and stronger with each passing year. And now, it's finally cracked. To be expected, I suppose. People change. Organizations change. The core of ComStar wants to remove the 'mystical' trappings that the blessed Blake gave us. I can't understand why some people think that by giving up ritual, things will improve. For those of us who trust Blake's vision, who want to remain true to the old ways, there was nothing to do but leave."

"Well, the Free Worlds League certainly appreciates your settling here. Between Word of Blake's strength and the money and technical information the group brought with them, your presence will be a great boon."

Precentor Blane looked down at the book on Masters' lap: *Le Morte d'Arthur*. "A good book?"

"Wonderful."

"What language is that?"

Masters turned the book over and looked at the cover. "The title is Old Terran French, though the book was written in English."

A woman's voice came over the cabin's speaker.

"Attention crew and passengers," the voice said. "We will be jumping to Gibson space in one minute."

Precentor Blane closed his eyes and lowered his head. After a moment he touched the wall of the cabin with his fingertips. Masters could not help but stare, and when Precentor Blane looked up again he met Masters' gaze. "A prayer of supplication," he said.

"Oh."

"I thanked the ship for traveling this far, and wished it well through hyperspace." Masters didn't know what to say. Precentor Blane obviously caught the look of confusion, for he went on to say, "When True Believers do this, we are not asking for the machinery to work. Contrary to what popular opinion says of us, we know that all machinery works without prayer. But we want to respect the machinery made by human hands. Since technology is a fundamental part of our life, we believe that paying respect to it is paying respect to ourselves. If we do not use technology with respect, we lose respect for ourselves."

The lights dimmed and the two men looked out the viewport. The stars changed. Without pause, they had traveled to the edge of the Gibson system. The two men looked at each other and smiled. Few travelers were so jaded that the miracle of hyperspace failed to make them giddy, or sometimes even physically sick.

Masters thought back on Precentor Blane's words. The ideas appealed to him, for he saw his relationship to his 'Mech in a similar light. He couldn't use his BattleMech as only a machine of war. That was exactly the path his mother had warned him against. "Precentor, if you don't mind me asking, when we were in the Captain-General's office last week the two of you began to discuss whether the progress of technology should be restrained. . . ."

Precentor Blane raised his hand. "I know you mean no offense, but I do mind. Such matters are of intense debate within the ranks of the True Believers. Our schism has separated us from the core of ComStar. But Word of Blake has yet to fully form. There are many debates raging within our ranks. My assistant and I are constantly at each other's . . . ears. Constantly talking and trying to prove our points."

"So there may be more schisms."

"Perhaps, but I hope not. I would not want us to follow the path of the Catholic Church. The Reformation, then counter-reformations, one splinter group leading to another. But there may be no way to prevent it."

"Is that why you wanted all the Word of Blake emigrés with you on Gibson."

"It was one of the reasons. We had a solid base on Gibson, a good relationship with the government. And yes, I did not want the True Believers dispersed. I believe that if our movement is not to simply fall off the tree of ComStar and become a rotted fruit, we must remain unified."

"Interesting that you use the metaphors of a fruit and tree—living things. I would have thought all your imagery would be based on machines."

Precentor Blane smiled. "I know. It would be simpler for all outsiders if we followed a stereotype of using only mechanical allusions. But things are a bit more complicated than that. Technology does not exist without the human spirit first envisioning it. Without human flesh, organic life, there is no machinery."

During the days of travel through the Gibson solar system to the planet Gibson itself, Masters re-read passages of Malory's book.

With that came Merlin on a great black horse, and said unto Arthur, 'Thou has never done, hast thou not done enough? Of three score thousand this

*day has thou left alive but fifteen thousand, and
it is time to say Ho! For God is wroth with thee,
that thou wilt never have done, for yonder eleven
kings at this time will not be overgrown, but and
thou tarry on them any longer, thy fortune will
turn and they shall increase. And therefore with-
draw you unto your lodging, and rest you as soon
as ye may, and reward your good knights with
gold and with silver, for they have well deserved
it; there may no riches be too dear for them, for
of so few men as ye have, there were never men
did more prowess than they have done today, for
ye have matched this day with the best fighters of
the world.*

He looked up from the book. *God is wroth with
thee, that you will never have done.*

How much is done, Merlin? How much is enough?
How do we keep God pleased with us, being only human, unable to sustain peace for very long at all?

All his life Masters had read about warfare, searching for ways to win. He had learned that on ancient
Terra, in an era when technology was no more than
the ability to make pots, warring tribes used to remove
the feathers they wore for accurate hunting of game. This
change made the war between humans much less le-
thal, for these primitives made a distinction between
hunting game and fighting humans. War was a dance,
with much sound and fury, but only a bit of death.
When a warrior was downed, both sides departed the
battlefield, one side to celebrate, one to mourn.

A good 'Mech battle was like that. The number of
ruined 'Mechs could usually be counted on one hand.
And the combat was carried out with respect. You
could see your opponents on the battlefield. You knew
you were fighting *someone*, not sending out random
bits of metal to smash into some unknowing soldier.

He closed the book, and looked at Precentor Blane, now fast asleep on the bunk opposite him. A new generation was coming up, spurred on by ancient secrets once held safe by ComStar and the True Believers. Soldiers had new toys to play with as technology in the Inner Sphere made its slow climb back up from the near-Armageddon suffered generations past. Little academy cherubs incubated in a time of peace knew only that war existed and was reportedly glorious. They wanted a piece of that. But they didn't know about the *beast* of war, the creature that could crawl through a population's spine and turn them from a people at war into ghouls craving blood and flesh.

Outside the cabin viewport the world of Gibson came into view as the JumpShip maneuvered into orbit. They approached from the night side, over the continent of Jakarta, where the Word of Blake immigrants had settled and where most of the war was taking place. Across the dark orb the lights of cities glowed like distant stars.

The DropShip separated from the JumpShip and descended toward the planet. It fell toward the city of Portent, the world's capital, the ship's bottom burning bright white. It fell quickly, and then touched down.

Precentor Blane and Masters walked along the passages of the DropShip. "I'll get my *Phoenix Hawk* off the ship and meet up with you outside," Masters said.

"Fine, fine. I'll arrange for our transport to the Principal's palace."

"The palace?"

"Of course. There's a party tonight. In your honor."

"I didn't know anything about it."

"A surprise."

Masters hated surprises. "I'd really rather get out in the field. Get to work."

"One night, Sir Masters. The countess, Principal

Hsiang, countless useless functionaries—they'll all be very disappointed. Come now. Let the people see their first real Knight of the Inner Sphere."

Masters couldn't argue that point. It was vital that the Knights make themselves known. They must become a palpable presence. "Very well. But first I must get my 'Mech off the DropShip."

"Meet me by the Officers Staff Pool. I'll have a car waiting." Precentor Blane looked at him awkwardly, as if unable to say something. "Welcome to Gibson, Sir Masters," he said finally. "It will be good to have someone here I can trust."

"You trust me, sir? I would never have guessed."

"There is much I must keep secret from you. But you are a friend of Thomas, and thus I know you are trustworthy." With that Blane turned and headed off.

Large crates filled the DropShip's massive cargo bay, and workers used forklifts to move the crates off the ship along a ramp to the starport's tarmac. At the far end of the metal cavern stood Masters' *Phoenix Hawk*. The 'Mech still shone with its fresh coat of red and silver paint, the new colors of the Knights of the Inner Sphere.

Closer still he saw Jen working up in the *Phoenix Hawk*'s cockpit. Jen was his Tech, one of the best he'd ever had. "Morning, Jen!"

She looked down, a smile for him on her tanned and wrinkled face. He couldn't see her eyes clearly at this distance, but he knew they sparkled with that peculiar, calm wisdom of hers. "Morning, Sir Masters."

He began climbing up the ladder hanging down the leg of the 'Mech. "Anything wrong with him?"

"No. Just wanted to give him a final tune-up before you took him out. Better now than having me run out with my tool kit in the middle of a battle. I also put in the communication codes for the Word of Blake and Gibson Loyalist forces."

He climbed up to the edge of the cockpit and watched her replace a few of the older wires. "Did you arrange for a ride out to the base?"

"Yes, though I won't be going out to the Tactical Operations Center, since I found out you're going to be stationed at a 'Mech lance outpost with a platoon of infantry attached. I'll be waiting for you there after you meet up with Arian."

"A 'Mech lance outpost?"

"They're keeping the units spread out and small," Jen said, without diverting her attention from her work. "It seems there are few large-scale engagements." She stopped and sighed and looked up at him. "It's the new war, Paul. The new ways leading to the old ways."

"Well, I'll see what I can do about that."

"I know you will."

"We've only been here ten minutes. You found all this out already?"

"That is, I believe, why you keep me around."

He laughed. "Right. Well, I've got a party to go to tonight . . ."

"Looks like this knight business certainly has its perks."

"Anyway, I won't be going out to the outpost until tomorrow. Go on out there and scout the situation for me."

"Yes, sir. And have a good time tonight."

"I doubt it."

When Jen was done Masters slipped around her and into the cockpit, while she began her descent down the ladder. The cockpit was in near darkness, the only illumination coming through the tinted faceplate, which filtered the cargo bay's light considerably.

He picked up his neurohelmet and pulled it down over his head and shoulders. The device allowed the

'Mech to use a pilot's own natural sense of balance to stay upright. The machine's gyros would serve for typical movement, but for quick maneuvering, the human ear was the best thing going. It also acted as the 'Mech's security system. After the computer verified his access code, the console controls lit up. The control panels washed the small cockpit red, blue, and green, and the screens before him flickered to life.

He placed his left hand on the throttle and pushed it forward just a bit. He felt the engines revving up and the grinding of the myomer bundles that mimicked human muscle. The left leg lifted, moved forward and came down with a heavy thud. The right leg did the same. Shocks ran up the 'Mech, and although the stabilizers mitigated most of the vibrations, Masters felt clearly the forty-five tons of walking metal beneath him. He smiled. He loved this.

He looked down and saw the cargo crews stop their work to stare up at his 'Mech. On their faces he saw amazement and not a little fear. He turned the 'Mech toward the door of the cargo bay, thinking how good it was to be a MechWarrior.

=== 7 ===

Masters brought his *Phoenix Hawk* to the BattleMech security area, where he left it before joining Precentor Blane at the Staff Car Pool. The Gibson sky glowed yellow overhead. In the distance long, dark clouds raked the horizon. The air was warm, but a tinge of cold evening air had begun to gather.

A black limousine with two small flags mounted on either side of the hood awaited him. The first banner showed a red chimera on a blue field, the flag created when Gibson broke off from the Principality of Regulus and joined with the worlds of Molokai and Clipper to create the Principality of Gibson. The second flag belonged to Word of Blake. It displayed a sword, pointing down, with a new version of ComStar's symbol incorporated into the sword's cross-hilt. Masters could see that a bond had developed between Hsiang's government and the True Believers, and it had formed quickly and with great strength.

A chauffeur stepped out of the car and opened a door for Masters. The man wore a black uniform and his eyes shone with a light that caught Masters off guard. He held the door carefully, as if it were the hand of a small child, something to be nurtured. A True Believer, Masters thought, even more ardent in his devotion than Blane.

Masters slid into the back seat where Precentor Blane sat pouring himself a drink from the bar. "Ah," said the rotund man.

"I'd like to change before the party."

"All been taken care of. A room is waiting for you at Castle Dystar, where the countess invites you to spend the night as her guest. You'll be able to dress and clean up there, and then be taken to the party at Hsiang's palace."

"Quite an itinerary."

"I imagine everyone will want a little piece of you, Sir Masters." Precentor Blane winked.

The car started up and drove through the narrow streets winding through the starport. Masters watched avidly out the window, noticing that the local populace wore a grab-bag mix of clothes from Terran cultures pre-dating Kerensky's Exodus—men in dashikis, women in turbans and dirndl dresses or kimonos. He'd heard that the various groups among the Gibson population had clung tenaciously to their ethnic Terran heritages and it seemed to be true. If he remembered correctly, the people of Gibson had broken away from the Principality of Regulus when the Regulan rulers wanted to impose Hinduism as the state religion. Even the Gibson Hindus had balked at the idea. "I noticed the Word of Blake flag on the car along with the Gibson flag," Masters said, turning away from the sights.

"Well, yes," Blane said, nearly coughing up his whiskey.

"The second flag is usually the House Marik bird of prey."

"Not our idea, actually. Hsiang suggested it, and then implemented it before we could respond. He said it's for the duration of the war. He's really quite fond of us. The arrival of the Word of Blake emigrés makes Gibson a very important world, and will probably make it very rich.''

Masters nodded. The situation disquieted him. He began to understand why Thomas wanted him here. For three hundred years, ComStar had controlled interstellar communications through their sole monopoly of the hyperpulse generators that sent messages across the vast distances of space. Now the splinter group, Word of Blake, had that power in the Free Worlds League. If there was anything dangerous brewing that involved Word of Blake, Thomas might not hear about it until it was too late. As of yet, nothing seemed particularly wrong. But that didn't mean it would stay that way.

By the time they left the starport, night had fallen over Portent, and stars glittered above. The limousine passed through an industrial district, then drove up a ramp to an express causeway where it picked up real speed. From the elevated road Masters saw the city's lights form an almost perfect, huge disk. The swift limo was at the edge, driving in toward the center.

Gazing down from the road he saw what looked like a small town built of wood scraps and cardboard. He looked at Blane. ''What's that down there?''

''What do you mean?''

''The shacks. The people standing around fires.''

''Crops.''

''What?''

Blane laughed ''Sorry. That's what we call them. Crops. Villagers and farmers who've moved to the city.''

They'd left the shanty-town behind now and Masters watched as the neighborhoods below seemed to improve in quality. ''Why would they move to the city?''

"Pacification program. We've been tearing down villages and towns to prevent the GFL from using them as bases."

"And they choose to come here?"

"Well, we encourage it. In the city we can keep an eye on everyone. We'd rather have control, especially around Portent. Out in the fields, well, we just don't know what's going on."

"And they live in shacks made of pressboard?"

A look of sadness passed over Blane's face. "Yes. Well, I suppose you could say that the program leaves much to be desired in many respects. But once we get everything settled . . ." His voice trailed off and he sipped his drink.

Looking down at the areas beneath the causeway, Masters watched the architectural styles flash by. They were like the rings of a cut tree, marking the phases of the city's growth. To the right he noted a style of construction that must date from the height of Merschmidt's influence. Further ahead was a run-down area probably built during the Regulan minimalist period. They were moving back in time, each style older than the last, until finally, far ahead, the stars suddenly vanished.

"Good god," Masters said softly.

At the core of the city stood the Old Walls, built by Gibson's first settlers, long before terraforming had turned Gibson from a waterless planet of orange stone into a world covered with giant yellow trees and grass. In the darkness of night, the Old Walls rose like a chunk of darkness hundreds of meters high, blocking the view of the stars beyond. As they approached, Masters saw that the Walls were made of thick, silver metal blocks. Closer still, and the white light of the moon revealed a deep aqua-green corrosion that had spread across the surface of the walls. The corrosion swirled and curled in and around on itself, forming fascinating patterns of alternating silver and thick, textured green.

Soon they came to the base of the wall, which seemed to reach for the sky. Craning his neck back, Masters suffered a moment of vertigo as the wall spun endlessly up. Then a ceiling crashed down on his vision as the limousine passed into a long, wide tunnel. A string of lights ran along the curved ceiling. The lights seemed to go on forever, but soon Masters saw a patch of darkness far ahead, marking the tunnel's end.

The air chilled quickly as they drove through the tunnel. Within five minutes they had entered a massive well form by the Old Wall. The roof of the Old Wall had been removed generations ago when Gibson's air had become breathable, and the stars shone clearly overhead. The walls within had been spared the corrosive effects of the planet's old environment, and glowed with smooth, silver light reflected from the city and the moon. Within was a three-dimensional maze of silver buildings connected by elevated tunnels. The causeway looped around the wall several stories off the ground, held in place with thick braces. Various exit ramps led down into the Old City.

"This looks big enough to be its own city," Masters said.

"Essentially it is. It's the Old City. It has its own service industries, tech support, and so on. It houses the core of the planet's civil servants and government offices. Everything that affects the planet is controlled here, so more gets done in less time."

"Is that the Countess Dystar's castle?" Masters pointed to a large gothic structure that clung to the Old Walls at the south end. The huge building grew out of the smooth silver metal, kept in place with thick flying buttresses that attached to the walls, roof, and base of the building. Dark and intricate, the castle looked out over the Old City like a brooding guard dog.

"Yes," Precentor Blane said. "And down below is the Principal Hsiang's palace." Masters looked in the direction indicated and saw a sprawling silver building with many tall columns. He couldn't be sure from this distance, but he thought he saw several large statues sprinkled along the roof and exterior stairs. At a glance the structure looked like another grab bag of "impressive" styles, each elegant enough in its own way, but garbage when tossed together.

"And on the other side—I don't know if you can see it—there's a large building complex." Masters saw it. It fit in with the rest of the Old City's style, built hundreds of years ago. Wide, squat buildings with few windows and little ornamentation.

"That's where the True Believer business offices have settled. We run everything from there, and make our contacts with the other corporations on Gibson. Our military—that is, the True Believer military—command center is also located there. However, Precentor Martial Arian has set up a Tactical Operation Center out in the field. He's usually there." Blane paused, then a pleased pride filled his voice. "The True Believers have been here less than two years, but I think we've already settled in well."

"And the people in the shacks at the edge of the city?"

"Excuse me?"

"Have they settled in well?"

"Sir Masters, I can't say I like your tone. We've come to Gibson with money to invest. The crops—the people out there—the farmers, don't know what's good for them. When the Star League collapsed centuries ago they adopted an agrarian-based economy, and have obstinately remained backward. It's time for them to move on. Everybody wants it to happen. Countess Dystar. Principal Hsiang.''

"And the farmers? Do they want it?"

Precentor Blane stared over his glass at Masters. "You just became part of a military ruling elite. Did you ask the people permission for that?" Masters started to reply, but Precentor Blane cut him off. "You and I both know that leaders must make decisions for their people. It is the way of the stars."

"Sir, I mean no offense in saying this, but you are not of these people."

"Wrong, Sir Masters! Wrong! We are now citizens of Gibson."

"Yet you have established a separate military, separate offices, have made direct ties into the government as Word of Blake."

"As we must if we are to survive." Blane threw up one hand in a gesture of dismissal. "Enough. That is enough. We will discuss this no further."

They traveled the last leg of the trip in silence.

The limousine left the elevated causeway and continued a short distance through the streets of the Old City, where Masters saw well-dressed people filling the walks of tidy, clean streets. Laughter mingled with the warm air. The evening reminded him of his youth; going out for entertainment with other MechWarriors, their uniforms sharp and pressed. The people of the Old City oozed that feeling, that buzz of anticipation. Well-dressed, well-fed, sure of themselves. Odd, he thought, that an entire city should remind me of my adolescence.

The limousine turned down a wide, empty road and drove into a fenced, well-guarded heliport. The guards checked the IDs of Masters, Precentor Blane, and the chauffeur, then waved them through.

Ahead a helicopter was warming up, its blade winding slowly around the engine. "I'll see you in a short while," Precentor Blane said coldly and politely as he and Masters climbed out of the limousine. The chauffeur stepped around and transferred Masters' bags to the helicopter.

Masters was equally polite. "Yes. I look forward to it."

Soon he was seated in the helicopter, riding high above the buildings, floating toward Castle Dystar. Masters kept his eyes fixed on the building, which was covered with tall spires and, yes, gargoyles. Directly ahead a massive terrace extended from the castle walls. Three other choppers rested there. A fourth was just taking off.

Lining one wall were large windows, ten meters high, their panes cutting the glass into large diamonds. A warm yellow light filled the rooms behind the glass.

The helicopter drifted toward the helipad and within minutes had settled down on it. The chopper's blades were still beating the air as Masters jumped out. The roar of the machinery filled his ears, and the air rushed around him wildly. He reached back in to pull out his bags, then took quick strides to clear the helicopter, which soon took off and away again soon after.

Even with the helicopter gone, the wind continued to whip around him. Masters turned and looked out over the Old City. Encased in the Old Walls, it looked like a miniature created with great care.

"Sir Masters!" It was a woman's voice calling from behind him. He turned back toward the castle and his mind tumbled in several directions. A woman stood in the doorway leading from the landing platforms to the castle. She looked to be in her early thirties, and wore a long, dark skirt and white blouse. Over the blouse she had on a waist-length tweed jacket, tapered to accentuate her figure. Three pins made of brass were pinned to the jacket over her right breast. Her body was slim and small, her flesh smooth and brown, her straight black hair cut to just below her ears. His thoughts finished tumbling and the first concrete idea that formed in his head was, "Please, please don't be involved with anybody."

"Sir Masters," she said again, walking toward him now, a hand extended in greeting. She moved with a long, confident stride and Masters could see both cleverness and puzzles in her eyes. "I'm Maid Kris. I've been sent to retrieve you."

He also extended his hand, gathering his wits and putting on a friendly smile "A pleasure," he said.

"If you'll follow me, please." She turned and walked toward the castle. With his bags in hand he followed her through the dark, chill corridors of the castle, their footsteps echoing with sharp precision. "Your trip was pleasant?" she asked without looking at him.

"Pleasant enough. Better now."

She looked at him now, an eyebrow arched interrogatively. He smiled at her, and she smiled back politely, then turned her attention forward once again.

After a few more steps she asked, "You are here as a Knight of the Inner Sphere?"

"Yes." When she had said nothing more for a long while, he asked, "Does that trouble you?"

"What do you fight for? If you don't mind me asking."

"I fight for my liege. Captain-General Thomas Marik wants the war to end, and I'm here to help end it."

The look she threw him said that he had no idea what he was getting involved with. "More soldiers will not end this war." Her voice was cold and final. "Your room, Sir Masters." She stepped up to a door and pulled a key from a pocket in her jacket. She unlocked the door and entered the room, looking about approvingly. Masters followed. There was a large canopy bed, an oak dresser, and a door leading to a dressing room and bath. The chamber was as sumptuous as his guest quarters in Thomas' palace.

He turned to her. "I don't suppose you want to tell me why you believe this war cannot be ended by military means."

"I . . . ," she began quickly, but suddenly stopped. "Is there anything else I can do for you right now?" She took two steps backward toward the door.

Masters followed her. "You can tell me why you think there is no military solution to the conflict on your world."

She stared into his eyes, defiant. "No, I can't."

"I am here to end this war. I will use whatever means necessary to do so, as long as it is the appropriate solution. I think you can help me. Am I right? I'm looking for information. What can you tell me?"

"Your knights are supposed to be a self-congratulatory, noble lot. Why don't you figure it out yourself?"

"Well, we don't see it quite that way."

"What do you have to offer that the Word of Blake MechWarriors cannot give to the cause of the war?"

"My loyalties are to Thomas Marik. And Thomas is a just man. I am here to bring his justice."

She looked at him carefully, searching his eyes. Then he saw her decide not to trust him. "No. I really can't talk to you about it." She turned and walked toward the door.

"Will I see you later tonight? At the party?"

She gave him a smile that seemed to wrap within it a hidden meaning. "Oh, yes. Everyone will be there."

8

The helicopter's blades beat the air with a rhythmic thrum as it floated toward Principal Hsiang's palace. Maid Kris sat in front next to the pilot. Sitting beside Masters was Countess Dystar wearing a strapless green evening gown with a plunging bodice. Twice she placed her hand on his right knee, and both times he gently removed it.

"Yes, the True Believers tell me they need more troops, and I've been hiring them as they request them," she said in answer to his question, clearly bored. After he removed her hand the second time, she looked away from him and out the window, a child showing her anger.

"Where are you getting them?"

"From many worlds. Most are not professionals, just men and women looking for work. Some are veterans who've been attached to 'Mech units before. I understand that some were even in the Wolf Pack, but only a few."

"Where do they get their training?"

"Right here. The True Believers have training camps

on Gibson. I'm told the war is going very well." Masters saw Maid Kris' shoulders jerk slightly at Countess Dystar's words, but he couldn't guess why they so affected her.

Soon the palace came into view, an ugly amalgamation of pillars, statues of naked, muscular men, and fountains. "Who did the charming decor?" Masters asked, shaking his head slightly at the sight of so many phalli. It looked like someone had been very desperate to impress.

"Principal Hsiang himself," Maid Kris said. "He redecorated after taking office."

"Lovely."

Maid Kris looked back at him with a rueful smile.

Once the helicopter had touched down on the pad, Masters helped the countess out. Maid Kris got out on her own, then stood, waiting patiently for any orders from the countess. Masters quickly realized that she was very protective and responsible to the countess whenever eyes were on her, but that her expression showed something just next to malice when she believed herself unobserved.

They walked through the night toward a large pair of open double doors, from which the sound of dancing music drifted out. The air was now cool, and Masters was pleasantly surprised that the temperatures could drop so much on the continent of Jakarta, even during the summer months. When they reached the doors, Countess Dystar turned to him and said, "Wait here, Sir Knight." She stepped through the door, followed at a discreet distance by Maid Kris, and the music suddenly ceased. Then came a burst of polite applause. When it subsided, he heard the strong voice of the countess saying, "Ladies and gentlemen, I am taking the floor tonight, on this very special occasion, to present to you, Sir Paul Masters, Knight of the Inner Sphere."

The applause began again, now loud and over-whelming. On cue Masters stepped forward and through the door, coming to the top of a staircase lead-ing down into the ballroom. He drew in a sharp breath at the sight of the huge room, with its gold-painted walls, giant chandeliers, and the hundreds of guests facing him, applauding and smiling. The moment swept him up. For his status of knight to matter to these people moved him deeply. He glanced at Maid Kris, who was gazing steadily out over the crowd, re-vealing nothing.

He raised his hand and the clamor eventually set-tled. With the sudden quiet he realized that something must be said, but he had no idea what. Opening his mouth he let the first words that came to him tumble out. "Good people of Gibson, I bring you greetings from Captain-General Thomas Marik. He wants you to know that he is apprised of the situation on your world, and that he has sent me to help bring peace back to your planet. By working together, we can bring this to pass."

Applause once more filled the room. The countess took his arm and let Masters lead her down the stairs. Maid Kris followed. When they reached the foot, well-wishers rushed forward, crowding around. They wore tuxedos, Gibson military uniforms, gowns, Word of Blake adept robes, and many other colorful and textured garments. They thrust their hands at him, clapping him on the back and shaking his arm vigorously.

The people followed him and for a good hour Mas-ters had little control over his movement or his focus. They approached him, sometimes alone, sometimes in groups, wanting to shake his hand and say hello. By the time the crush ended, however, the first exhilara-tion had changed to sadness. So many of these people demanded his attention simply because he was now famous, not because of what he represented. He could tell by the way they greeted him that it was simply the countess' introduction that made him seem valuable, not that he was a member of an elite group of Mech-Warriors backed by a vision.

Eventually he secured a corner by a table well-stocked with bottles of champagne. Every once in a while another person would come over to greet him, but he ended the conversation quickly after a polite shaking of hands. An hour and a half after his arrival Masters looked up from his champagne bubbles and saw Precentor Blane on the other side of the room. Blane appeared to be arguing with a tall man who had a pencil-thin mustache and was wearing the white robe of a Word of Blake adept. They spoke with great animation, and finally Precentor Blane turned on his heel, looking upset. He went up the steps Masters had so recently descended, leaving the party.

A short oriental man in an olive green suit suddenly blocked his sight of the adept. Behind the man was a tremendously tall redhead, her right hand on the short man's shoulder. Both were obviously on their way toward Masters. Though dressed expensively, the tall woman radiated something cheap. Masters thought they could be a pimp and a prostitute who might have bribed some corrupt official to let them into the ballroom to drum up business.

The small man walked directly up to Masters and smiled broadly. "Hello, Sir Masters, Knight of the Inner Sphere." He opened his small arms as expansively as he could. "I've thrown a very big party for you. Do you like it?"

A terrifying realization snapped across Masters' mind as he suddenly recognized the short man's face from newscasts. "Ah, Principal Hsiang," he said, extending his hand. Hsiang shook it. "A pleasure to meet you. Yes, the party is lovely."

As he turned toward the red-haired woman, she

caught his eye. The tip of her tongue appeared between her lips. Hsiang caught Masters' expression, and said, "You like, eh? My wife. Ha!"

"Ah. Yes. Very lovely. A pleasure to meet you, Madam."

As they shook hands she pressed the tips of her long red fingernails against his wrist. "The pleasure is all mine," she said smoothly.

He disengaged his flesh from her nails and turned back to Principal Hsiang. "I'm honored, sir."

"All for you. It cost me ten thousand Marik bills."

"Your wife?"

"The party."

"I'm honored."

"Good."

"And well you should be," said a new voice. The man who had been arguing with Precentor Blane now appeared next to him with disturbing abruptness. "Adept Starling. First-Assistant to Precentor Blane. Principal Hsiang can be very generous, but he only lavishes such attention on people he truly believes deserve it."

Hsiang bowed his head in false humility.

"I'm honored," Masters said yet again.

"You should be," said Hsiang's wife.

"I am."

"Good," said Starling. He eyed Masters up and down. "So, Sir Masters, to what do we owe the honor of your presence on Gibson?"

"To whom," Masters corrected him. "I am here at the command of my liege. He asked me to come to your lovely world to help your forces bring a swift peace to Gibson."

"We have the matter well in hand," said Starling. "The war is well on schedule. It will be over within three months, with or without your help."

Masters stared at Starling. "Sir, if I didn't know

that you and your people were on the world of Gibson as guests of my liege, I'd think you were being rude."

"Not at all. Just prideful. A failing among religious zealots. Or hadn't you heard?" said Starling. Hsiang laughed three sharp barks, and his wife gave a wry smile. "What faith do you practice, Sir Masters?"

"I no longer follow the religion of my parents, but they raised me a Catholic."

"I have a theory regarding cases such as yours. Would you like to hear it?"

"As I'm sure it would please you to speak it, certainly."

"The old religions are kept in motion these days through inertia. Yes, the old Terran religions—Christianity, Judaism, Buddhism, Islam, and others—have survived down the centuries from their in-the-mud origins. But they were written without the knowledge of what humanity would one day create, that we would one day become symbiotic with machinery."

Masters blinked. "Are you referring to biocomputer interfaces? I've heard of some experimental work being done along those lines for BattleMechs. . . ."

Starling gave a soft, condescending chuckle. "Oh, no, no, no. Nothing so elaborate. I refer only to the fact that . . ." He paused in thought, his eyes looking upward. "Well, if you were to walk through this city, you would see only objects that are made by man. In fact, given the peculiar nature of the Old City, you would not even see the natural horizon. The limits of our vision are contained by the massive and impressive Old Walls. We are all, right now, standing in an environment almost entirely manmade. Even the air we breathe was arranged by human hand."

"We have a park," Hsiang said in a sad and disappointed voice.

"True enough. A park. There is a grove of Gibson's lovely trees standing at the center of the city. Planted and arranged by people. Perhaps the only organic spot in the entire metropolis.''

"And what has this to do with religion?"

"Well, to the Word of Blake, everything, for our faith exists in the space between humanity and machinery. What does it have to do with the old Terran faiths? Very little. And that's my point. If you look at the imagery in the old religions, they speak of gardens, trees, flowers, animals, deserts, rivers. What has any of this to do with us, the human race, which travels through the cold, empty distances of space?" He laughed loudly. "In the New Testament, Jesus ascends to the heavens—not his spirit, you might recall, but his actual body. Well, where did it go? Did it travel sublight? If so, it is still floating in a straight line through the Milky Way Galaxy after three thousand years, with hundreds of thousands of light years yet to travel. Or did the Christian God have a jump drive back then to snap his son to 'heaven' as soon as Jesus cleared orbit?"

Masters shrugged, not sure where the discussion was going.

"You don't know? Well, neither does anyone else. And why not? Because a body floating up through the heavens doesn't have the same meaning anymore. When *we* float through the heavens it's in our faster-than-light ships. The first idea is simply false. We don't think that way anymore because we've learned the truth about the nature of space, physics, biology. The old religions have tried to shed as much of their extraneous baggage as possible, but their roots are still mired in the past, a past without technology, a past without science. How familiar are you with the history of the Christian Church?"

"Not very, I'm suddenly afraid to admit."

"Well, some time ago on Terra, the Church promoted the belief that Terra was the center of the universe. The idea was, apparently, that the rest of the universe was simply for show. Well, after a great deal of experimentation, calculations, torture, and excommunications, the Church had to admit that it had made a mistake. So it rewrote its beliefs to keep up with the times. My point is that these religions cannot keep rewriting themselves fast enough to keep up with reality. Just as the Church held onto its beliefs long after the time to give them up had passed, so people today cling to the old faiths. But with time, Word of Blake will claim the souls of the Inner Sphere.''

"Aren't both ComStar and Word of Blake too exclusive to attain such goal?''

"The time has not yet arrived. The time is getting closer, however. The split in ComStar is the beginning. The signs are here. And we have your liege's hospitality, and the hospitality of Principal Hsiang, to see ourselves through to the fruition of our faith.'' He nodded to Hsiang, who again returned the nod.

"You are here to help us, to aid us at the orders of the Captain-General,'' the little man said. "What do you need from us?''

"All I need now is to get out into the field. I've got a bed waiting for me at Castle Dystar, and with some sleep, I'll be gone in the morning.''

"Excellent!'' cried Hsiang. Then, with the same enthusiasm, he asked, "It is so terrible outside of the city. Are you sure you would not prefer to stay here?''

The question caught Masters off guard, but he said, "No, I really want to get to the battlefield. I'm looking forward to it. That's my job.''

"Most of my commanders live here,'' Hsiang said happily.

"And they do a fine job,'' Starling added quickly. "But other soldiers must be in the thick of it. Correct, Sir Masters?''

"Exactly," said Masters slowly. He looked down at Hsiang. "Why are your commanders here?"

"Brave men must be ready to defend the Principal, don't you think? If the city is taken, there is nothing left."

"Ah." Things were getting a bit strange now, but Masters was simply too exhausted to pursue the matter. "Well, if you'll forgive me, all this talk of rest has reminded me of how tired I am. Thank you very much, Principal Hsiang. It was a pleasure to meet you, Mrs. Hsiang. First-Assistant Precentor Starling."

After each had said goodnight in turn, Masters made his way across the ballroom to the large double doors leading to the helipad. As he went, he could not shake the feeling that three sets of eyes were boring into his back.

He stopped and bid the Countess goodnight. Her hand rested on the arm of a young soldier in the Loyalist Gibson forces. She smiled to him, as if to say she'd exchange the boy for him in a moment, but he smiled back, shook his head, and continued on.

Back outside he found Maid Kris speaking with a man in overalls stained with dirt and grass. Seeing Masters approach, the man suddenly assumed a mask of humility and slumped his shoulders. Turning sharply Maid Kris caught sight of Masters, but she neither greeted nor acknowledged him. She said a few more words to the man, who then walked off into the shadows of the trees, throwing Masters a slightly idiotic smile as he went.

"Who was that?" Masters asked her.

"Is it your place to question to whom I speak?"

He put up a hand and said, "I'm sorry."

She decided to tell him anyway. "That was Cao, one of the palace gardeners."

"But more than that."

She looked at him, her eyes cold and steady. "I wouldn't know what you're talking about."

"Maid Kris, despite your hostility, I believe you may be the only person here whom I can trust. Everyone else . . ." He waved his hand, unsure of exactly how to express it. "Precentor Blane is fighting with his first assistant. Both Blane and the countess claim to have little knowledge of the war. Hsiang looks like a pimp. . . ."

Maid Kris laughed loudly.

"What?"

"Nothing. That is exactly what many of us think of him. Maybe I might like you after all. After a while."

He dropped his tone. "Maid Kris, I need help *now*. I think you know what's going on. There are layers of—"

"No," she said firmly, and looked away.

He grabbed her arm. "We don't have time for this."

She turned quickly, facing him, and he thought she might call for help. But when she spoke it was in a voice full of quiet anger. "Let go of me or I'll kill you."

He didn't know if she could do it, but he was certain she'd try. He let go of her. "I'm going to the war tomorrow."

"And?" She kept her eyes on him, wary of any movement he might make.

"I'm here to find out what's going on. Won't you help me?"

"You say you're here to find out? Then go to the war. See the war. You'll be the first person to leave these walls and do that. Go see the war, and you'll understand more than I could possibly tell you on this night, on the grounds of this palace, under the spell of romantic dance music. Go to the war, go to the killing, and you'll know what I know. If you are what you claim to be, noble knight, you will see more than enough.''

She turned and walked back to the party. He saw her body change, the tension released from her shoulders and spine, the fighting spirit soften for courtly presentation. Whoever she worked for was very, very lucky.

Masters continued on toward the helipad. How had she phrased it? ''Go to the war, go to the killing.'' Yes. Tomorrow he'd be back in his 'Mech. Finally home and where he belonged.

Part 2

KILLING

9

Masters' *Phoenix Hawk* strode across the countryside, the low morning sun casting the 'Mech's shadow
long and thin across a sea of yellow grass. To the west
rose terribly blue mountains, craggy and tall. Ahead,
to the north, lived a vast forest of giant trees covered
with yellow leaves.

With his early start, Masters would reach the Nagasaki Valley and meet up with Precentor Martial Arian by early afternoon. Though it was his 'Mech that
did the actual walking, he felt that his being expanded
to fill out the metal form of the machine, and that it
was actually he who walked—but he walked as a giant.
The technology did not do this; his neurohelmet did
not connect sensation from the 'Mech to the pilot. It
was Masters' imagination at work.

Inside the cockpit the red, green, and blue lights of
the rocker switches and controls washed colors over
his face. He wore the MechWarrior's typical piloting
clothes, the shorts and cooling vest that was all one
could stand in that heat that built up inside a 'Mech
during battle.

Walking along and taking in the terrain, Masters decided to reconfigure his weapons. Though his own experience was mainly in 'Mech combat, he knew that the Gibson Freedom League depended on guerrillas working their way through forests. That meant he had to change his strategy a bit. On his first weapon trigger, a blue thumb-button on the joystick, he aligned his extended-range large laser with his short-range missiles. That would let him chew up trees and remove the guerrillas' cover. He then set his pulse laser and his machine guns to the green thumb-trigger. He'd use these to sweep over exposed guerrillas and remove smaller trees and remaining debris. His anti-missile system he left on his red finger-trigger. Unless he met Countess Dystar's renegade 'Mechs, he probably wouldn't need them.

He glanced at his display, currently set for long-range. Jen had loaded the programs for the terrain around Portent and the Nagasaki Valley, and he watched computer graphics of forests and rivers roll by on the screen as he traveled northwest.

When a red blip appeared from the west edge of the screen, he punched a button and got an ID. It was a Loyalist-controlled Earthwerks T-420 hovercraft, currently used by the First Squad out of the lance outpost Masters was going to command. The former lance commander, Captain Verner, had been killed two weeks earlier in a surprise raid.

Masters touched the glowing radio stud on the console. "First Squad H-craft, First Squad H-craft. This is Phoenix Hawk One."

The speakers in the neurohelmet crackled to life, producing a rich and jovial male voice, somewhat muffled by the whine of the hovercraft's engines. "This is First Squad H-craft. Pleasure to have you planetside, sir. Sergeant Jacobs here, though most folks call me Chick. Ah, there you are. We weren't picking you up right away. Good to have you here, though. We'll attach to you as soon as you arrive.''

Masters glanced at his display. The blue blip had grown close now. ''Just out of curiosity, First Squad H-craft, what are you doing out here?''

''Phoenix Hawk One, we lost a patrol out around here last night. Picked up a fierce firefight over the comm, but then nothing from them. Now we're just trying to help the wounded and claim the bodies.''

''How many soldiers?''

''Twelve in the squad. Haven't heard from any of them.''

''Want some help?''

''Yes, sir.''

''Just tell me where you want me to look.''

Chick gave coordinates, and Masters accelerated his 'Mech toward the area. Once there he slowed down and began a careful search. The trees in this forest were so large that the lowest branches were at cockpit level, and he could maneuver his 'Mech easily around the thick trunks. The branches grew long and twisted and around each other in maze-like knots. Huge yellow leaves, twice the size of a hand, grew from the branches. Every once in a while a leaf floated from a tree, releasing white spores as it wafted one way and then another. Under these great trees stood smaller ones and extensive underbrush.

Masters wandered through the forest in his *Phoenix Hawk,* twisting his 'Mech's torso and head every so often to look left and right. After forty minutes he saw a patch of forest floor that had been chewed up by grenade blasts. He thought he might be in the area of the fight, but didn't want to call Chick until certain.

Just after passing around a thick group of trees, he saw the bodies—two women and one man, their chests cut open by machine gun fire. He saw that they wore the gray-green fatigues of the Loyalist army. ''First

Squad H-craft. This is Phoenix Hawk One. I think I've got your dead here.''

"How many, sir?''

"Right now, just three. There may be more in the area.''

"Sir, if you don't mind me saying, just stay in your tinman and wait until we get there.''

"Right,'' said Masters, but he paid no attention to the warning. He popped the canopy and dug an Imperator submachine gun out from behind his seat. Taking the gun, he climbed down the 'Mech to the forest floor, where he looked around and listened. Hearing a scraping noise to his right, he turned and saw a dark rodent scurry across the dirt. The animal paused briefly for one moment, looked Masters in the eye with its soulless black pupils, then rushed up the tree trunk. It disappeared into the vast maze of the tree's yellow leaves.

Waiting a bit longer, he heard nothing else, and so walked toward the bodies on the ground. Closer now he saw white maggots roiling within the revealed guts of the corpses. The eyes of the soldiers looked up, their stare blank and unseeing. He saw too that bits of flesh had been taken out of the bodies, the work of forest scavengers.

As an officer Masters had often confronted death or, for the sake of the group, been forced to send soldiers on missions that promised almost certain death. But he had never become used to it. He knew some soldiers who did, having learned to turn off all feeling once in awhile, becoming nothing more than BattleMechs without pilots. But few could accept a shredded corpse easily. Even the corpse of an enemy, once emptied of a soul and no longer a threat, had too much in common with the living observer to be dismissed completely.

He found the ruined bodies before him particularly

distressing. A 'Mech battle usually involved a few dozen 'Mechs at most, the damage being kept to a minimum because of the machines' heavy armor. In 'Mech combat the true test was of the soldier's piloting skill under pressure, not a soldier's random fate: would he or would he not get caught in a hail of bullets when rushing for cover in the middle of the night?

Masters stepped away from the bodies, scanning the ground for more soldiers, his ears alert for the approach of danger.

The six pairs of legs dangling two meters off the ground caught his attention out the corner of his eye, and for one desperate moment he hoped it was only that he'd spooked himself into seeing things. But when he looked back, the reality pierced his eyes: six corpses hung by their wrists from belts wrapped around the low branches of a small tree. Someone had spread the corpses out along the trunk like macabre ornaments. The heads lolled forward over the ruined bodies, and their uniforms and flesh, ripped open with automatic fire, were now no more than meaty pulp. He saw *within* the bodies clearly.

Masters lowered his gun, his muscles suddenly very weary. He had never seen such a sight. Before him stood the work of madmen. Psychotics. Not soldiers.

Shocked, his hands trembling, he stepped toward the nearest suspended corpse, a black woman, the small sharp features of the right side of her face still perfect in horrible contrast to the ruined face on the left. He felt an overwhelming need to touch her, to know that the body before him actually existed, and was not some perverse creation of his thoughts.

He walked right up to her, the stench of her death rushing in at him, her yellow fat peeled back and exposed, a deep cavity of darkness cut across her ribs. He raised his hand to her flesh. . . .

"I wouldn't do that if I were you."

Masters froze, his fascination with the corpse—an oracle, a portent of his own mortality—diverted by the voice from behind him. He turned, his hand still upraised toward the body. A sergeant and three privates dressed in green flak armor stood a half-dozen meters off. The red chimera patches on their uniforms identified them as Gibson troops hired by the Countess. The sergeant was a burly man with tired eyes. His face looked very serious.

"Sir Masters? Sergeant Jacobs. Step back, please. The body might be rigged." He spoke with the directness of a teacher to a student.

Masters' hand wavered, uncertain, his soul spiraling down into something uncertain and dangerous. "Rigged?"

"The body, sir. Rigged with a bomb. Please. Step away."

Masters looked up. He saw no explosives either on the corpse or hooked up to the belt buckle tied to the tree branch. Nothing. "I don't see anything."

"Inside, Sir Masters. They sometimes put mines inside. We try to recover the bodies—and pow!" His hands came together and then parted; the universal symbol of oblivion.

"All right." In a daze Masters stepped backward, retracing his steps.

When he'd cleared six meters he reached the sergeant. They shook hands, and the other man's thick, muscular hands felt wonderfully reassuring.

Two soldiers, a man and a woman, walked up to the bodies. Their eyes were cold and strained and fixed as they stared silently at the corpses. Finally the man cursed softly. They looked around, as if searching for something, then eventually gave up and returned to join the sergeant. The man said, "I ain't never seen this one. I don't know how to check. Too high up."

"Got to get them back. Contract," said the sergeant. "All the bags go back full."

"Maybe. But no way to do it. I'm not fishing my hand in there on tippie-toe." Masters saw a bead of sweat roll down from the man's temple, though it was not hot at all. His face, however, betrayed no emotion.

Chick thought for a while and said, "All right. We'll shoot them down, one by one. A body blows, we know. It don't, we check it." The man and the woman nodded and walked away. "Wix!" Chick shouted.

"I don't understand," said Masters.

"Sorry, sir. Ugly little war here. They like planting mines for us. You walk along, bam! Off go your legs. Got some that bounce up when you step on the trigger, explode at chest height and rip through your heart. Sometimes they mine the bodies. Sometimes they skin them." He nodded. "I've found some skinned."

"Why?" Masters didn't see the point. They were dead. Let the field be cleared.

Chick laughed in response. "So we'll think we're in hell, sir." He offered no more explanation, and a pink-skinned girl arrived with a sniper rifle. Chick mumbled some words to the girl, and her pink turned to white as she looked to where Chick pointed. She nodded and looked around for a position from which to shoot.

"Sir, you might want to come over here."

"Of course." The two of them walked behind a tree. Masters peered out and saw the girl brace herself against a large trunk. She took careful aim, and shot.

A belt snapped in half and a body dropped to the ground, feet first, collapsing like a sack of dirt. Nothing happened.

Another shot, another snap, another body. Nothing. Three more times.

The last body was the black woman. The gunshot popped, the belt snapped, the body stabbed the ground, followed by an explosion that sent shrapnel and bone splinters flying everywhere. Everyone waited, frozen, as if more explosions might suddenly erupt. When silence fell, they breathed again. "Saunders, go to it."

The man wandered back to the corpses.

"What is he going to do?"

"Check the bodies for mines. They might not have gone off, and I'd hate for some high-tolerance trigger to get snapped on a bump while we're in the Fourtwenty."

Masters nodded. He had no idea what to say next. He looked back. The man was on his knees, dipping his fingers slowly into one of the wounds. Slowly, slowly he pushed his hand into the body. Slowly he was in up to his wrist. Slowly his forearm entered the corpse. His eyes remained unfocused. Eyes wouldn't help. He blinded himself to the world, just waiting for an odd touch.

Masters turned and walked back toward his 'Mech.

He heard someone say to another mercenary, "I don't give him two weeks."

The second man said, "He's Blake. Got a tinman. Those tabs live forever."

He ignored them and sat down under the shadow of his *Phoenix Hawk,* resting his back against the machine's giant right foot. Soon his breathing returned to normal. Without a word to Chick or the squad, he climbed back up his 'Mech, started it up, and headed off to the Tactical Operations Center.

As he traveled across the yellow landscape toward TOC, Masters admonished himself for his naïveté. Certainly incidents such as this had occurred before. He'd read about them in his studies of wars of the past. Such horrors had occurred both on ancient Terra and in the history of the Inner Sphere.

But not recently. Or at least not that he'd heard

about. It was nothing he'd ever personally encountered, nor had he ever expected to. It was obvious that
whatever was happening on Gibson went beyond his
current reach of understanding. An age of barbarism
was descending upon the Inner Sphere. The work of
thousands of years of history, countless lives wasted
in warfare, and just as many surrendered in the name
of peace, might well come to nothing.

As the reverberations of the 'Mech's footsteps passed
up his spine, his determination to aid Thomas' dream
became stronger and stronger. Thomas had seen it all
coming. It was his gift. His friend looked at the events
around him and saw patterns of danger the way another person might see dark clouds on the horizon and
declare the imminent arrival of rain.

After another hour of travel, he had calmed down
further. All he had seen were the actions of the GFL.
It was not unreasonable to assume that they were bar-
barians, and the Word of Blake and Gibson Loyalist
forces were waging the best war they could under arduous circumstances. Perhaps the GFL guerrillas were
simply farmers gone mad, as everyone back in Portent
seemed to believe.

He began to feel better. He didn't know the full
story yet. Perhaps things were not as bad as they
seemed.

=== 10 ===

Nagasaki Valley, Gibson
Principality of Gibson, Free Worlds League
23 January 3055

As soon as Masters walked his 'Mech into the TOC compound and popped the hatch to his cockpit, he began to worry again. Low in the sky, the late afternoon sun blinded him momentarily, but he could hear the drill below clearly enough. "Kill, Kill, Kill, Kill!" shouted a dozen soldiers over and over in rhythmic chant. He shaded his eyes and saw two squads running around a parade ground. Every time their left feet hit the deck, they shouted out the word.

It was an obsolete technique, dangerous when it had first appeared during the old days on Terra, and certainly more dangerous now.

The barbarism had crawled into his own camp.

He pulled out a pair of trousers and a long-sleeved shirt from behind his seat, and slipped them over his shorts and cooling vest.

Precentor Martial Arian was a bullish man in his fifties, his face worn with many wrinkles, the flesh hard and frozen. When he moved his right arm, it was always with a bit of an extra roll from the shoulder, as if the joint no longer hinged properly. He listened to Masters politely, letting him speak for a long time.

For his part Masters alternated wildly from impassioned stretches that involved a great deal of pacing, to low, slow tones where he stood almost completely still. He had a great deal to say, most of it presumptuous and some of it awkward. He lectured Arian for a good twenty minutes about the dangers of training troops to be killers rather than soldiers, until he finally spent himself.

Arian stood up from behind his desk. He paused, composing his thoughts, then smiled politely. "If you wish to leave, I'll understand completely," he said.

Masters felt as if someone had just tried to trip him. "What?"

"Well, if you wish to leave, please do so. Return to Atreus, with our thanks to the Captain-General for your efforts. I do not wish to draw you into something you find repulsive."

"What are you talking about?"

"You, Captain Masters. You. You have just come into my office and told me we are training the Countess Dystar's mercenary recruits in completely the wrong way. Well, to your sensibilities, this may be true. You are a cultivated man. We all know of you. . . . You are a Knight of the Inner Sphere, for goodness sake. You represent the Captain-General personally. Meanwhile, I am waging a war on a backwater world filled with farmers running wildly around the forest. Our tactics, tactics forced upon us by the enemy, do not mesh with your sensibilities."

"The sensibilities of any decent soldier."

"Ah. Well, yes." Arian looked down, almost as if personally hurt. "War is like that, I suppose. Sometimes we become indecent."

"Yes. Sometimes. And the tendency must be resisted. And overcome when it occurs."

"You see, here it is, right here—this is where you and I part ways. Right now *we* don't have a choice. You want me to stop training the mercenaries to kill—"

"To kill mindlessly. I don't want you turning them into killing robots."

"But the nature of the war . . ." Arian spread out his hands. Oblivion.

"The nature of the war demands that you turn your back on hundreds of years of civilization?"

"I am a MechWarrior, too, Sir Masters, and I, too, would prefer that the Ares Conventions be maintained. But I don't control the situation." His voice tightened and he clenched his fists. "I fought the Clans, sir. I know what war, total war, can do to people." He casually brought his hand up to his damaged shoulder and touched it lightly, as one might touch one's hair. "If these people on Gibson were civilized, that would be one thing. If they all lined up in neat rows for those 'Mech battles I believe you would like to see, that would be one thing. But they don't do that, Sir Masters. They run through the forests like damned animals. We have to split up our units to track them down. We've done studies, however, and found that when we split the soldiers up, they don't fire their weapons as often as they would in a group. Thus, we have to train them to kill automatically."

Masters lost his patience, and rattled off his words as if afraid of being interrupted. "We all know this! The first studies on the need for keeping soldiers in groups were made before the Exodus, during Terra's world wars. Without the peer pressure of fellow soldiers around them, soldiers chose not to kill. A person raised in a civilized society is told killing is wrong. When dumped out on the battlefield, the taboo against killing doesn't just go away. If no one is around to notice, a soldier usually chooses not to kill. The studies showed that only fifteen percent of trained combat riflemen fired their weapons at all in battle. We've known this for centuries. But the solution isn't to drill civilization out of your troops!''

He crossed to the window, and even through the glass he could faintly hear the words of a drill sergeant to a group of mercenary recruits at attention. ''You want to rip his eyeballs out, you want to tear apart his love machine, you want to destroy him!''

Masters turned from the window and calmed himself. ''Precentor Martial. The problem with your tactics is that the soldiers you are creating out there won't be able to do much except be killers. You're brainwashing them to become killers.''

''I want them to be killers!'' Arian sla   is hand down on his desk.

''A soldier kills because it is his job. A killer kills because he wants to. There is a tremendous difference.''

''A difference, Sir Knight, that you can afford to live by, judging us from the safety of Atreus.''

''I'm not on Atreus. I'm right here.''

''In any case, you are under my command. If you stay, you take orders from me. I shall take your concerns under advisement. Is there anything else you'd like to say.''

''One question. Why is the countess recruiting all these mercenaries? There are billions of people on this planet. Why do you need mercs?''

''We don't. There have been some problems working with the locals. They seem uncomfortable with fighting the war.''

''What do you mean? It's their planet.''

''Sir Masters, I have a great deal of work to do. You have entered our war. If you wish to leave it, do so now. If you wish to stay, you have your assignment. If you take it, you will follow our procedures.''

Masters thought about it. His skin had begun to feel

odd on him, as if he'd entered a dream. But he knew
he had to stay, to find out what was actually going on.
"I'm here. I'll stay."

"Fine. You'll be taking over the lance unit in the
north quad of the Nagasaki Valley."

"Yes. My Tech gave me the rundown."

"Good. Well, good day."

They saluted each other, and Masters started toward
the door. He knew that protocol had been broken. Arian should have given him more instructions, but he
could acquire the information from the base, via radio,
to avoid more direct confrontation with Arian. Probably best for now.

At the door he stopped and turned. "Precentor
Martial?"

Arian looked up from a map on his desk. "Sir Masters?"

"Is it working? The training? Is it helping the war?"

Arian looked out the window for a moment. "No.
Nothing seems to be helping, frankly."

"What?"

"The war—it's going very badly."

Masters' spine stiffened. "Do you know that First
Assistant Precentor Starling says otherwise? He told
me just last night that the war is going very well. And
Countess Dystar echoes that point of view. Only Precentor Blane seems concerned about the direction of
the war."

An odd look came over Arian's face, a look that
Masters was beginning to recognize as Word of Blake
in-fighting. Arian said, "Blane is an alarmist."

"But you just said . . ."

"No matter what, it can't possibly be as bad as that
man says. Good day, Sir Masters."

"Good day."

He turned and walked out the door.

Returning to his 'Mech he saw more mercs at prac-

tice on a rifle range. Their Word of Blake drill sergeant
had them screaming how much they wanted the Gibsonians to die before they pulled the trigger. Masters
was so distraught by the rote killer-training that it took
him a moment to sift out the other concern that had
entered his thoughts. They weren't brainwashing the
troops to kill only the enemy. They were telling them
to kill Gibsonians. But weren't True Believers also
Gibsonians now? Where was the line being drawn?

The lance outpost rested on a flat hilltop with
roughly four sides. Three sides dropped sharply, and
allowed for better defense. The fourth was a slope with
a gentle grade that made it possible to walk 'Mechs
up to the outpost, as well giving hovercraft a means
of exit and entry. Coming up the slope with his 'Mech,
Masters spotted a sign by the gate that said, "Masters'
Lance."

Entering the compound he saw three other 'Mechs
standing there: a *Blackjack*, a *Shadow Hawk*, and a
Hatchetman. Together they looked like metal giants
gathered for some meeting of mythical creatures. All
had two legs, a torso, a head, and arms, though some
of the arms were obviously cannon or large lasers. The
Hatchetman was exceptional for the massive three-ton
axe it carried in the right hand, used against other
'Mechs when in close combat.

Eight 420s also rested in the compound. A dozen or
so soldiers sat on the dark-green metal of the hovercraft, relaxing in the day's fading light. They propped
themselves up and looked at the *Phoenix Hawk* as
Masters brought it in. He saw that the Gibson Loyalist
troops wore black uniforms, while the countess' mercs
wore the green uniforms he'd seen earlier that day. The
two groups kept their distance, only one set of uniforms to a hovercraft.

He brought his 'Mech up with the others, popped

his hatch and climbed to the ground. Once down he spotted Jen walking toward him. "Heard what happened on your way in," she said. "This place is very cold."

"Where's the CP?"

"Come on."

As he walked past the troops, some of the mercs made half-hearted attempts to salute, others simply nodded. The Gibson Loyalists, however, delighted in saluting, and did so with snap and flourish. It looked like the Loyalists were playing at it.

The CP was made of sheet metal. Jen stopped by the door and said, "This is it. Your counterpart is waiting inside."

"My counterpart?"

"A Gibson Loyalist captain. In charge of his half of the post's infantry. You're essentially Blake, he's Gibson. They're working this war together."

"Right. What's his name?"

"Captain Ibn Sa'ud. Arab descent. And like most Gibsonians he's got his Terran culture draped around him."

Masters nodded and entered the office.

The maps caught his attention first. They completely covered the walls, and the pins and arrows all over them suggested a swirl of war movement and activity. Fighting everywhere, everything in conflict. Beneath the maps sat Ibn Sa'ud, sound asleep in his chair, feet propped up on his desk. He wore the black Loyalist uniform, but also a dashiki. His beard was thick but well-trimmed, his flesh dark, his face large.

When Masters rapped on the metal wall, Ibn Sa'ud gave a massive snore and then began to fall back in his chair. He opened his eyes, realized what was happening, and rocked himself forward to prevent crashing backward. "WHAT!" he shouted as his hands hit the desk. Then he looked at Masters, his face suddenly alight. "Are you Sir Paul Masters?"

Masters saluted, and Ibn Sa'ud did the same. "A pleasure to meet you," Masters said.

"No. The pleasure is all mine. Here, sit here." With a gnarled stick that might have passed for a riding crop, Ibn Sa'ud gestured to a seat next to his. Both men sat down and then they faced off. Ibn Sa'ud took on a very serious expression, his eyes attempting something close to cunning. "So. Now we will make war."

For a moment Masters thought he might laugh, but he restrained the impulse. "I thought the war had been going on for nearly a year," he said.

Ibn Sa'ud stared back, his face blank, then burst out laughing. "Yes, yes." Then immediately he became serious again. "But now we will truly make war. We will drive them into their graves."

Ibn Sa'ud's words were vague enough that Masters almost asked exactly who it was they were going to drive into graves, but he decided to hold his tongue. "I was told by the Precentor Martial you would explain procedure to me."

"Oh, yes? Well, tonight we go on a search-and-destroy. Excellent strategy." The man almost bounced up and down in his seat like a child.

"I've never heard of it before."

Ibn Sa'ud smiled and brought his stick down on the desk with a sharp thwack that made Masters jump. Ibn Sa'ud stood. "Ah! The key, you see, is the enemy."

"The key is the *enemy*?"

"Yes. We don't know where they are, how they move, what they are up to. So we send the mercenary squads out into the forests to find them." He placed his pointer against one of the maps, and moved it across the surface as if demonstrating the search. The tip of the stick ran through the city of Portent, and, according to the scale of the map, the troops searched a good three hundred kilometers in a straight direction.

"You just said we don't know where they are. How can our troops find them?"

"They find us." He gave a smug smile.

"They find us?"

"They're quite good at it, actually."

"We send patrols out at night to be found?"

"And then we know where the guerrillas are."

"What does the GFL do when they find our troops."

Ibn Sa'ud looked at Masters carefully. "Well, they attack, of course."

"So we send our troops out. The GFL finds them and attacks. Now we know where they are."

"Precisely."

"We send our troops out to be ambushed?"

"Yes!" Another thwack of the stick against the desk.

"Is that it?"

"Tsk, tsk. Not at all. Then you, with your BattleMech lance, rush in, and cut the enemy down. Your firepower is most impressive, and you always win against the remaining Goffels."

"The *remaining* Goffels?"

"Of course. You don't think they'll just wait around for you to show up and cut them up do you?"

"Of course not."

"Precisely!"

"What about our troops?"

"What about them?"

"What happens to them?"

"They leave as soon as you arrive."

"But before that."

"They engage the enemy."

"They wander around the forest, get attacked, defend themselves as best they can until the 'Mechs arrive?"

"Yes."

"That's insane."

Ibn Sa'ud suddenly looked tired, his enthusiasm leaving as if he'd sprung a leak. "It is an insane war."

The fury worked up during his talk with Arian boiled within Masters again. "Yes, because we're making it insane!"

"No. It is simply insane. We are only following suit."

"How can it *simply* be insane? Someone has to make it so."

"Who would do that?"

Masters cocked his head and looked at the man. He seriously wanted to know. "We are doing that."

"Why would we do that?"

"I don't know. I just arrived."

"Then how do you know we are making it insane?"

Masters opened his mouth to speak, but his vocal chords panicked, uncertain of how to proceed, and he emitted only a gravelly squeak.

"Would you like some water?"

"No. Thank you. What do your men think of the plan?"

"Which plan?"

"The search-and-destroy."

"They think it is marvelous. Many Goffels are killed."

"So they like being used as bait?"

"Oh, no. My men don't go on the search-and-destroy."

"They don't?"

"The mercenaries go. My troops are too valuable."

"They are?"

"I have orders from Principal Hsiang. We are not to engage the enemy."

"WHAT?" Now it was Masters' turn to slam the desk, his hands open and flat.

Ibn Sa'ud jumped back. "Is something wrong?"

"What does Precentor Martial Arian think of this?"

"Think of what?"

"All of it? The fact that you don't engage the enemy. The fact that you're taking orders from Hsiang. What does Hsiang have to do with any of this?"

Ibn Sa'ud looked solemn and raised his eyes heavenward. "He is my king."

"He's an elected leader."

"He is *my* king."

"All right. Why did he tell you not to engage the enemy?"

"We must be ready to fall back to Portent in case the Goffels attack."

Masters blinked three times. "Then why are you here?"

"To work with the Word of Blake forces. It *is* our war, after all."

"Yes." Masters paused, uncertain how to proceed. "Doesn't this affect the mercenaries' morale?"

"Who cares?" Ibn Sa'ud leaned forward, whispering slyly. "Word of Blake and Hsiang and Countess Dystar are all rich."

"All right. I've got to go now. I'll see you later."

Ibn Sa'ud looked upset. "Where are you going? We're officers. We work together. Here. In the office."

"I've got to go check on my 'Mech. Make sure it's all right."

"Are you sure?"

"Positive."

"Well, then." Ibn Sa'ud stood and saluted. "See you later." Masters did the same.

As Masters walked out the door, he turned for a last look. Ibn Sa'ud was already back in his chair, sound asleep.

═══ 11 ═══

He found Chick at the outpost's mess hall, a small tent containing three tables lined with benches. Chick was sitting with a group of mercenaries, and from the way everyone was leaning in toward him, it looked like he was telling a story. The group exploded in laughter, then they noticed Masters, and the laughter stopped. "Could I have a word with you, Sergeant?" Masters asked.

The group looked at Chick expectantly, as if sizing up his loyalty. Chick looked back at them as if to reassure them, then said, "Yes, sir."

Masters led him out of the mess and to a clear area away from all ears.

"Sergeant, these search-and-destroy missions, could you give me your impression of them."

"Sir?"

"Please. I'm new here. I need to learn as much as possible about how the True Believers are fighting the war."

"I'm not sure what you want to hear, sir."

"I don't *want* to hear anything, Chick. I want your

evaluation of the search-and-destroy missions. Do they work? How do they work? Are they bad? How are they bad?''

Chick shifted nervously, reminding Masters of Maid Kris back at the castle.

"Sergeant, I'm not trying to trick you. I need to know more about how the war is being waged. Pretend I know nothing about it, because I'm new here and know very little.''

Chick looked into Masters' eyes, trying to decide whether to trust him. "You're not taking this to them?''

"Them?''

"Word of Blake, sir. Or the Loyalists.''

"You're all on the same side, right, Sergeant?''

"I'd much prefer it that way, sir. But I can't say that's always the case. Or we—the mercenaries—don't always see it that way.''

"No, then. This is just for me. I have to learn because if I don't, whatever is happening here on Gibson is going to keep happening.''

Chick licked his lips like someone about to confess to a priest. Then the words rushed out, low and soft, with careful glances to make sure no one was near.

"Night movement. It's a suicide patrol, sir. It's the worst patrol you can go out on. The purpose is for us to walk up on Goffels and get hit by them, and then for the 'Mechs to come up and wipe them out. We're bait to draw them out. That's all we are. Bait.'' Chick's hands shook as he continued. "Captain Mort, before you, sir, before Verner bought it, he sent us out there to find a regiment. He knew one was out there. He wasn't looking for a handful of Goffels. He wanted us to hit the big time. The Goffels would wipe us out, and then he'd come running in with the 'Mechs and waste the Goffels. One night it worked. I lost almost everybody. He got a huge body count. Got sent up the ladder with a medal.''

''Body count?''

Chick looked at him with surprise. ''Didn't anybody tell you which circle you stepped into, sir? Body counts are how Blake is keeping score. Here.'' He rummaged around his front pocket and pulled out a worn sheet of paper folded into quarters. Masters unfolded it and turned it to the light.

''Promotion Tabulation Chart,'' it said at the top. Then the words, ''Points awarded for the following'' and a list:

    10—each possible body count
    10—each 50 kilos of rice
    10—each 50 kilos of salt
    20—each mortar round collected
    50—each enemy individual weapon captured
    100—each enemy crew-served weapon captured
    1,000—each prisoner of war

The next line read, ''Points deducted for the following,'' and another list:

    20—each mercenary wounded in action
    40—each Gibson loyalist wounded in action
    50—each True Believer wounded in action
    200—each mercenary killed in action
    400—each Gibson loyalist killed in action
    500—each True Believer killed in action

''What is this?''

''It's the scorecard, sir. The Blakes use it to reward infantry and MechWarriors. Blake officers get promotions based on these scores.''

''No.''

''Yes. They go nuts when the bodies don't come in

fast enough. Mort, he pushed us hard. We went on search-and-destroys constantly. Competition's stiff. There's a shortage of positions for career-minded officers. You got just over a hundred True Believer-run battalions for some seven hundred-fifty lieutenant colonels. They're knocking themselves out sending us out to collect body counts."

Masters searched Chick's eyes. "What are you people doing here? This isn't your fight. What are your mercs doing on Gibson?"

"Well, I'll tell you. Most of these kids aren't pros. I've got combat experience way back. But these greens, some of them never saw a gun before."

"What are they doing here?"

"They're hungry. A lot of them got families back on their home worlds. They took a job. The pay's good. They figure, Word of Blake against a bunch of farmers, no problem. But it's a problem, cause these tabs don't give a damn about them. These kids are rungs in the ladder for them. If they lose a few along the way, what the hell does it matter? Buy a new ladder, that's all. Me, I spend as much time as I can just trying to keep them alive."

"I'm surprised there aren't mass desertions."

"Where're they going to go? They're on another *world*. There's nowhere to go."

"What do you do when you engage? On these search-and-destroys."

Chick snorted. "Engage? Sir, there are only twelve of us. We get sent out in small groups. Cover more ground that way. Like dogs out hunting, flushing game out of the brush. We do the only thing we can. We radio for help. We try to stay alive."

"We're supposed to be going out tonight."

"I know, sir."

"What do you think about that?"

Chick only shook his head.

"All right. Thank you very much for your time. Where can I find the other MechWarriors."

Chick smiled. "Well, Belgrade and Valentine are probably in that shack over there. And Tinman—well, I think you better talk to them about him, sir."

"Tinman?"

"Spinard. We call him Tinman. He's fond of his 'Mech. You might find him in his 'Mech or with Belgrade and Valentine."

"I'll see you in an hour."

"Yes, sir."

Chick walked off toward the mess hall, and Masters crossed the compound toward the MechWarrior quarters. The sky had darkened completely and the stars were shining brightly. He looked up at the sky and remembered the night of the ceremony. Where was Atreus? He didn't know the stars in Gibson's night sky. Perspective changed too much with space travel; one trip through hyperspace and you couldn't find your way home.

He knocked on the door.

"Come in!" shouted a woman's voice.

He opened the door and entered. A man lay on a cot reading. On another cot a woman played solitaire. Each one looked up casually, saw Masters, and scrambled off their cots to attention. Both saluted.

"At ease. Sir Masters. Pleasure to meet the both of you."

"Private Belgrade," said the man.

"Lieutenant Valentine," said the woman.

They were in their twenties, well-scrubbed and bright-eyed. True Believers.

"Where's . . . Spinard?"

"Here, sir," a voice said from the shadows.

From a dark corner of the barracks a man emerged. He was stocky and carried himself as if set to block a punch. From the look of him, he'd either just awakened or else gone without sleep for a week. "Are you all right, Private?"

"Sir, yes, sir." His voice was tired, but without any trace of concern for himself.

Masters believed that Spinard truly thought he was fine. He glanced at Belgrade and Valentine, who merely shrugged their shoulders when they met his gaze.

"All right. We're going out on the search-and-destroy in under an hour. I want everyone in their 'Mechs at ten-forty-five."

"Yes, sir," the three MechWarriors said.

"Belgrade. Could I have a word with you?"

Masters left the barracks and Belgrade followed him a short distance from the building. "Is Private Spinard all right?" Masters asked.

"In what capacity do you mean, sir?"

"What capacity do I mean? What are my choices?"

"Lieutenant Spinard is one of the most effective combatants we have had at this post. His body count totals often surpass—"

"His well-being. His mental well-being. How's that?"

"He is a fine soldier. . . ."

"What is his mental state?"

"Borderline schizophrenic, off the top of my head. Sir. But I really don't know much about—"

"Do you consider this a problem?"

"For him? Or for his capabilities as a soldier?"

Masters raised a hand to his face and rubbed his forehead. "We're obviously from two different schools. It's possible for a man or a woman to be a wreck but be a competent soldier?"

"He's not a wreck, sir."

"I'm using an extreme case, Lieutenant," Masters said tersely.

"Well, I suggest once again that Lieutenant Spinard has an excellent kill record. I hardly think his abilities as a soldier are currently impaired."

"So you're judging his performance as a soldier completely by his number of kills?"

Belgrade cocked his head slightly to one side, truly curious. "What other objective standard is there to judge by, sir?"

"Never mind. Get set. Let's see how this all works."

Belgrade left. Masters stood alone for a moment. Before he could complain to Thomas about the absurdity of the war, he'd have to see it all with his own eyes.

Masters walked across the 'Mech holding field. Valentine was waiting at the base of her *Blackjack*. Belgrade was climbing up the ladder to his *Shadow Hawk*'s cockpit. Spinard's *Hatchetman* already hummed with mechanical life.

Reaching his *Phoenix Hawk*, Masters placed his hands on the rungs. They were smooth to his touch, well-worn after many years of use. Hand over hand he climbed to the top of the 'Mech and slid through the hatch into his cockpit. He got into his cooling vest and neurohelmet, then spoke the secret code that would allow him to operate the machine. As the control console came on, a swath of colored lights—reds, greens, and blues—cut across the darkness and washed over his hands. "All right. Let's do it."

Chick's voice came over the radio. "First Squad H-craft ready, sir."

Sergeant Donald said the Second Squad was ready, and Peterson reported in for the Fifth.

"All right. Move out."

Masters tapped a button that brought up his short-range screen. Blue dots appeared for the hovercraft moving north from the center of the screen. He looked out his cockpit faceplate and saw only the moonlit tops of the trees around the base. Looking back at the monitor, he saw that the hovercraft had already split up. After four hundred meters he clicked his screen to long-range.

"Masters' Lance, this is Phoenix Hawk One. Let's get down the hill and wait for contact."

He pressed the left pedal lightly and the 'Mech turned to face the slope leading down from the base. Then he pushed the throttle forward to walk the *Phoenix Hawk* toward the slope, one massive footstep after another. Passing the infantry troops guarding the base's gate, he thought they looked terribly fragile and tiny in the dim lights of the base.

Glancing at his screen he saw the other three 'Mechs, blue squares on the screen, following tightly behind him. He opened a channel to them. "The report I read said we're looking for a GFL platoon in this area."

"That's what we understand," said Valentine, her voice calm. "They raided a town called Homs last week. Destroyed a portion of a production facility."

Amazing. It was as if the people on this planet had never heard of the Ares Conventions. "Valentine, was it the Gibsonians' habit to attack industrial facilities before or after your people arrived?"

"I really don't know, sir."

"You don't know?"

A pause. "I don't think so, sir."

"How can you not know? Didn't you bother to find out?"

"The fighting, I believe, had been going on for some time before Word of Blake's arrival. I really don't know how the fighting was conducted before our arrival."

"Before your arrival? I thought the arrival of the True Believers was what set off the war."

"Sir," said Chick. He spoke very softly, and Masters had to turn up the volume of his speakers. "We're at our drop points now. We're taking it on foot." Now the display showed the three hovercraft stopped several kilometers out from the base.

"All right, lance, let's make our way up."

"Sir," said Belgrade. "We usually wait here for the call. It increases our chances of surprise."

"How many bloody guerrillas do you get by the time you run all the way to the point of the ambush?"

"Quite a few, actually. Sir."

"Well, today we're doing it differently." Masters took his 'Mech toward the forest, the other three 'Mechs following. When they reached the dark trees, they looked like mechanical monsters stalking through an enchanted forest.

Masters thought of Chick and his men making their way through the woods, cut off from other soldiers, uncertain when their support would arrive. It was nonsense. Absolute nonsense.

As he worked the *Phoenix Hawk* through the night forest, the 'Mech's speakers crackled with soft-spoken reports from the squads. He could hear the fear in their voices. Soldiers were never supposed to be cut off like this. Electronic communications did not make up for the isolation this kind of fighting imposed on soldiers. The Ares Conventions had marked the end of such warfare: senseless, stupid wars where troops had no idea what they were supposed to be doing.

He remembered reading stories of the Terran world wars. The first of the two, at the beginning of the twentieth century, did things to men he could hardly believe. Gone were formations, gone the power of soldiers working together. Gone was movement, a soldier's sense of purpose. Once the Germans and the French had dug into their trenches, the war barely moved either way for month upon month. Soldiers sat in water-filled trenches that ran almost non-stop from the English Channel to the border of neutral Switzerland.

His thoughts drifted into those trenches as he imagined living under such conditions. Across a desolate, bomb-shelled field the enemy waited in a similar trench sometimes only three meters away. Could he see a helmet there? Was that a man, waiting as Masters waited? Should he try to take him, charge across the field? How? Rifles would cut him down before he moved a few steps. The rifles let soldiers sit endlessly, guarding large stretches of worthless ground.

Masters imagined the muck of the trenches rising up over his boots. Countless cases of—what was it called?—trench foot, yes trench foot—soldiers crippled just from standing in a water-filled trench. How much longer before trench foot set in and his foot had to be amputated? He imagined a corpse, a friend, dead in the water beside him. Wounded days earlier. He tried to keep the rats that swam through the water away from the body, but couldn't. Had to sleep sometimes. The rats came for him then. No one came to help. No one else is in sight. Troops are strung out for hundreds of kilometers. Not knowing when he'll see someone from his side again. Sometimes a full week, sometimes longer.

The helmet again, just over the lip of the enemy trench. Should he shoot? No. It's the only person he can see right now. If he shoots, all he's left with is a dead friend in the middle of desolation. If he kills that man, he'll be truly alone. Waiting alone in the trench with a corpse and the rats, out in the middle of nowhere, not knowing why he's there. Insanity could not be far behind.

Chick's voice came over the radio. ''We're going to

be slowing down a moment here. Tennison found a trip wire. We're checking—''

The words broke off as a loud explosion cracked from the speakers, almost drowning out the sound of a scream.

=12=

Nagasaki Valley, Gibson
Principality of Gibson, Free Worlds League
23 January 3055

The sound of the explosion and the scream slammed at Masters' ears and sent him back against his chair and clutching at his neurohelmet. Glancing down at his screen, he saw Chick's squad moving due west. He slammed down on the joystick and turned his *Phoenix Hawk* in a wide arc to the left to meet up with them.

"Phoenix Hawk One," came Valentine's voice. "We shouldn't leave yet. We don't know if they've engaged the enemy."

Masters didn't let up on his speed. "Well, the enemy certainly knows they're there now!"

"Sir, respectfully, they might only have hit a mine. We don't even know if the Goffels are around. But you'll chase them off if you go in now with your 'Mech."

Masters pulled back on the throttle. Trying to decide what to do, he realized his left hand was shaking on the throttle's large grip; this inaction was unnerving. Valentine was right, he supposed, but he couldn't be sure. He had no way of knowing how things worked on Gibson. The strategy and tactics revolved around too many odd concepts. Where was the engagement? Where was the enemy?

Chick's voice came over the speakers. "Phoenix One, this is First Squad H-craft. We've lost Tennison. Quiet now. No idea—"

A rapid popping of machine gun fire came over the radio now, followed by Chick's voice. "Deploy! Deploy! Sir, we got em! We got 'em!"

"Let's go, lance!" shouted Masters. He slammed his 'Mech forward once again. At a full trot it would take five minutes or so to get to the First Squad. But through the trees, maybe an additional four minutes. "Second Squad, Fifth Squad. Move back to the base."

"On our way, sir," Donald said.

"Same here, sir," said Peterson.

A roar of automatic fire ripped over the speakers. First Squad's heavy machine gun came up loud, tearing through the night air. "Any time you want to show up, 'Mech lance, we'll be more than willing to hand this over to you," Chick shouted.

Masters ran his *Phoenix Hawk* through the forest, the leafy canopy becoming thicker and the forest darker as he went. He clicked on his infrared screen. The window itself became tinted, showing Masters the objects outside according to their heat signature. The trees gave off a faint heat trace stronger than the air temperatures, appeared on the IR screen as faint pillars of dark green outside his window.

"What've you got, First Squad?"

"Two, three squads, sir. One up north, the other to our east. Don't know for . . . Chub!" A loud burst of autofire filled Masters' cockpit.

"Chick!"

He wound his 'Mech through the trees, turning wildly left and then right, desperately looking for openings in the heavy woods. Even with the IR, piloting at high speed was difficult. He slammed into smaller trees and tore them down, making far too much noise and putting unnecessary wear and tear on his machine. It might not matter at the moment, for a BattleMech was very tough, but in the long run the damage might be enough to spell doom if someone hit him just the right way. The air in the cockpit warmed as he pushed his 'Mech harder. Reflexively he checked the heat monitors. The heat sinks were doing fine; they absorbed most of the heat the machine generated and kept the 'Mech from frying out from under him.

"Sorry, 'Mech lance," said Chick. "We're here. Fine." The automatic fire continued. Then Chick screamed, "Fall back! Fall back!"

Masters glanced down at his screen. Almost there. The rest of the lance had fallen back. "Masters' Lance!" he shouted into his microphone. "Where are you people?"

Valentine answered quickly, awe mixed with the sound of her quickened breathing. "Frankly, sir, we're not used to going this fast through forests."

"Well, learn now! Valentine, Belgrade, split off west and come around the northern Goffels. Spinard, stick with me. We're going to plow right through the center of the eastern group."

"Confirmed." Spinard's voice sounded metallic and soulless. It chilled Masters just briefly, but then he saw flashes of red through the IR filters of his window— patches of heat as the GFL guerrillas moved through the shadows of trees for cover.

With his right hand he pulled up his joystick and watched the cross hairs float up and over a group of glowing red figures moving due east through the forest. His 'Mech's left arm rose up and pointed ahead. He let his thumb slide over the blue fire-control button, waiting for a clean shot. Not yet, not just yet. Too many giant trees blocking the line of sight.

He led the cross hairs a bit to the right, trying to

anticipate the movement of the guerrillas. He couldn't be sure, but he thought the cross hairs were targeting a path that would intercept the guerrillas. He glanced down and checked to see that Chick's beacon was not about to run across the front of his 'Mech; they were over to the west, everything was clear. The guerrillas came up to his cross hairs, about a dozen of them. He gave them a meter or so more lead, and then lowered his thumb against the blue fire-control button.

A roar began as two short-range missiles streaked from his 'Mech's outstretched arm and the large laser fired into the group of guerrillas. The laser bolt ripped through smaller trees and crashed into the center of the group like lightening hurled by an ancient god. It killed some of the guerrillas instantly, and sent others to the ground.

Meanwhile, an intense spray of golden fire rushed from two missiles racing toward the guerrillas. The red forms scrambled up and began to make a break for it, but too late. The missiles slammed into the ground at the center of the breaking group and sent the guerrillas flying through the air, the metal shards of the missiles ripping through their bodies.

Masters tossed the throttle forward and began stomping through the trees again. His face taut with concentration, Masters slid his thumb over the green fire-control button. He jerked the joystick to the right, targeting a group of guerrillas running for a heavier section of woods.

He pressed down on the green button and a thick hail of bullets and pulse laser beams cut through the forest. The pulse beams slashed through the trees, chewing them up and knocking them down. The bullets rushed past the fallen trunks and cut into the guerrillas. Masters saw the red forms spin momentarily and fall to the ground.

Spinard came up behind him. A few of the guerrillas

were continuing west, and Masters told Spinard to pursue them. Then he turned his 'Mech back toward Chick's squad. Valentine's and Belgrade's blue squares were moving around quickly, probably pursuing guerrillas in close chases.

"First Squad H-craft, this is Phoenix Hawk One," he said into his microphone. "What's the status?"

Chick's voice was soft. "First Squad H-craft. We're down a few. Tennison, Fowler, Hunter. Maybe more. The Goffels have broken up, though. We've got what sounds like missile fire from the west. Think it's Valentine. . . ."

Masters spotted a group of four guerrillas moving quickly north; distant flashes of red drifting in and out behind trees. As he listened to Chick give status, he turned his 'Mech and began pursuit. The guerrillas stopped for a moment, probably looking back at the juggernaut rushing toward them, then began running at a faster pace. Masters turned at a clump of trees and bore quickly down on them, the adrenaline of battle pouring through him. The cabin had warmed up, and he felt his body melt away as his spirit rode the BattleMech.

He raised the cross hairs, and jabbed the green button without aiming precisely. Machine gun fire raked over the bodies of the guerrillas and sent them quickly to the ground.

"Phoenix Hawk One, this is First Squad H-craft. Sir? You there?"

"Here, Chick."

"Everything seems wrapped up. We've been hurt bad."

"Valentine?"

"Yes, sir?"

"Status."

"Got mine. About five."

"Belgrade?"

"Three, sir."

"Spinard?"

"Four, sir."

"And ten or twelve or so for me. Let's . . ."

"We'll need an accurate count, Sir Masters. And a count from Chick's squad when they were engaged."

"Four," said Chick.

"Estimate or actual?" pressed Valentine.

The airwaves held a long pause, and then Chick said in defeat, "Estimate."

"What are you talking about?" Masters asked. "I said about a dozen. Chick said about four. It's night. We got them. Let's get out."

"Sir. We need accurate counts. It's how we determine our progress."

"I say we're getting out of here and back to—"

"Precentor Martial Arian will be expecting accurate body counts, sir. It's standard operating procedure."

"So we're going to stand around here in the dark and count bodies?" Masters made no attempt to hide his contempt.

"Sir. Yes, sir. If you *will* allow it."

He didn't want an argument in the middle of the field, nor did he want to countermand standard operating procedures without first talking with Arian. "Fine. Let's get it done quickly. Spinard and Belgrade, to the First's beacon immediately. We've got to check our trophies."

The four 'Mechs stood guard around the wounded of the First Squad, waiting for the hovercraft, which would arrive momentarily. As Masters climbed down his 'Mech, he glanced below and saw flashlight beams floating around ten bodies from First Squad, the soldiers lined up neatly on the forest floor.

He continued down the ladder. Valentine assured him the guerrillas never attacked after a firefight—as long as a strong force remained in place. She wanted to come down and supervise the body counts while Spinard and Belgrade remained in their 'Mechs. Masters agreed, wanting only to get back to the base quickly.

Reaching the bottom rung, he stepped onto soft ground and walked over to the prone men, where Chick was tying a wounded man's arms with a tourniquet. Some of the men groaned. Others were completely silent, their eyes open and glassy, catching light from the flashlights and reflecting it brightly.

"Chick," said Masters softly. "What happened? I thought you said you were down three men."

"I didn't know at the time, sir," Chick said, still wrapping up the man's arm. "I had no idea what had happened. Most of these guys ain't going home." He stood up. "Finished. Eight dead. Two wounded and stable. They'll be able to walk themselves into the H-craft."

"Eight?"

"It was a bad one, sir. I get the feeling we stumbled on them as much as they stumbled on us. They had us outnumbered three to one, though, and—" Chick moved his eyes, indicating he wanted to step away from the men.

They walked a short distance away, the branches of the underbrush illuminated harshly by Chick's flashlight. "It seems like you want to know these things, sir, so I'll tell you. Morale here is terrible. When the attack came, they all folded. They're so strung out, they don't even know what to do when the Goffels come in after them."

Masters began to ask a question, but Valentine came up, a flashlight in one hand, a comp pad in the other. Chick immediately shut up, and half-turned, pretending he had somewhere to go. He didn't, so he simply stood there.

"Looks like we got the squads we were looking for," said Masters.

"Yes, sir," she said, but paid him little attention, seeming anxious to get on with the body count. "GI-Div was right. One platoon out here. We found them and bagged most of them."

"And we lost eight men. Two more wounded."

Her back stiffened, but Masters did not think it was because of the loss of the soldiers. Masters' Lance would suffer a huge debit.

"Well, we'll probably even out against the guerrillas by the end of the month."

Valentine wandered toward the 'Mech perimeter, her flashlight bobbing along in the darkness. Masters unslung the Imperator from his back and followed. "Come on, Chick, let's get this done."

A stillness hovered over the forest now. Apart from a few birds and the buzz of insects, all was at peace. Not Masters, though. On edge, he peered out into the darkness. First, he felt exposed, wandering around a combat zone outside of his 'Mech. It made no sense. Why travel around in a dark forest with nothing more to protect you than a thin wall of flesh? Second, his mind was once again seized by the madness of this war. First they sent men out to get shot up as decoys, then they waited around to count the bodies. The GFL must be laughing at them from behind nearby trees, waiting for a clear shot.

He imagined how they saw the war from Portent. What seemed like insanity in the middle of the war—the search-and-destroy, the body counts—helped make it manageable and understandable for the bureaucrats back in the city. They weren't counting bodies in the middle of a forest at night; they did it from nine to five in the safety of the Old Walls, tabulating the reports the soldiers sent in. For them the war was very clean, very precise, very logical.

He glanced at Chick, who was eyeing the trees suspiciously, also waiting for an attack.

Valentine had no such concerns. She kept her attention focused on the ground, the beam of her flashlight flitting about the forest floor.

"Ah!" she said softly.

Masters looked to where her light pointed and saw a thick trail of blood leading along the grass. "What?"

"Blood trail," Chick said flatly.

Valentine punched a number into the keypad.

"Does that count?" asked Masters, amazed.

"Yes," said Valentine, already moving on.

"Whoever left that there might not be dead. Just wounded. He could be ready to fight tomorrow."

"Counts. Policy." Her voice made it clear she had nothing more to say about the subject.

They moved on. When they found a body or a blood trail that went on for more than five meters, Valentine tabulated it. "What if the blood trail belongs to a person whose body you've already counted," Masters asked at one point.

"We acknowledge the presence of statistical errors. They are all calculated into our final results."

Masters didn't know how to respond to that, so all he said was, "Oh."

Then they came upon the main group of men Masters had attacked with his short-range missiles, pulse lasers, and machine guns. In truth, these men and women were not whole. The weapons had chewed them up and scattered bits of their bodies throughout the forest area. Some of the corpses were so badly torn up that Masters could barely distinguish the flesh from shredded trees and foliage.

A dizziness came over him as he viewed the carnage. *He had used his 'Mech to do this.* He had attacked infantry before, of course. Back in the Fourth Succession War, when he had just begun piloting a

'Mech, the soldiers on Procyon threw themselves at the 'Mechs of his unit in a suicidal frenzy. Even that had pressed his sensibility of the warrior code to the limit. But it had at least been a true battle, with 'Mechs fighting 'Mechs. The infantry had made their attack in a last, desperate gesture. Hundreds of troops had attacked. It might have worked. It was an assault.

But this. Using 'Mechs to hunt down soldiers wearing nothing more than flak jackets. What was the point? Yes, from a technical standpoint, the 'Mechs were safe in the assault, and the enemy would suffer heavy losses. Thus, technology won out.

But where did the soldiers fit into this? One might as well return to the days of atomics, finger-fighting wars without the need for direct conflict. Or poison gas.

Where was the honor?

He looked down at the mangled bodies. Soldiers should not die like this. They had in the past, but hadn't progress been made? Why was it all happening again?

Valentine calmly walked amid the gore, tapping away on her comp pad. Masters looked around, thinking it was impossible to tell how many people had been killed here. Some of the bodies were no more than pulp, tossed and slammed together, their ruined forms mangled beyond all recognition. "What are you *doing*?"

"Sir, as I've explained—"

"NO! What are you doing? You can't possibly know how many dead are here. You can't."

"Sir, I've told you—"

"That arm, right there!" Masters pointed at a dismembered arm. "What does that count as?"

"A body, sir. One Goffel body."

He rushed over to a splintered torso. "And this? This woman's chest?"

"A body."

He pointed to a head. "That man's head."

"A body."

The flesh around Masters' eyes began to feel prickly. "This is ridiculous! You're *pretending* your war is ver- ifiable by statistical analysis. You're *pretending* there's a scientific basis for your actions." He felt reality slip- ping out of the edges of his thoughts. "And . . .," he sputtered, "and attrition is not a valid method of gauging a war anyway. What do you people think you're doing?"

Valentine's spine straightened dramatically and her eyes sparkled with the holy faith of the True Believers. "Sir, I am a true follower of the Word of Blake. No one who lives outside the truth of the Word of Blake may question my understanding of the ways of the uni- verse. You use technology as a mere tool. The True Believers live in tandem with technology. We are part of it. It is in our soul. You do not know of what you speak. You do not understand the universe. You also do not understand this war. This is our war. Not yours. If you have questions about how we conduct it, I sug- gest you take them to Precentor Martial Arian."

Masters tried to think of a reply, but when he opened his mouth, it was dry and no words came out. What she said frightened the hell out of him. If she could justify any action by her faith, and her superiors were willing to do the same—a blind faith based simply on *being right*—what effect could he possibly have?

They finished the count. By the time they were done, Valentine had tabulated seventy-two guerrillas. Mas- ters knew that the number was far too high, but all he said was, "Well, that certainly makes our losses more palatable."

Valentine did not answer.

* * *

The call came in just as they reached the 'Mechs. Belgrade and a private from the first were loading bodies into the hovercraft when the radio unit on the ground spit out a panicked cry: " 'Mech lance, this is Second Squad H-craft! They've got us. They found us. Sweet Jesus, they found us!''

Nagasaki Valley, Gibson
Principality of Gibson, Free Worlds League
23 January 3055

Masters ran for his *Phoenix Hawk* and threw his hands one rung after another up the ladder. Spinard, already sitting in his *Hatchetman*, took off, cracking thick branches off the forest's lower trees as he headed toward Second Squad's location. Belgrade moved next, and before Masters could reach his cockpit Valentine had also taken off in her 'Mech. Just before opening the hatch of his own cockpit, Masters shouted down to Chick and the private, "Get the bodies in and follow us! Don't get ahead of us!" Then he pulled the hatch shut, and followed the rest of the lance.

He moved quickly through the trees, putting pressure on the foot pedals to circle around trees and make narrow shortcuts. His mind raced with questions. Hadn't intelligence said there was only a platoon in the area? Hadn't they just taken out a platoon? For a well-run war, full of tabulations and tables, their data seemed woefully inaccurate.

The sounds of fighting that came in over his speakers from Second Squad sounded furious and overwhelming. He heard a new voice, not Sergeant

Donalds', come over the speaker. "They're all over the place!" Then the channel fell completely silent but for a light static.

Masters looked down at his screen. The Second's blip rested a third of the way up the screen, three minutes at least through the forest at current speed. Too long. He pushed his throttle forward, and the thrum of the extra heat sinks kicked in. A thick group of giant trees loomed ahead. He pulled back on the throttle and slowed the 'Mech, but Masters still would not clear them easily if he didn't stop—which he did not want to do.

He turned the 'Mech sharply, and he felt the *Phoenix Hawk* lean left. A moment of panic hit him, as it always did whenever his 'Mech began to tilt. While seated on top of forty-five tons of metal, it always seemed that the beginning of a fall was doomed to end in impact. A fall could do major damage to the 'Mech, even internal injury. With countless rounds of machine gun ammo as well as short-range missiles packed away, such damage could set off a conflagration that would broil him even as he fumbled for the cockpit latch.

But Masters was saved by his neurohelmet. Linked to his body through sophisticated sensors, the helmet used his own inner ear to compensate for the 'Mech's lack of balance. The gyroscopes made quick, tiny, but ultimately vital adjustments. The right foot slammed down at just the right spot, the impact sending Masters up out of his seat. Then the 'Mech pulled its left foot forward and finished balancing itself. Without waiting for the relief to hit him, Masters pushed the throttle further forward and continued toward the beacon.

He still heard nothing from his speakers. On the screen Spinard had almost reached Second Squad.

"Hatchet Man One? Phoenix Hawk One. What do you see?"

Silence.

"Hatchet Man One?"

Silence.

"Spinard?"

"Nothing, sir. Don't see anything."

Masters checked his screen again. Spinard's red square now rested on the Second's beacon. How could he see nothing?

"What about Second Squad? Can you see any of our troops?"

"Their bodies are here, sir," Spinard said, speaking as if in a dream. "If that's what you mean. But nothing else."

Masters swallowed hard. Dark trees rushed by, the high branches full of shadows and strange twists. "Spinard," he said slowly, "What do you *mean*?"

But no answer came.

He saw the *Blackjack* and the *Shadow Hawk* just ahead of him in the forest. All three of them reached the site of the beacon at just about the same time. Ahead he saw the *Hatchetman* standing in a clearing. A few strides later he saw the *Hatchetman*'s open cockpit. He walked his 'Mech up to the *Hatchetman*, and Valentine and Belgrade joined him in taking up a defensive position.

Masters clicked on the floods on the legs of his 'Mech. Blood washed the underbrush like raindrops, and torn scraps of cloth hung from bushes.

And down amid the carnage walked Spinard, as if in a daze.

"Valentine, Belgrade, stay in your 'Mechs and keep guard." He popped the cockpit open and made his way down the rungs. The gore had a distinct odor, an alien scent against the fresh leafy smell of the forest. Now he could see grenade burns and mortar craters covering the area. Bullets had shredded tree bark at about chest level, leaving the bare, exposed trunks sparkling with metal rounds. Whatever happened here was on a much larger scale than the attack on First Squad. The Second had been slaughtered. Unused to gauging infantry action, Masters couldn't be sure, but it looked as if they'd been cornered by a company at least. The assault had been swift, and then the GFL dispersed back into the woods. His men might be able track them. Maybe not.

"The enemy is the key," Captain Ibn Sa'ud had said. True enough. It was the GFL's game, and Word of Blake didn't know the rules any better than he did.

He looked over at Spinard. The man stood beside a bush, staring down at it, and moved his jaw, as if speaking. Masters crossed the distance to the man. As he got closer he thought Spinard looked like a child in prayer, the way he was staring intently at the bush before him.

"Spinard?"

Nothing.

"Private Spinard?"

Now Spinard spoke his words with breath, as if to block out Masters, so softly that Masters could barely make out the sound. He stepped a bit closer and heard, "Ninety-seven. Ninety-eight. Ninety-nine. One hundred. One hundred-one. One hundred-two."

Carefully Masters brought his hand down on Spinard's shoulder. The counting stopped. "Spinard, what are you doing?"

Without turning his gaze from the bush, Spinard said, "Counting. One hundred-three. One hundred-four."

Masters squeezed Spinard's shoulder. "What are you counting?"

"The leaves, sir. One hundred-five. One hundred-six. One hundred-seven . . ."

Behind him came the low hum of the First's hovercraft. Masters turned and began walking toward it, while behind him the counting continued. As he crossed the site of the battle, blood and dirt clung to the soles of his boots. Around him now he saw the corpses, fallen under bushes and lost in the forest's shadows.

He didn't know any of the soldiers. They'd all died the day he arrived and he knew none of them. He clung to that thought and it comforted him.

Chick came out of the hovercraft. "Frak," was all he said as he looked around. The private stepped out behind him. Masters saw an emotion suddenly shake the man's shoulders, but then the soldier put on a casual face as if to say, "Oh, this again."

"There was more than a platoon in the area."

"I'll say," answered Chick.

Chick noticed Spinard. "What's up with the Tinman over there?"

"He's . . . he's counting the leaves on a bush."

For a moment Chick's face drew blank, then it lit with a smile of realization. "Counting! I've been wondering what the hell he's been doing for the last five weeks."

"What?"

"I've seen him muttering to himself for over a month. Sometimes he'll just stare at his 'Mech and mutter. Sometimes at mess he'll look down at his vegetables and mutter. I suppose he was counting the whole time. Counting, counting, counting. Counting bolts in his 'Mech, counting kernels of corn on his plate. Word o' Blake counting away." He glanced up at the BattleMechs standing tall around them. "I hate these guys."

"Sergeant?"

"Bust me if you want, sir. But you're not one of them. You see it too, don't you? You know this whole thing is a worthless corpse factory. Saw it on your face earlier. See it now. Knight of the Inner Sphere, right?"

"Yes."

"All right. What do you want to do with the bodies?"

"Check . . . at least check for survivors. We'll come back. . . " He looked around. "During the daylight we'll collect the tags. Nothing until then."

"What about the Tinman?"

Masters looked over at Spinard. "I'll take care of it. Get in the H-craft. We'll take off in a minute." He walked back to Spinard, who by this time had moved to another bush. "We've got to go now."

"All right." With that Spinard turned and began moving toward his *Hatchetman*. Masters stepped back, surprised. He'd expected to have to use some sort of sympathetic logic to get the man to give up his methodical task. Yet Spinard returned to his 'Mech with even, measured steps and then began to climb back up.

The days that followed were filled with the same activity, though the kills against the GFL never reached the same level. Countess Dystar's bankroll easily provided replacements for fallen soldiers, and Masters had the strange feeling that even if he did not call in for replacements, they would arrive, factory-ordered, ready to be delivered into the heavy yellow forests.

Whenever they shot up a few GFLs, Captain Ibn Sa'ud's face glowed with pleasure. Each night on the patrol's return he would pull out a thick ledger and draw up the lance's profits and debits. "The other night was very bad," he would say, shaking his head. "We will have to make up for that soon." As the days passed his joy lessened, and he became more and more concerned that the losses suffered on Masters' first night out would never be made up by the end of the month, when Precentor Martial Arian tabulated each outpost's results.

Masters, meanwhile, spent day after day trying to

get through to Arian, to demand that the nightly
search-and-destroys be stopped. He also wanted to relieve Spinard of duty. Spinard had taken to spending
more and more of his time in his 'Mech. He slept in
it. He only left it to eat or when ordered. When Masters mentioned his concern to Ibn Sa'ud, the captain
only laughed and said, "Not to worry. He'll snap out
of it. I've seen it a trillion times."

When Arian finally got back to Masters, he was furious. Furious that Spinard's abilities were in question
when the man had one of the best body-count records
in the Word of Blake. Furious that Masters had the
gall to suggest that a well-thought-out strategy should
be scrapped. Furious, Masters guessed, at being sad-
dled with a troublemaker who couldn't be easily dis-
posed of.

They talked by phone, arguing a full forty minutes
until Masters agreed to leave the issue of Spinard's
capabilities alone as long as Arian let Masters stop the
night search-and-destroys. Then Masters drew in a
long breath and asked for a company of Gibson Loyalists. Arian wanted to know what the hell he wanted
them for, and Masters explained that he wanted to go
into the woods to win against the GFL.

Arian wanted to know what the hell was wrong with
using the 'Mechs to clean out the woods. Masters explained that the 'Mechs might be invulnerable to the
firepower of the guerrillas, but they weren't doing as
effective a job in the woods as infantry would. The
'Mechs were already slow, but moving through trees
slowed them down even more. The guerrillas could
undoubtedly hear them coming from minutes away and
thus could clear out long before the 'Mechs became a
threat. Arian sputtered something about overwhelming
firepower, the superiority of technology, and Masters
let him go on. When Arian paused for a breath, he put

in, "But those things aren't working. I'm sure the Captain-General will see my point of view."

Eventually Arian relented, saying he'd get the troops to the outpost some time in the future. Captain Ibn Sa'ud, who was also in the room, stared at Masters with unabashed horror. When Masters hung up the phone, the captain asked in a high-pitched voice, "What are you doing? Why do you need Loyalists?"

"To fight the war, Captain. To fight the war. The correct means must be used for the proper circumstances. Right now we're dithering around out there. We're not using our troops effectively. They're not on patrol, where they'd be allowed to stay out of sight. They're not out to engage the enemy, because we're not sending them out in units strong enough to win. We're tossing them out like bait. Enough is enough."

"But the BattleMechs are invulnerable."

"Yes but they're not doing the job. I've only been here a week, and that's obvious. The BattleMechs are not winning the war. By the time we arrive to pick up the pieces of our soldiers, the guerrillas are probably laughing their heads off that our metal giants can't touch them."

"You . . . you're a MechWarrior. How can you say such things?"

"*Because* I'm a MechWarrior. Precisely because of it. BattleMechs are not deus ex machinas sent down from heaven to solve every military problem. They are *a* solution for *some* problems."

"Duxa whats?"

"Forget it. We're bringing troops in here, and we'll train them correctly and we'll start taking apart the GFL."

That night Masters tried fitfully to fall asleep. When he did, he dreamed of men and women filled with bombs. But it wasn't wartime. All the people walked

around in a city, going about their business, like in
Portent, well-dressed and purposeful. And none of
them knew they carried bombs within them. But Masters knew. Only he knew. He wandered the city and
people glared at him strangely because he looked at
them strangely. but he did so because he could see
wires and cables through their flesh. He realized they
were all small BattleMechs—dressed up in costumes
of flesh. But nobody piloted the little 'Mechs. Everybody thought, "I look like a person, I don't need a
pilot." So they all walked around, not noticing that
they were overheating because all lacked pilots.

Every once in a while someone who looked completely normal suddenly fired all his weapons, shooting everybody around him without meaning to. Like
a burp. They cut everybody around them to pieces.
The people near the scene of the violence, who wit-
nessed it and survived, shook their heads. It happened
over and over again for what seemed like hours. The
people kept walking along the streets, and either hic-
cuped lasers and missiles, or got shot to shreds by
someone who overheated and went insane.

Masters ran up to a woman, a beautiful woman—
Maid Kris, he realized after he touched her—and said,
"Stop. You've got a bomb in you."

She laughed and said, "Oh, now, you stop it."
Whereupon she turned into Countess Dystar. The
Countess stretched out her hands and touched Masters
on the cheek. Her touch burned hot, so hot he felt his
skin melt. But it felt wonderful, too.

Suddenly, he was at the tree where the mercenaries
had been strung up. The Countess was with him, and
he wanted so much not to feel anything for the people
hanging in the tree, blood streaking their faces, their
bodies torn open by harsh metal.

"I can give that to you," the Countess said. "I can
make you forget. I can make you not feel." The touch

of her flesh became hotter as she traced her fingertips along his stomach and chest. He looked down and saw that under his flesh, his muscles were changing into myomer bundles, his flesh into metal. "Do you want it?" she asked. "All you need do is be happy and content forever, and spend the rest of your life working hard to distract yourself. . . ."

She leaned in to kiss him, and just as her beautiful, warm lips pressed against his, he heard a horrible scream.

"Paul!" someone said near him, far above him, through the deep water of dreams. "Paul, wake up!" He realized it was Jen standing over him in the darkness. In the distance, somewhere on the outpost's grounds, the screams continued.

"What?" he stuttered.

"Come on," she said. "You better deal with this."

$\equiv$ 14 $\equiv$

Nagasaki Valley, Gibson
Principality of Gibson, Free Worlds League
6 February 3055

The screams came from behind the latrines. When he rounded them a silvery pool of bright blood lit by a lamp caught his eye. Then he saw a man, his head in the pool of blood, his throat cut. From his rough, dirty clothes, he looked like a farmer.

Several Gibson Loyalists were holding onto two more farmers. Captain Ibn Sa'ud stepped toward one of them, a large knife in hand. Chick was there, visibly shaken, observing, but not participating. "Jesus," said Jen. "I didn't think. . . ."

"What the hell's going on?" shouted Masters as he stalked up to Ibn Sa'ud.

"Ah!" said Captain Ibn Sa'ud, very pleased to see him. "My men caught these Goffel sympathizers in a nearby village. Now they must give us information." He stepped up to the second man, who silently pleaded for his life with terrified eyes. For a moment Masters thought the Captain would only threaten the man with the blade. But just as he remembered the corpse on the ground, Ibn Sa'ud grabbed the man's hair, forced his head up and back, and ran a deep cut across the throat. The second farmer's blood rushed from the wound, and he struggled for a moment to breathe. Ibn Sa'ud signaled his men to let the farmer go, and the dying man fell to the ground, clutching at the dirt.

Dazed and taken aback, Masters shouted at Chick, "Tell him to stop that now!"

"It's the way he interrogates people."

"Ha! You see," said Captain Ibn Sa'ud, "this one is now truly frightened." As he stepped toward the last man, Masters lunged for Ibn Sa'ud and knocked his hand down. "I said to stop it!"

The Captain dropped the knife and looked at Masters like a hurt child. "What are you doing? This is my job. This is what I do."

Masters ignored him and turned to the Loyalist soldiers holding the last prisoner. "Lock him up, but don't hurt him." The soldiers looked for authorization from Captain Ibn Sa'ud, who was looking down at the ground, oblivious to what was happening around him. "Do it or else I'll knock your ass all over this base," Masters said. The soldiers dragged the prisoner off. "You and you!" he said, pointing to Jen and Chick. "My quarters. Now."

Back in his quarters, Jen sat down on Masters' foot locker. Chick stood. Masters dropped down on his cot.

"What the hell was that?" he said to Chick.

"It happens. I told you, it's how they interrogate."

"He was killing them."

"Welcome to the war."

"Cut the crap!"

"I think you should see this," Jen said, and pulled out a sheet of paper. "I was going to show it to you in the morning, but . . ."

He took it as she fell silent. The paper contained a long list, and a few items caught his attention immediately:

Wrap in barbed wire
Head in mud— 1⅓ minutes
Knife strapped to back
Shoot through ear

"What is this?"

"It's a list I made up while listening to the Loyalist soldiers. There were laughing about what they do to prisoners."

He looked back down at the list . . . When stomach is filled with water, beat to induce . . . "This can't be."

"It is," said Chick. "Both the GFL and the Loyalists torture wildly." He looked up, searching. "They're from the same planet. I don't understand it."

"What about the off-planet mercs, Chick?" When Chick looked away, he insisted, "Tell me now."

"It's hell here, sir. The things they do to us. . . ."

"I can't believe this!"

Chick continued. "You should know that sometimes we just go into villages. Shoot them up."

"What?"

"They call them Free Fire Zones."

"What?"

"Free Fire Zone. Everything in the area is a target."

"It's a battlefield?"

"No. Not really. You might think it by the way we talk about them. They're just areas designated as belonging to the enemy. Huge areas. The rule is, anything in the area is enemy. Should be killed."

"Body counts," Masters said, his voice barely a whisper.

"Direct hit, sir. I have no idea who determines the Free Fire Zones or how they're determined. For all I know, villages bribe people like Captain Ibn Sa'ud to *not* declare their village a Free Fire Zone.''

''Are you serious?''

''Absolutely, sir. I've got no proof. But I have yet to figure out what the hell makes a Free Fire Zone and what doesn't. Except that you need enough warm bodies to drive up a lance's body count. We just kill people, and Blake and the Loyalists assure us we're doing the right thing.'' Chick raised his fingers to his eyes. He gave a sharp sigh, then said, ''I keep shooting, but you know, you kill enough ten-year-olds . . .''

Masters could not even speak. He simply looked up at Chick, his face wracked with despair.

Chick dropped his hand and he glared back. ''Don't get on me about this. Those kids—they'll *kill* you. I've seen it happen. They walk up to you and toss grenades into the H-craft hatches. This isn't a war. It's just killing. Everybody is screaming about religion. The Blakes want their religion. Everybody else wants their religions. They all think they're right. So they get to kill anybody they want. I don't care anymore who I kill or don't. . . .'' He drew in another sharp breath. He looked about to cry, but stifled it. ''Sorry, sir.''

An awkward silence filled the room. ''All right,'' Masters said finally. ''I'm going back to Portent tomorrow. The Captain-General has considered negotiating with the GFL. I'll go talk to Precentor Blane about this, and send word to Thomas Marik that things are out of control here. Because they are. This is madness.''

The next morning, before he could leave for the city, a call came in from TOC. Countess Dystar's two renegade 'Mechs had been spotted in the Nagasaki Valley the night before. Masters decided to forego his trip, for two wild 'Mechs were too dangerous to leave loose.

He scrambled his 'Mech lance and the mercenary hovercraft squads.

Inside his cockpit Masters glanced at his display. On the long-range screen he tracked the other three 'Mechs in his lance, then he touched a button changing the screen back to short-range. His 'Mech companions disappeared and he saw only Chick's hovercraft. Out his viewscreen Masters saw the hovercraft rushing through the tall grass like a boat through water, keeping pace with him five hundred meters to the right.

He punched up the radio and said, "Hatchetman One, Blackjack One. This is Phoenix Hawk One." Both Spinard and Valentine responded, and he continued. "Take the area around Padang. The 'Mechs might be based there, or at least in the vicinity." The two MechWarriors confirmed the orders, then he called up Belgrade. "Shadow Hawk One, stick with me. We'll head up Cyclone Ridge and double back." He looked down at his screen and watched the dots break off.

If only they could find the 'Mechs . . . That would be more like it, though still lacking in complete form. Heralds would be required for a proper battle, the field chosen by both sides, the 'Mechs lined up, the battle fought.

People he spoke with, civilians, often thought that such battles, mimicking the ritual combats of such ancient Terran societies as feudal England or Japan, left little room for tactics or individual talent. Such was not the case. Perhaps it might have been so generations earlier, when soldiers marched in tight block formations and smashed at each other like waves against rocks. But better weapons and better armor allowed each warrior to matter more.

That was the test of ritual combat: the fight was all out in the open. It demanded that each warrior be an improvisational artist. If a surprise were to occur, it had to happen right under the nose of the opposition. Shifts in the battle demanded quick, fluid thinking under arduous circumstances. This was the test of the warrior—to outwit the enemy in a moment of action.

Tools of destruction from the past—poison gas, the atomics, and others—had been outlawed because they were inhumane. War was inherently inhumane. War, which demanded that humans kill each other, was inherently inhuman. No. The key was that gases and atomic fireballs were simply unleashed—they ruled out the skill of a warrior. If no skill was required, there was no job. And without that, people like him had no place to go.

There was, he knew, in his blood, something that demanded making decisions under fire. He felt most alive when piloting his 'Mech, targeting his opponent, commanding his fellow warriors all on the brink of the ultimate chaos. But he knew his taste was limited, unlike the thirst so many other people had. He knew that after most civilians had their first experience with combat, there was no stopping them. The war quickly became a matter of state pride, and the atomics could soon follow.

"We've got Padang up ahead, sir," said Valentine.

"Keep me posted."

"They're on the move, sir. We're going in."

"Who's on the move, Blackjack One?"

"The townspeople, sir. We have confirmed Goffels."

Masters felt the situation spiral out of his control once again. "*Confirmed* Goffels, Blackjack One? How did you confirm them?" He looked at his display and saw Valentine's and Spinard's 'Mechs rushing forward full-throttle.

"They're moving, sir."

Something was definitely wrong, and he spun his 'Mech around to meet up with Valentine and Spinard at the town. "Shadow Hawk One, stick with me. Blackjack One, what the hell do you mean, they're moving?"

"They're moving, sir. I can see it from here, half a klick off. They're running around between the buildings."

"As if in response to two large 'Mechs rushing toward their home?"

"Exactly, sir. We'll be engaging in five seconds."

"Belay that, Valentine!"

"Negative, Valentine," piped in Arian's voice, swirling into the conversation as if by magic. "Proceed as usual."

Masters was stunned. What was Precentor Martial Arian doing on the channel? Sophisticated communication gear allowed senior officers to involve themselves with field combat, but it was a terrible idea. Getting immediate commands from someone outside the fight only complicated matters.

"Precentor Martial Arian," Masters said quickly, "Blackjack One just told me they're running as if in fear. Isn't that normal when a 'Mech rushes toward you?"

Arian said, "Sir Masters, think it through. Loyal Gibsonians have nothing to fear from us. It's only the Goffels who would panic."

"I think you're crediting . . ."

"We're on," said Valentine, and a rush of missiles sounded through the speakers.

"Jesus." Masters slammed the throttle and rushed the *Phoenix Hawk* forward, the 'Mech ripping up huge patches of dirt underfoot. "Blackjack One, belay that! Belay that! That's an order!"

"Captain Masters, you are jeopardizing the entire . . . ," Arian said, and continued in a similar vein, but Masters paid him no heed. He topped a ridge that overlooked Padang and slowed to a stop at what he saw. Like Portent, the village of Padang formed a circle made up of several hundred wooden buildings. Farmlands began at the edge of the village and continued out for kilometers.

Spinard's *Hatchetman* stood in the center of the village. Wielding the three-ton hatchet in the 'Mech's right hand, he swept it through the buildings, splintering them. Bodies flew out of the homes, sometimes lifted meters into the air, then smashed into the ground or other buildings. Every once in a while he fired the autocannon mounted on his 'Mech's right shoulder, the shots going to the edges of the village and ripping apart people trying to escape. Masters saw no one who offered resistance, and everyone still alive looked like they only wanted to flee.

Meanwhile Valentine's *Blackjack* tirelessly circled the village, searching for villagers who had made it to the edge of the town proper and were trying to make a break for it. She shot down dozens of people with her lasers.

He pushed the throttle forward again. Charging down the hill, he jabbed the comm button. "What are you bastards doing? They're not fighting back!"

"It's a Free Fire Zone, sir," Valentine said. "Everyone here is Goffel."

"How do you know that?" Masters screamed. He rushed into the village, cutting down a wide avenue, trying to avoid villagers as they ran wildly for shelter. He drove his *Phoenix Hawk* right up to the *Hatchetman* and with his 'Mech's left arm grabbed the handle of the axe as it started to swing down. The massive arms of the two 'Mechs pushed against each other, sending a grinding whine through the air. Masters felt his 'Mech begin to lose balance as momentum brought the *Hatchetman*'s arm back down.

He couldn't risk getting knocked over, so he pulled his 'Mech's arm away. The *Hatchetman*'s arm continued to swing down until the axe slammed into the ground and shook the earth fiercely. Reacting quickly, Masters brought his 'Mech's hand down on top of the axe. Gravity was his ally now, helping him pin the *Hatchetman*'s arm in place. "Stop! Stop it now! They're finished. They're not fighting back!"

"Captain Masters!" Valentine shouted, "What are you doing?"

"What is going on out there?" demanded Arian.

The *Phoenix Hawk*'s cockpit had warmed up since his run and his attacks against Spinard, not nearly hot enough to be dangerous, but enough to feel it. "They're not fighting back," Masters said carefully, slowly, for he was suddenly unsure if he'd really stated this simple truth out loud.

Valentine stopped firing, but then Masters saw her training her weapons on him. She did not fire, perhaps for fear of hitting Spinard, or possibly because she was simply not yet ready to shoot at her captain. He spotted Belgrade on a ridge overlooking the village, a witness to the proceedings, but not yet a participant. And only a few meters off was the dark cockpit of the *Hatchetman*, with Spinard invisible behind it.

Down below all movement had stopped. Masters saw not a single person standing, but hundreds and hundreds of bodies were scattered about like tossed dolls. Some lay in the street, others within ruined buildings, the structures shattered by missile and cannon fire or the terrible power of Spinard's axe. "They're not fighting back," he repeated. "It's time to stop. We tend to the wounded now."

"What?" asked Valentine, drawing the word out like a child denied dessert. "They're animals! In a Free Fire Zone. We don't—"

"Do as Sir Masters says, Lieutenant," Arian broke in. "And get me a body count. I'll be back on in a moment."

Masters let go of the *Hatchetman*'s axe. He remained on guard for a sudden riposte, but Spinard backed his 'Mech up a few steps, then powered down.

"First Squad H-craft," Masters said into his microphone.

"Here, sir," answered Chick.

"Let's move the squad in, check for wounded. Check for GFL weapons and guerrillas."

"Yes, sir."

"I'll expect the other H-craft squads to do the same." There was a pause, then each of the squad sergeants confirmed.

Masters sat back in the command couch and wiped the sweat from his forehead. First he'd assaulted a Regulan officer during peacetime at the party, then he'd threatened his Loyalist counterpart the night before, and now he had just struggled with MechWarriors under his command. Was he completely out of touch with the world, or had the world gotten completely out of touch with reality?

Below he saw the squads beginning to disperse through the remains of the town. He spotted Chick kneeling beside a pile of bodies, and then saw the man call his radio operator over.

"Sir," came Chick's voice over the speakers, "we've got a lot, I mean *a lot* of people that are just hanging on by a thread. We don't have the supplies or the means to take care of this many injured, and no help's going to come. What do you . . . what do you want us to do about them? Sir."

Masters rubbed the bridge of his nose and closed his eyes. Where were the ideals he and Thomas had conceived? When did the war start getting clean?

"You're suggesting there are no options, Chick?"

"Not at this time, not for most of these people. But they're in misery."

"All right. But only the extreme cases. Make sure everyone understands that. Save who you can."

He opened his eyes and looked down below. Chick pulled out his Mydron auto pistol and pointed it down at a small body—a child maybe, or half a man—Masters couldn't be sure from the distance. One bullet, and the body on the ground jerked once, then went still. Chick lowered his head.

Valentine climbed down the side of her *Blackjack*, a bag slung over her shoulder. He knew that inside were the tools of her true trade; not weapons of war, but a calculator. His loathing for her and the Word of Blake dried his mouth and made his tongue feel thick against his teeth. He had to get word to Thomas. Whatever he had been told, whoever had passed the lies on—whether it was Countess Dystar, Hsiang, Word of Blake—it didn't matter anymore. This situation was a horror. It was exactly why MechWarriors had to seize the means of war, *noble* MechWarriors who knew their job.

As soon as he'd finished supervising the cleanup, he'd head straight to the city. Masters popped the lock on his hatch and began the long climb down his 'Mech.

15

Padang, Gibson
Principality of Gibson, Free Worlds League
6 February 3055

Padang looked like footage ready-made for an anti-war documentary. Though Masters hated what he saw, he had to remind himself that he did not hate war.

War, first and foremost, tested a person's will. Above any strategy and any technology, soldiers had to hold their positions, carry out their orders, work together. No matter how brilliant a general's maneuver on a map board, what counted were the soldiers' decisions once they were on the battlefield—when other people started shooting at them. A military unit lived or died by its ability to continue operating as trained. The trick was to be calm and determined enough to make the opposition break ranks. Nerve and will. That was where a battle was really fought. If just one soldier turned and ran, it opened a gap for the enemy. And once a line opened, the gap rarely stayed small. At that moment the battle would turn.

Of course, technology had put a major crimp in that philosophy of war. High-tech weapons permitted wars to be conducted from too great a distance. With a mere press of a button someone could launch a missile, all the while remaining far from the *threat* of destruction. Without fear, there was no test. Any idiot could press a button.

It was quiet now in the village, quiet and still. And hot. It was only ten hundred hours, but the air already shimmered with heat. Flies buzzed around the corpses, the pieces of bodies, the women torn in half, the children shattered against the walls of huts. He imagined the slow pan of a camera over the corpse-filled scene. "There! See! Death! War is bad and shouldn't be fought!" What the filmmakers always forgot was that the person waging a war believes that such atrocities are necessary, and thus acceptable. Illogical? Yes, but by the time negotiations collapsed, the time of logic had passed.

Here on Gibson, the same problem. The True Believers needed a home after splitting off from Com-Star, but the people of Gibson refused them. Should Word of Blake simply wander the stars until they all died in the cold of space? No. They had been invited here by Thomas Marik, Captain-General of the Free Worlds League, and promised a haven. And if they had to fight for that haven . . .

The people of Gibson saw the writing on the wall. The True Believers quickly became part of Hsiang's inner circle, with contracts and tax money going directly to them. Would the True Believers some day ask more of Hsiang? Would they someday impose their religion on the people of Gibson? The people had no wish to sit still and wait for the zealots to rule their souls. They wanted to force the True Believers off their world *now*.

And so mutilated bodies lay strewn about the splintered homes. It was the way of it. War killed people.

But did it have to kill so many civilians? No, but this one had by now become a guerrilla war, with civilians on the front line.

How did one win a guerrilla war?

History showed one didn't.

Around him the squads gathered the wounded who had a chance to survive. They carried them to Chick's hovercraft, where the medics had set up a quick and dirty first aid facility. None of the farmers would be whole, and many would die within a few weeks.

Masters saw that the soldiers seemed to be working slowly, and often gave him dark looks when they thought he wasn't looking.

He spotted four men from Fifth Squad standing around a pile of bodies, smoking cigarettes. "Move it!" he shouted. They turned their eyes languidly toward him, shook their heads, and tossed their cigarettes aside. One of the men leaned down and dragged a weeping woman out of the pile of bodies. Blood covered her flesh, and Masters couldn't tell if it was from other bodies or if her skin had been ripped off by shrapnel.

Valentine walked by, her casual gait incongruous with the carnage. She avoided looking at him as she passed, but he asked, "Where's Spinard?"

The moment she turned, a fury began to bubble out. "Where do you—?" But she caught herself, cleared her throat, and said, "He's in his 'Mech. Sir."

"I told him to come down."

"Yes, sir. You did. But I'd give you really long odds on him showing his face outside of that *Hatchetman*." She walked on, scanning the area and punching some numbers into her comp pad. Masters looked around. He wasn't certain how he would tell a villager apart from a Goffel, and he told her as much.

"Well, for the purposes of this count, I'm counting them all."

He stood stunned for a moment. "What?"

"I'm counting them all. We found a crate of arms under one of the huts. Anti-tank. Don't know where they're getting them, but they got them. This village was hiding them.''

"Some*one* in the village was hiding them.''

"And the rest of the villagers said nothing. They all count.'' She looked down at the calculator and nodded.

"I take it the tabulations on this body count will make you and Spinard look quite good. Arian will be able to walk into Blane's office and prove the war is going well.''

"It *is* very good for the war's progress. We attacked a GFL village and rendered it inoperable. The survivors will think twice before they work against us.''

"Survivors?'' He gestured at the carnage and laughed in spite of himself. "This village is ruined. All you found was a crate of six rocket launchers. Don't you think our time would be better spent tracking down the source of the GFL supplies than mutilating some old farmer who probably had the weapons shoved into his home at gunpoint.''

She ignored him. "The village is ruined,'' she said, as if repeating a religious catechism. "Now they'll move to a city. Probably Portent. All the better. We can keep a better eye on them there. The guerrillas are still crawling all over the countryside. Can't do spunk about them. In the city, they're ours.''

Masters raised his hands in front of his chest and touched his fingertips together. He remembered the shanty town at the edge of Portent and the conversation with Precentor Blane in the limousine on the way from the starport to the Old City. *"This* is the pacification program?''

"You've heard of it.''

"Yes. Though it's not what I expected.''

"Well, whatever.''

She wandered away, her fingers flying over the buttons on the keypad. "Valentine,'' he called after her,

"has it occurred to anyone in this army that the reason
the ranks of the GFL keep growing despite your attrition programs is because of stunts like this? You're
driving neutrals away from the government and into
the hands of the guerrillas!" Her fingers flashing over
the keypad, she paid him no heed.

Masters heard the voices of children. Looking to his
right he saw two little boys, about eight or ten years
old, tugging at the sleeves of two soldiers. The boys
wore kimonos splattered with dirt and blood. Deep
cuts ran along their faces, and one boy kept wiping
blood from his right eye. Both kept gesturing toward
the edge of the village as if trying to persuade the
soldiers to go there.

The troopers were merely waving the boys off, and
when the children persisted, one of the soldiers drew
his gun and pointed it at the younger one.

"Private!" Masters shouted.

The boys pulled back in fear. Seeing it was Masters,
the private lowered the gun reluctantly.

"Find out what they want," Masters ordered.

"Sir, they say their parents are trapped under a
building," the soldier called back.

"Well, go get them out!"

"It's a trap," the trooper shouted with exasperation.
Then he looked down at the ground, embarrassed. "It
might be a trap. Sir."

The words echoed in Masters' ears. Certainly it
might be a trap. Such things happened. Chick had told
him. Was that it then? *No more help for children. It
might be a trap.*

"You two," Masters called as he walked toward
him. "We're all going." When he reached the group,
he said, "Your parents are over there?"

"Yes, sir. Please," said the older boy. "They need
help. They're dying!"

"Take us to them," Masters said. The two soldiers,

one a sandy blond, the other dark-haired, looked at him as if they'd like to assign him a death sentence.

The group made its way across the ruined village and soon reached its edge. A thin trail of dirt led on for another fifteen meters to a collapsed hut. "They're in there," said the older boy. "Dying." He almost whispered the word as he looked up into Masters' face.

The boys continued to lead the way, followed by the blond soldier, Masters, and then the second soldier. As they walked, Masters and the two troopers scanned the surrounding area for snipers and mines, but spotted nothing.

Then, just a few meters from the house, Masters noticed the boys beginning to take odd steps. Not exceptionally odd, just odd enough, a slight extra kick as they stepped forward, as if avoiding a wire across the path.

A wire across the path.

Masters grabbed the blond soldier just as he was about to run his ankle against the trigger. He pulled the soldier down and away from the wire, the two of them sprawling onto their backs. The older boy turned, saw what was happening, and rushed back to the trip-wire. As Masters was twisting around to get up, the boy jumped toward the trigger, hoping to catch Masters and the soldiers while they were still near it.

Masters grabbed the blond man's shoulders and dragged him further back, the two of them rolling over each other several times.

When the mine exploded it was like a blur of dirt, but the dull pop followed by a shrill scream were unmistakable. The soft sound of needle shots followed immediately. Looking toward the noise, Masters saw the dark-haired soldier standing farther back down the trail from where they'd come, his face splattered with the older boy's blood. The soldier was holding his needle rifle and squeezing the trigger again and again.

The weapon fired fine metal shards that caught the sunlight for an instant as they exited the barrel of the gun.

Masters saw the younger boy running as fast as his small, thin legs could carry him. On the third shot the soldier's needles cut the boy across the back. A scarlet ribbon spread out along the small of his back and he doubled over, his spine severed. Without a sound his small form tumbled to the ground.

A terrifying quiet fell over the area. As Masters and the first soldier waited a moment on the ground, their breathing slowing, he stared at the remains of the first boy. It was a powerful mine; he'd almost got them.

The second soldier stepped up to the first and extended his hand to help the man up. Then, without a backward glance at Masters, the two walked back up the path toward the village.

A child, no more than ten, had just tried to kill them. Was the entire village GFL after all? Once more, but more clearly than ever, Masters realized he'd arrived on Gibson with no idea of what was going on. He looked after the two soldiers walking away from him. Past them stood the *Hatchetman,* standing tall and threatening amid the carnage. What he had first seen as indiscriminate slaughter now might be considered payment in kind. Slaughter for slaughter. An eye for an eye, in the older parlance. Could he fault Word of Blake for their war?

Damned straight. And he would. The more vicious the enemy, the more crucial that a soldier never stoop to his enemy's tactics.

As he reached the edge of the town Chick came up to him. His face showed intense concern, but his body betrayed no tension or fear. He walked up alongside Masters as if all he had in mind were a few mundane details to discuss.

"Sir," he said softly, "I think you should know that

while you were gone orders for your arrest came in from Precentor Marshal Arian." Masters turned in surprise toward Chick, who said, "Ah, don't do that. They don't know I know, so they don't know you know."

Masters returned his gaze to the ground, and nodded casually. He noticed a fly trapped in a pool of blood on a corpse's chest.

"I've talked about it with some of the men in my squad," Chick went on. "Those I trust. If you want to make a break for it, we'll get you into the H-craft, and then take off for the forest."

"You do have a full grasp of what you're suggesting."

"Sir, I can't keep doing this anymore. The men and women I've spoken to can't keep doing this anymore. If we help you, and live, we'll expect a pardon from the Captain-General. Just as you live outside the bounds of mindless authority as a Knight of the Inner Sphere, so will we."

As they walked into the center of town, Masters thought it over. If they arrested him, he'd have little chance of contacting Thomas directly or of getting his full report out. And he found the idea of imprisonment by these bastards completely repugnant. Surrender to them? No. Never.

"All right."

"Very well, then. Here's what I can give you. My troops are at the H-craft ready to go. All we have to do is wander over there before Valentine spots you. She's got the orders. We get in—"

"No. Thanks, but I need my 'Mech."

Chick paused. "Sir, you're outnumbered three to one. The hovercraft is fast enough to get us out of here."

"No, give me enough fire so I can get to my 'Mech

and then take off. I'm a MechWarrior. I fight with my
'Mech. I escape with my 'Mech.''

"Very well." Chick pulled a smoke grenade out of
his belt. "Here. This might help. You're going to be
exposed for a while."

"Thanks."

"Captain Masters," called Valentine. He looked up
and saw her standing beside a pile of corpses. The sun
was high overhead now, and the beams of shattered
buildings pointed up from the ground like spikes ready
for sacrifice.

"Good luck, sir."

"To you too. No firing unless they shoot at me first.
If we can, let's meet up at the north end of the valley."

"Yes, sir."

Valentine walked toward them, and Chick split off
and headed toward the far end of the town and his
hovercraft. Increasing his pace Masters walked directly toward Valentine, who stood between him and
his *Phoenix Hawk*.

"Captain Masters," she said when he came closer,
a smile playing at the right side of her mouth.

"Yes, Lieutenant," he said, walking right past her
without breaking pace.

This startled her for a moment, and she took some
big steps to catch up with him. "I've just received a
message from Precentor Martial Arian."

"Well, that is exciting. What a delightful bit of
news. A message. Good, good, good. Can't expect
anything better than that." The *Phoenix Hawk* stood
fifty meters away.

"He told me . . ."

"Yes, what did he say? What has the Precentor Martial to say for himself? Excited about the body count?
What did we bag today, five hundred, six hundred desperate, ruthless guerrillas? Oh, there's a nasty one,"
he said, pointing to the shattered corpse of an old

woman holding a small, dead child in her arms. "Good work."

Forty meters.

"He said—"

"No, don't tell me, for I'm so proud to have been part of today's operation. We've all been given three-day passes . . ."

"Actually Spinard and I did—"

"Really. The absurdity is rather easy to predict around here when one allows oneself to wallow in the logic."

"Sir!" she said, and stopped.

Thirty meters.

He kept walking.

Over his shoulder, he said, "Ice cream for the troops this weekend? Children getting gold stars? Little bonuses toting up for all our big, grown-up murderers?"

"Sir, the Precentor Marshal has placed your arrogant ass under arrest!"

"Well, there's a problem with that, Lieutenant. I am a Knight of the Inner Sphere. As such, I live by the rules of my heart, not those of you bloody bean-counters!"

Twenty meters.

"Harris and O'Donnally, disarm and subdue Captain Masters!"

With that, Masters stopped walking and began to run toward the *Phoenix Hawk* as fast as his legs would take him.

=== 16 ===

He heard one of the soldiers—Harris, he thought—shout, "Captain Masters! Stop!" Then came the thin sound of gun bolts pulled back and the explosion of machine-gun fire from his right. He ran on toward the *Phoenix Hawk,* his Imperator slapping against his back. Suddenly the sound of heavy machine gun fire cut loose to the left and behind him. He heard screams from his attackers as Chick's squad fired the Dryfus support machine gun mounted on the hovercraft, sending everyone behind him running for cover. For a moment he felt a splinter of relief. Then the roar of more weapons cut through the air and bullets passed him, ricocheting off the thick legs of his 'Mech. He whirled around and pulled up his Imperator, letting loose a broad spray of fire. He saw a half-dozen soldiers, including Valentine, dive for cover behind the piles of corpses.

Chick's hovercraft hummed to life and rushed toward the center of the fray, firing the laser mounted on the top of the vehicle in random arcs. Masters took the opportunity to begin climbing up to his cockpit.

In his rush to get up, he took the first few rungs too quickly and his right foot slipped. His hands held tight to the rungs above, but his right shin slammed into a rung and a red pain shot through his leg. He cursed his age and continued up.

The sound of gunfire continued, as well as a great deal of shouting. The soldiers below, many of whom had no idea that Arian had authorized his arrest, tried to figure out what was going on and drew up quick alliances.

As he worked his way up the rungs, a bullet slammed into his left side and tore through meat just above his hip. He did not fall, for his muscles all tightened at the moment of impact and his hands clung tightly to the rungs. His teeth clenched, and he said reflexively, "Come on, come on."

He glanced up, and the cockpit seemed tremendously far away. Bullets were ricocheting all over the surface of the 'Mech. Another bullet caught him in the shoulder and he found himself dangling from a rung by one hand. As he swung around, like a weather vane in a changing wind, he saw the forces scattered about below, with Chick's hovercraft coming in for another pass. Now, however, the mercenaries seemed to have broken up into several groups, shooting at each other, Chick's hovercraft, and Masters. Some men were shouting for the fighting to stop, and Masters spotted a makeshift white flag made from a dress once worn by a citizen of Padang.

As some soldiers continued to shoot at Masters, he remembered the smoke grenade Chick had given him. With his wounded arm he pulled the grenade from his belt and brought it up to his mouth. The action cost him, for the bullet wound in his shoulder stung deep. He gripped the ring in his mouth, the taste of the metal cold and flat against his tongue as he pulled the grenade forward. He swung around, still clinging by one hand to a rung, and shoved the grenade into the 'Mech's knee joint.

The grenade billowed out a thick white cloud. The sulfur and smoke, thickest near Masters, fogged around him and made his eyes tear. Between the tears and the smoke he could see nothing, but he positioned himself to continue up the ladder. With his right arm and left hip both wounded, every movement up the rungs sent pain through his body. But the smoke screen worked, and though bullets slammed into his 'Mech, he was no longer a prime target.

As he topped the smoke that floated up from the grenade, he saw the *Hatchetman* lumbering toward him, its huge feet make the ground shake with every step. As it approached, the right arm raised and lifted the huge axe.

Masters scrambled painfully up the last few rungs and hurled himself into his cockpit and pulled the hatch shut. He grabbed his cooling vest and snugged the neurohelmet over his head just as Spinard slammed the axe against the rear torso of the *Phoenix Hawk*. The 'Mech started to fall forward even as Masters began to voice the secret code.

As the 'Mech's engines fired up, his fingers flew over the controls. The horizon rushed past as the machine toppled, the ground looming closer and closer. He threw one of the *Phoenix Hawk*'s legs out to break the fall, then pushed the throttle forward, using the momentum of the fall to get into a quick run. Masters knew a three-against-one fight would be difficult, but he also knew he could outmaneuver all the other MechWarriors. He might make it.

He glanced at his monitor and saw only Spinard's *Hatchetman* moving; Valentine and Belgrade probably hadn't gotten to their 'Mechs yet. Should he take the opportunity to damage their 'Mechs before they were even in them? It wasn't the warrior code he and

Thomas honored, but it seemed a shame to let the opportunity pass. Smiling to himself, he decided they were ruffians—red knights who deserved a few bad breaks.

Continuing across Padang's fields Masters turned the *Phoenix Hawk* from the waist up. Then he dropped his targeting cross hairs over Valentine's *Blackjack*. All he wanted was to damage its movement enough that he wouldn't have three 'Mechs on him. When the cross hairs was over the *Blackjack*'s right leg, he pushed the blue button and a red laser bolt shot through the air.

While the bolt hit the leg and was burning away some armor, he pressed the green button on his joystick, firing two short-range missiles. The missiles struck home, and the outer armor of the *Blackjack*'s leg flew off, revealing a shredded actuator.

With the temperature in the cockpit rising sharply, Masters checked his heat monitors. He could still take a few shots at Belgrade's 'Mech and then be off. Even if he ran, within a matter of minutes the heat sinks would take care of the extra heat from the shots, if he managed it correctly.

Suddenly laser bolts shot past him to his right. Looking back he realized Spinard was shooting at him. Then an autocannon shell exploded against his 'Mech's back, tossing him forward. He hadn't strapped himself in, and the blow slammed him into the thick window of the faceplate. The impact made his right shoulder go numb. As he struggled to disentangle himself and get back into the seat, the *Phoenix Hawk* ran forward blindly, the throttle still halfway up.

He repositioned himself and brought the 'Mech's speed down by half and jabbed the left foot pedal. The 'Mech turned sharply and he saw another autocannon shell fly past him. He accelerated again, rushing past the *Hatchetman*, thinking to get a shot at Belgrade's *Shadow Hawk* before the other man could fight back.

In the distance he saw Chick's hovercraft flying away, pursued, or followed, by the Fourth Squad's hovercraft.

As he came back toward the town proper Masters saw Valentine's *Blackjack* come alive, its arms lifting up to shoulder level. From launch tubes built into the monster's chest she fired four short-range missiles. Masters dragged his throttle back and tapped the reverse button. Valentine's missiles rushed straight at him, at cockpit level, and he saw them as blue orbs with red-orange auras. He pushed the throttle forward and the 'Mech took two quick steps back. As he'd expected, she'd given them a good lead, and the four missiles rushed by, one so close it left a wide, faint smoke trail across his window.

Without pause he pulled the throttle back again and tapped the reverse button once more. Now, as he pushed the throttle up, he moved forward slowly, giving the opposition a false lead, then suddenly he slammed full throttle. The *Phoenix Hawk* raced across the fields of Padang, the soft soil giving way every so often, a sudden lurch here and there.

Now Belgrade's 'Mech woke from its mechanical slumber. Masters' plan hadn't quite worked out—the 'Mechs were all up. Time for the straight run. His only chance lay in getting far enough away from the 'Mechs that they couldn't hit him. He pushed his throttle full forward and raced for a sea of yellow-leafed trees. Valentine's 'Mech would be slowed, so the other two could either wait for her or come after him by themselves. Two-to-one odds were better than three to one, and so far his situation was good.

He took a moment in his straight run to slip on his harness. The wound in his side stung, but didn't seem serious. His shoulder, however, hurt like blazes, and moving around to pilot the 'Mech aggravated the pain.

He glanced down and saw blood, far too much of it, trickling down his arm, covering it like paint.

More shots flew by him, red lasers and fiery tails of missiles. A straight run would give them too easy a lead on targeting, so he cut his speed by a quarter and began veering left and then right. The turns came wide, but they were enough to keep the shots away from him. Then, before they could get used to his new movement, he cut his speed again, and made tighter turns more frequently.

He glanced at his monitor. Belgrade and Spinard ran together, leaving Valentine further and further behind, the shots to her leg a drag on her speed. He rushed toward the tree line, hoping to find some escape route within the maze of massive trees. He had no guarantees, but neither had he any other choice.

A terrible thought occurred to him. Like the mercs hired by the countess, he was trapped on Gibson. Where could he possibly go?

No time. He rushed into the woods, the bright sunlight suddenly dimmed by the thick canopy of yellow leaves high overhead. The giant tree trunks formed winding avenues, most of which ended in dead ends. He could knock down the trees if he found himself in a natural cul de sac, but the trees looked strong and deeply rooted. Too many blows would eventually wear down his armor.

Laser bolts ripped into a tree to his right, followed by more shots as portions of the trees to either side of him exploded in pulpy shards. Taking a quick look at his monitor, he saw Belgrade and Spinard closing quickly.

A series of blasts rocked his 'Mech. Punching up his armor display, Masters found that laser fire had chewed up half his rear torso armor. The boys behind him must have been heating up their 'Mechs pretty fierce to get so many shots off. In response he threw his 'Mech into high speed, hoping the excessive heat would hamper their speeds and piloting ability.

At the higher speed he had less control over the 'Mech's turning ability, and so the *Phoenix Hawk*'s shoulders and head sometimes slammed into low branches as he raced it through the woods. Leaning his own body back and forth and side to side with the 'Mech, Masters strained to keep his eye on as many facets of the terrain as possible: massive roots lying across his path, deep gullies, and piles of large, loose stones.

Twice, and then a third time, he nearly slammed full into a tree. The first time he veered just in time. Next he stopped just short of the tree, then turned and moved past it. The third time, he misjudged his approach slamming the 'Mech's shoulder into the tree, uprooting it slightly and sending a violent reverberation through the cockpit. The collision nearly knocked him over, but he regained his balance and kept moving.

On the monitor Masters saw Belgrade and Spinard quickly losing ground, with Valentine already far behind. It would work. If the forest was just large enough, he'd be able to get far enough away to be out of range, power down, and hide. He switched off his communication and sensor system, there being no one he wanted to talk to. The three 'Mechs behind him vanished from the display. That didn't matter. He didn't care *where* they were, just as long as they were behind him. What did matter was that they couldn't see him on their screens, either. They were trapped using visuals to find him, and soon he'd be out of their visual range.

But then, ahead, he saw that the forest grew lighter, and more than that, actually was sparkling. A tremor of fear ran through his chest as he realized the woods were about to end only a few hundred meters away.

He stormed out of the thick trees and found himself on flat, open swamp land at the edge of a broad lake. He craned his neck, looking over the terrain. The swamp extended around the lake, and was bracketed by steep, rocky hills. His shelter had vanished. If he was going to make it, he'd have to clear the hills before his pursuers arrived. That might do it.

The *Phoenix Hawk*'s heat was completely under control. Now, with no chance of staying out of sight, he decided to use his jump jets to cover more ground between here and the steep hills. He turned west and hit the controls. With a growing rush, the rockets built into his 'Mech's legs accelerated, forcing him deep into the command couch. The *Phoenix Hawk* blasted up and forward, cutting through the air in a low arc, the jets burning white as they lifted away from the shallow swamp water. Masters relaxed, letting his balance take over. As it did, he maneuvered the 'Mech's legs slightly forward to brace him as he came down.

The *Phoenix Hawk* landed with a smash in the shallow water, the 'Mech sinking up to its knees in the swamp muck. That was both good and bad. Good because the water helped dissipate the heat from the jump quickly. Bad, because it would take a moment for Masters to leverage himself out of the holes he had just dug and to make another jump.

Anyone nearby would be able to see him clearly as he flew through the air, so he decided to turn on his sensors and find out how the opposition was doing. As the monitor flickered to life, he saw the blue squares representing Belgrade and Spinard's 'Mechs adjust their course and head after him through the forest. He had to switch to the long-range screen to find Valentine, who was far behind, but not far enough.

He used the neurohelmet's control abilities rather than the throttle to get his legs out of the mud, because the helmet allowed finer control of motion. As he thought about the motion he wanted the 'Mech's legs to make, he made slight, similar motions with his own legs. He did not need to completely mimic the actions he wanted, just enough of them for the neurohelmet to receive the impulse of movement from the brain. It was tricky business; too much movement and thought, and the 'Mech's motions became erratic and wild, a high-step kick reminiscent of a showgirl—and likely to send the 'Mech tumbling onto its back. Too little movement and thought, and the 'Mech remained still and silent. A MechWarrior had to know just how much motion and thought was required in any given circumstances. Right now, with several meters of 'Mech plunked down in the mud, he needed more than the usual movement, but he would have to slow down once the leg cleared the mud.

With his years of 'Mech piloting to guide him, Masters quickly cleared the mud and stepped onto higher swamp ground. He sank a little, but not much. Two more jumps would get him to the hills. Once more he thumbed the jump jet controls, and again flew into the air and again sank into the mud.

The shots against his back came unexpectedly even as he sank. They were coming sooner than he'd expected, missiles raining against the *Phoenix Hawk*, rocking him back and forth. Somewhere in the barrage a good hit got through, making a red light on his board start to blink on and off. It was paramount that he get moving. He was far enough away still that he'd be a difficult target if he could get free, but as long as he remained in the mud . . .

They closed on him, covering the distance carefully, avoiding the predicament in which Masters found himself. Closer and closer . . .

Masters brought up his 'Mech's right leg and placed it down ahead of him. Laser fire crashed in around him. The shots tore up his back so much that he had to stop his progress in the muck to twist his 'Mech's torso toward Belgrade and Spinard in a way that put his fresher armor up against their shots. And as long as they were in view . . .

He brought up his cross hairs against Belgrade, needing only to float the yellow circle a little as the 'Mech walked toward him. Masters might be trapped and standing still, but Belgrade's direct approach offered an almost equally sitting target. He depressed each of the joystick's triggers in succession, sending a barrage of missiles, heavy lasers, and pulse lasers at the other 'Mech. Belgrade had already begun to break to the right, which was exactly where Masters had expected him to go. The shots slammed home, sending a wash of sparks out the 'Mech's right arm.

Having done some damage to the opposition, Masters returned his attention to getting out of the mud. He concentrated, calming himself against the shots being fired at him, focusing only on his 'Mech's movements. First the right, then the left.

He was free.

He looked at his monitor—What?

Four more 'Mechs had suddenly appeared, and somewhere off to the left—.

Instinctively looking in that direction, he saw only water. But no, there was something, a slight shimmer in the lake. And then steam began to rise off the surface of the water, like heat off a gun. . . .

Part 3

BATTLES

$=17=$

A 'Mech lance waited hidden in the lake, revealing itself now as it warmed up quickly.

Another series of shots rocked Masters' *Phoenix Hawk*, a red light flashed, and he saw that Spinard had severed the power cables to his large laser. He assumed the new 'Mechs were Word of Blake, and knew he had to get out *now*. As he sent his 'Mech sprinting across the swamp, three-meter-high plumes of dark water splashed up and around the legs. He torso-twisted to get a look at the lake again. Four 'Mechs rose out of the water, a *Crusader*, a *Catapult*, a *Rifleman*, and a *Quickdraw*. Water cascaded down their metal surfaces, obscuring their colors. But after a moment, Masters saw orange and black swirls—Regulus!

Each 'Mech had small differentiations in patterns, indicating four different regiments, but each was from the Principality of Regulus. What were they doing here?

Even as he continued running his 'Mech for the hills, Masters' mind continued to puzzle out the question. What if Regulus was backing the GFL, as the

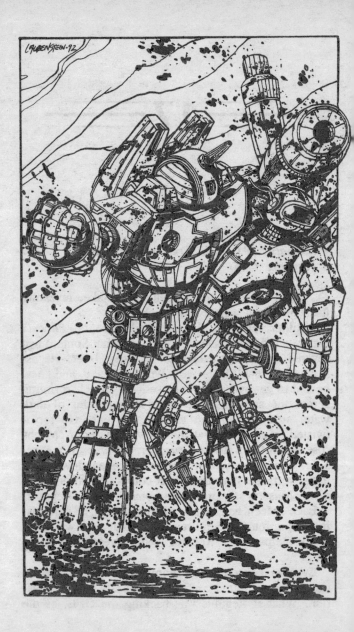

Countess had joked, expressing the Regulans' opposition to Thomas through a backwater fight on Gibson. It would make a kind of sense: Gibson and the True Believers were a testing ground for Thomas' policies.

The water around the *Crusader* boiled fiercely and the 'Mech rose straight out of it on its jump jets. It lifted slowly at first, then sailed up and through the air to close the distance between the lake and Masters in his *Phoenix Hawk*.

Masters turned forward again and raced as quickly as he could, but the *Crusader* splashed into the mud just ahead of him. He made a sharp left to avoid the 'Mech, but before he could get out of range, the *Crusader* swung up its right arm and slammed it into the *Phoenix Hawk*'s cockpit. A terrible CLANG! reverberated throughout the cockpit, and Masters was thrown first to the right and then the left. As the *Phoenix Hawk* began listing to the left, he slowed the 'Mech to keep it under control.

More shots slammed into his 'Mech's back, and a series of red lights blinked on the command console.

With the damage he'd already taken, it didn't look good.

Turning back around toward the *Crusader*, Masters saw the other three Regulan 'Mechs engaging Spinard and Belgrade. He just had time to see a series of autocannon shots rip into Belgrade's already damaged leg.

Masters charged the *Crusader*, reconfiguring his weapon systems as his 'Mech ran forward. He knew that the latest model *Crusader* was equipped with antimissile systems which would render his missiles nearly useless, so he plugged all his lasers into the green and blue thumb buttons.

The *Crusader* fired a laser barrage, which flew way off to the right of Masters' cockpit. As he closed on the *Crusader*, he pulled back on the joystick until the cross hairs dropped down onto the *Crusader*'s head. He knew he'd get only one good shot on this pass, and decided to close to where he could not possibly miss. His breathing was even and relaxed, every action smooth and calm. But even with all his training and experience, he muttered the word ''Please'' in a kind of little sigh of a prayer as his thumb hovered over the triggers.

The massive head of the *Crusader* loomed next to the *Phoenix Hawk*, filling the window of his faceplate. Jabbing the green and blue buttons on the joystick, he fired the 'Mech's large laser and pulse lasers directly into the *Crusader*'s head. The beams ripped through the armor and tore huge rifts across the cockpit. As Masters passed the *Crusader*, a bright orange flash erupted beside him.

He traveled another hundred meters and turned a wide arc back toward the other 'Mech. The *Crusader*'s head burned with bright flames, and the body wobbled slightly. Then the left torso exploded, torn open by a tremendous fireball. The 'Mech fell over backward, huge waves of dark water splashing up around it.

Masters turned quickly back to the other 'Mechs. Spinard's *Hatchetman* was already down. The other three Regulan 'Mechs ran wildly around Belgrade, blasting him with a barrage of missiles and beams.

Masters felt torn in two directions: either he could make another attempt at escape or he could help Belgrade. Much as he wanted to escape from the Word of Blake 'Mechs, he didn't want to leave them in the hands of the Regulans.

After a brief moment of deliberation he charged into the melee. At the same moment, the *Rifleman* turned toward him and raised its large lasers. As Masters made a sharp left, the blasts glanced off his armor. Beginning another zig-zag run, he saw Belgrade's 'Mech collapse.

The monitor showed him Valentine rushing forward in her *Blackjack*. With his back torso armor hanging on by the rivets, Masters decided a retreat was in order. Piloting back toward the forest, he jabbed the blue comm button and said, "Blackjack One, this is Phoenix Hawk One. We've encountered Regulan 'Mechs."

"This is Blackjack One," Valentine replied in a distinctly dry tone. "Whatever you say, Phoenix Hawk One." He knew she didn't believe him. She had no reason to think he wasn't working with the Regulans at this point. On his monitor he saw her change course, moving to intercept him.

As he rushed into the forest, the Regulans continued to assault his back with a storm of beams and missiles. Stray shots sent branches down on his 'Mech and across his path.

As he ran on, Valentine got closer and closer.

"Blackjack One. Phoenix Hawk One. Listen to me. We're outnumbered three to two. We've got to work together until we've dealt with the Regulan warriors. We can win if we do that."

But no answer came. He'd made good progress against two of the Regulan 'Mechs; one of them, though, the *Rifleman*, stayed on his tail. He decided to stop and engage his shadow before Valentine and the other two Regulans arrived. But even as he slowed, his radio crackled: "Masters. Captain Masters?" The voice sounded familiar, but he couldn't place it. "Imagine being caught all alone out in the middle of nowhere."

Colonel Roush. From the knighting celebration.

Masters ran for cover behind some trees, but even as he did, Roush got off two good shots that ripped through the *Phoenix Hawk*'s remaining back armor and went internal. Half of Masters' computer displays went out, then the engines made a horrible noise as the 'Mech ground to a halt.

Instinctively he slapped one hand toward the eject button that would launch him free of his 'Mech. But he stopped centimeters above the red button, for he remembered the thick canopy of large branches overhead. If he ejected, he might not make it past them. He might not die in the flight as he smashed into one branch after another. He knew, though, that he had to get word of the Regulan presence on Gibson to Thomas. There really was no choice.

He jabbed the button and the eject thrusters fired underneath him. The cockpit rumbled wildly, and then the faceplate blew out as his command chair lifted with a rush. He felt his flesh and muscles forced down as a wash of yellow passed before him. The chair smashed into a thick branch, then another, and then another, each impact accompanied by a solid knock that echoed in Masters' ears with nightmarish volume. The chair leaned right, and then he spun upside down. He couldn't keep his focus, and everything around him looked like a blur of yellow and brown. He slammed into something that stopped his progress cold, and then felt his landing begin. His thoughts slid away as he fell toward the forest floor, and then he remembered nothing more.

When they gripped him by the arms, he didn't know who they were. They dragged him out of the command chair and into the forest's dim sunlight. Then Masters remembered Gibson and the war and the GFL. He didn't struggle. He had no strength left.

"Well, *Sir* Masters," said Roush. He wasn't drunk now but his eyes showed the same loathing from the night of the party on Atreus. Without warning, he brought up his fist and slammed it into Masters' jaw. The pain sliced like a knife, and he thought for a moment he might pass out once more. Then Roush said, "You're the lucky one. We've got something for

Word of Blake that's going to make them wish they'd never accepted Marik's offer.''

They carried him back to a cave entrance, where Roush told the guerrillas to keep Masters safe until he returned. With a guerrilla on either side of him, Masters was led down a series of tunnels. They tripped him and shoved him into the walls of the cave; a few even came up and glared at him, brandishing knives and promising their ''time with him.''

They left him with his back to a jagged wall, his hands bound with coarse rope. He had no idea how to get out again, for he'd been too weak when they brought him in. But sitting and waiting in the tunnel for what seemed hours, he gathered his strength and resolve.

Some time later the guerrillas brought Spinard down the corridor with his hands also tied behind his back. His faced crawled with cuts and bruised skin. They dropped him alongside Masters, then one of the guerrillas, an Arab, laughed and said, ''He doesn't have Regulan protection like you. Until the colonel gets back, he's ours.'' The man then leaned down and placed his knife underneath Spinard's right eye. ''This is what might happen to you,'' he said to Masters. The tip of the blade pressed into Spinard's flesh, but did not puncture it. ''Come to our world, eh? Come to our world with Blake? You want to kill us all, don't you?''

Masters, wanting to deflect the situation, said, ''He doesn't want to kill—''

But the man grimaced and revealed yellow teeth. ''Shut up, *Knight*. This isn't your war. You're just on the sidelines, letting the Blake people run over us. You and your Captain-General. What have any of you done for us?''

''The countess—''

''Shut up!'' The man turned his attention back to

Spinard's flesh, just below the eye. "What do you say, *True Believer*?"

Masters watched the guerrilla carefully, ready to struggle to his knees and defend Spinard as best he could if the guerrilla actually cut him. But then something strange happened.

As the guerrillas leered at Spinard, his smile faded.

Masters looked at Spinard, and saw Spinard's eyes looking past the guerrilla, revealing a terror, something quiet and private, so deep it seemed Spinard could never reveal it, nor anyone fathom it. Masters turned back to the guerrilla. "Let him be," he said softly.

"Shut up!"

But the guerrilla stood and backed away. "We'll come back later," he said, without taking his eyes off Spinard. The other guerrilla eyed Spinard with equal trepidation, then the two of them left.

Masters cleared his throat. "Spinard?" Nothing. "Private Spinard?"

"Yes." Spinard's voice creaked like an ancient tank's hatch opening, an ancient tank complete with the skeletons of dead soldiers inside.

"Private? Are you . . . ? How are you holding up?"

"Not, sir."

"Not? You're not holding up?"

"No, sir." When Spinard spoke, he kept his gaze fixed ahead, his voice flat and monotone.

"They beat you?"

"Yes, sir."

They remained silent a long while. Guerrillas walked up and down the corridor past them. "I might be able to get something for you," Masters said. "Do you want something?"

"No." He remained silent for a moment. "If I could have my metal back, sir."

"Metal?"

"My 'Mech, sir."

Masters almost laughed. "You want your 'Mech back? I don't think we can pull that off right now."

Spinard ignored him, continuing in his monotone, but as if they were talking casually, perhaps in a mess hall after a good meal, looking at a very red sunset out the window. "I'd rather have my metal. We've got this skin that can be pierced. You know, they can get you, right, sir? The world, I mean. Everything. Everyone. You don't know what they're going to do to you, and you don't want to . . . feel. You don't want to feel it. It's better to be inside the metal, where it's safe."

"Spinard?"

"See sir, I figured it out. There's this death, and it keeps piling up and piling up, and I have this thought in my head of all these bodies, like the stars . . . you know, the stars . . . when you look at them at night . . . from space, I mean . . . and they're all there, and it seems like they go on forever, they must never stop, so many of them. And there are some stars you can't even see, some so far away they're too faint—those are the kids, see, sir, those are the kids I keep killing. And then there are the stars that are blocked by other stars, those are the grandparents and grandmothers. They're eclipsed by the closer, hotter stars. And so even though it seems like I could count all the dead, there are more and more, more I can't even keep track of, cause there are as many dead as there are stars. Which is hard to keep in your head. And they keep piling up, the dead, like stars seen from space, overlaid and piled up, and counted and catalogued. . . ."

"Private?"

"And, see, sir, I don't want to feel them, cause that's the thing. I need the heat of my 'Mech. I need the wall of my metal between me and the cold dead. I don't want to feel the world. I don't want to know . . . I wish . . . That cold will come get you, you know,

it'll come and hurt you. You think you can trust someone, you think you might want to feel, but you can't,
you know . . . . You know what I wish, sir?''

"No. What do you wish, Private?''

"I wish I could be metal. You know, sir? See? When
I got in my 'Mech, if . . .'' He sighed, searching for
the words. "If my flesh could grow and melt into the
metal of the 'Mech. I wish that. I wouldn't have to get
in and out. I'd be safe, metal, feel nothing. I could
hurt, kill, do what I had to do, but feel nothing.''

Unable to stop himself, Masters said, "That's
wrong, Spinard.''

"No, sir. See, we're killing people like they're . . .
bushels of apples to be harvested, if you know what I
mean. They're not people. See, people aren't people
anymore. Or, we were wrong about people. We used
to see people as special, with souls. That's wrong.
We're just things to be ground by the paperwork, because the paperwork works, people are too complicated. It's easier. But being alive still hurts. If people
are just animals, like a dog or a cat, how come I feel
so sad? It shouldn't hurt, see. So if I could *be* my
'Mech, safe in metal, killing and safe, I'd be all right.
I wouldn't feel bad anymore.''

Spinard stopped and stared off ahead, then closed
his eyes very tightly.

Spinard's words chilled Masters, planted the seeds
of a paranoid notion that Spinard's insanity on Gibson
could spread, a kind of mimetic disease. He had to get
to Portent, to the hyperpulse generator, without anyone from Word of Blake finding out about it, so that
he could get word to Thomas about the war. Or maybe
Precentor Blane. Maybe he could be trusted. But this
couldn't wait. Thomas had to know that things were
falling apart on Gibson.

He tugged on his ropes again. Still tight as ever.
The only thing he had going for him was that his hands

were behind his back, hidden from the sight of people passing by. He began to tug on the ropes gently, squeezing and probing the knots around each wrist. Unfortunately, he'd never paid much attention to knots before, and he realized that although he could touch the entire surface of the knots, he had no clear picture of them in his mind. For a very long time he pulled on pieces of the rope and wriggled his fingers through the gaps between the ropes. He rubbed his fingertips raw against the rough hemp, never certain he was doing anything more than tightening the knots. The whole while Spinard sat silently beside him, eyes closed. After an hour or so Masters' mind wandered and his manipulations of the rope took place without conscious thought. It became a habit more than an attempt to get free.

Then the knot around his right wrist slipped a bit.

Not a great deal, but enough that he might be able to actually free his bonds. He became alert once more, and worked another half hour, his fingers sore and tired. As he felt a long stretch of rope come loose, he gave out a startled sigh. As he pulled it through the knot, the rest of the knot quickly fell away. His hands were still behind him as he set to work on the knot around his other hand when a pair of black boots stepped up before him.

"Hey," a dark-skinned man said. "What are you doing?"

18

The guerrilla wore black fatigues, and carried a Valton machine gun strapped over his shoulder. Masters saw no one else in the corridor and decided the moment was at hand. "Trying to escape," he said. "That's what I'm doing. Trying to escape."

"That's what I thought," the guerrilla said and laughed, his white teeth gleaming. "Get up and let me check your knots."

Masters rolled over slightly and got up onto his knees, keeping his arms tight behind his back, as if still bound. He put on a show in his efforts to rise, and finally said, "I'm sorry . . . My arm, I was shot in the shoulder. I can't . . ."

The guerrilla leaned down and grabbed Masters fiercely by the left shoulder, the signal for Masters to suddenly swing his arms out in front of him. He grabbed the guerrilla's shoulder with one hand, and rammed his other fist up into the man's stomach. The guerrilla gave out a tremendous exhalation, and doubled over. It wasn't enough to put him out of the action, however. As Masters tried to stand, the man gave him a swift kick in the jaw, knocking him into the wall.

"Prisoner escape!" the guerrilla shouted. Masters rebounded and threw himself into the guard with a sharp leap that slammed the two of them into the other side of the tunnel. Masters turned the guerrilla around and grabbed him from the back. Seizing the loose end of the rope still tied around his waist, he brought it across to the guerrilla's mouth, trying to shut him up before anyone else heard the scuffle. The guerrilla struggled and the pressure on Masters' wounded right arm made the pain fresh and new.

Out the corner of his eye he spotted a second guerrilla coming down the corridor. Almost at the same instant she pulled up her gun to shoot, but Masters whirled the first guerrilla around to block the shot. The sound of machine gun fine ripped through the air and the guerrilla in his arms shook wildly for a moment, his scream garbled by the rope cutting across his mouth.

Keeping the lifeless body propped in front of him as a shield, Masters lifted the gun that hung from the corpse's shoulder. He pointed it toward the second guerrilla, spraying several rounds down the corridor that sent her diving for the ground around a bend in the tunnel. Masters had just pulled the corpse out of the way as the second guerrilla came in view again. This time, aiming, he fired a full burst that she answered with a loud and terrible scream. Blood shot up from her back, splattering the tunnel walls like dark raindrops.

Masters looked down at Spinard. The Word of Blake MechWarrior had not budged when the shooting began, and now sat forever still, his skull shattered by a stray bullet from the second guerrilla's gun. Masters sighed heavily, wishing immediately he had more power, more of what he needed to do everything he wanted to do, to protect those who needed protecting. "We do what we can," Thomas had told him once.

He unlooped the machine gun from the guerrilla's shoulder, then let the body drop to the ground once more. Then he ran over to the other dead guerrilla, grabbed the clip out of the woman's gun, and continued on his way. He had no idea how to get out here, could only hope that constant motion would lead him to better circumstances.

It wasn't long before he encountered more guerrillas, all of them alerted by the sound of machine gun fire in tunnels. Three times he engaged in a fire-fight, but he had no choice. Either die in combat or die of torture at the hands of the guerrillas. So each time he raced forward, charging the guerrillas, his determination shaking their confidence. Dirt flew off the tunnel walls as bullets slammed all around him. The guerrillas watched in surprise as Masters rushed at them, apparently undaunted by their overmatched firepower. Each time they hesitated, uncertain whether to press the attack or to run for support, and it was in those moments of indecision that Masters was able to take down one guerrilla after another.

As he ran and fought, he kept changing his spent gun for one taken from the dead and wounded. One gun after another passed through his hands as he sped down the tunnels.

Soon, though, the guerrillas began to come at him too quickly and in numbers too great. When six at once had him pinned, he had to retrace his steps and cut through passages he had passed by earlier. Not knowing which way he was going, Masters knew he could just as easily be running in circles. Would he soon be trapped by guerrillas on both ends of a corridor, cut to pulpy shreds in a tremendous cross-fire? A wave of fatigue and fear washed over him.

Turning yet another corner, his spirits suddenly

lifted when he saw bright sunshine filling the tunnel a hundred or so meters ahead. He broke into an open run, chanting over and over again, "Come on, come on, come on . . ."

He cold see now that he was approaching a large cave that led outside. Passing the tunnel's opening into the cave was the silhouette of a guerrilla. Apparently this section of the tunnels had yet to be alerted.

Masters ran up to the end of the tunnel and peered into the cave. It was broad and low, leading directly outside down to a lightly wooded area. The cave apparently served as a vehicle depot, for he saw half a dozen guerrillas working on light all-terrain vehicles. Some of the ATs had support machine guns mounted on their backs, others small lasers. It wasn't the best way to move valuable heavy weapons around, but probably all the guerrillas had.

Spotting a stack of crates covered with heavy cloth, he hustled over to them, getting closer to the ATs. As he ducked down behind the crates, he saw the writing on a crate where the cloth had been pulled slightly out of place. He made out a portion of stenciled label that said "Davey." Something clicked in the back of his brain at the sight of the word, but he heard a footstep off to his right just as he was going to pull the cloth back to see the whole label.

"Hey!" shouted a technician. Masters turned and saw a man pointing at him. From behind the tech, a group of guerrillas was closing on Masters. He leaped out from the shelter of the crates and sprayed the air with bullets, sending the guerrillas diving for cover while he rushed for an AT containing no weapons. Something unencumbered to get him moving as quickly as possible.

He raced through the parked vehicles, using the ATs and their mounted weapons as cover from the guerrillas' bullets. Coming to an open AT sitting in the front of the cave, he jumped into the driver's seat, hoping desperately that it would have a key. It did. He touched the ignition stud, the engine fired up, and he drove the AT down the base of the hill. Behind him came the sound of other engines, and he pushed the AT into higher gear.

The way he traveled was a dirt road that cut a path through a yellow forest. As soon as he passed the first bend, he drove the AT off the road and behind some trees and killed the engine. A few seconds later three ATs roared past down the road. The ruse had worked, but the guerrillas wouldn't be fooled for more than a few moments. Masters jumped out of the jeep, grabbed the gun, and sprinted through the trees. He expected to hear the shouting of guerrillas any moment, but their voices never came. For a good hour he ran, forging deeper and deeper into the woods, seeking safety in distance.

After an hour he began sucking in air deeply, gulping at it like a drowning man. He slowed his pace, but didn't stop. As the sun dropped toward the horizon and the stars came out, he slowed to a walk but kept on and on. No one seemed to be pursuing him, but Masters had no idea if the guerrillas knew which way he'd gone. One way or the other he couldn't risk slowing down. Long after the air had turned cold, his muscles stiffened and his wounds became numb, he continued walking into the night. It was many hours later when his eyes became so tired that he began to stumble over roots and rocks. Finally he tripped, falling to his knees and feeling a dull ache spread up his legs from the impact. He laughed softly, thinking there should be more pain. He told himself he would lie down for just a moment, just to rest his eyes, ten minutes at the most. Stretching out on the grass-covered ground, which was much warmer than the night air, Masters gratefully closed his eyes.

* * *

The voices and the sunlight slammed into his senses at the same moment, and he rolled over quickly, startled, fearing danger.

Looking up he saw an oriental man and a young girl of about twelve, perhaps his daughter, staring down at him. The girl jumped behind her father, but her father's gaze, curious and concerned, did not waver. Masters realized that he had fallen asleep on a patch of grass running between two fields. In the distance he saw a large wooden farm house with smoke rising from a stack. He thought of Padang, of the blood, and closed his eyes.

"Are you all right?" the man asked.

"No. My shoulder." He raised his fingers to the wound and touched it. It stung terribly, and the flesh felt soft and ruined.

"All right. All right. Don't worry. Relax. Lin, go tell mama to get the emergency supplies together."

"But . . ."

"Go tell mama you found a wounded soldier who needs some help."

Masters remembered he was wearing his uniform, and felt a shudder of fear. The girl ran off.

The man leaned down to help Masters up, but stopped when Masters asked him, "Which side are you on?"

The man's smile spoke eloquently of ease and serenity. "I'm not on any side. I'm not a soldier." He leaned down further and helped Masters up by his good shoulder, while Masters reached for the Imperator machine gun he had grabbed from the last guerrilla he'd shot.

"No. But who do you want to win?"

"I want the war to end. That is all. Word of Blake is bad. Very bad. Arrogant. And they support Hsiang, a corrupt, fetid lizard." The man took in a breath after virtually lifting Masters to his feet, and the two of them walked toward the house. "And the GFL are bastards who would sell us back to the Principality of Regulus. I don't want a winner. I want peace. Winners breed losers. And losers breed the next war." The old man walked Masters carefully to the house, taking care none of his neighbors could see him taking in a Word of Blake warrior. "The GFL's in the village," he explained.

"What?"

"Don't worry. I won't tell them you're here."

Inside the house the old man cleaned out the infections already beginning in Master's flesh, dressed his wounds, fed him, and gave him a mat on the floor. Masters wanted to leave before the day ended, but the farmer insisted he stay. He was in no shape, the man said, to set out alone. He must wait until he was stronger.

"Why are you doing this?" Masters asked, sincerely confused.

"Wouldn't you do the same for me?"

"I suppose. . . ."

"Well, even if you wouldn't. No matter. I'm doing it for you."

"What about the GFL in the village?"

"Oh, they'd kill you."

"No. I mean, why are you doing this with GFL in village? Are you GFL?"

"No. Father, farmer. Sleep now. You need rest."

He slept.

Masters stayed with the family for twelve days. Lee, the farmer, insisted he stay inside, for fear the GFL would spot him. "Can you give me their names?" Masters asked.

"No, no. I don't tell them about you, I don't tell you about them."

Masters did find out that he was about a week's walk

from Portent. And during long talks with the farmer that went late into the night, he learned even more.

"What's this about Hsiang being corrupt?"

"He is. He cancelled the limit on his term of office."

"I thought that was by a public vote."

"No, he fixed it. He fixes everything," Lee said. The image of the pimp with his wife-whore came back to Masters from the night of the party. He also remembered Maid Kris' insistence that he couldn't understand what the fighting was about. "Lee, the GFL is fighting against Word of Blake, right?"

"Now it is."

"What do you mean?"

"Word of Blake's arrival was a stroke of luck for the GFL. It gave them an enemy from offworld against whom they could unite everyone on Gibson."

"The GFL was fighting a war before Word of Blake arrived?"

The farmer cocked his head to one side. "I thought you said you were from Atreus. That you were from the Marik Commonwealth."

"Yes."

"For years now, we have been sending messages asking for help from Atreus. The GFL was founded to get rid of Hsiang. We weren't at war then. We wanted to avoid a war. But the Countess wouldn't listen. So we tried to get . . ." His shoulders slumped. "Are you telling me the Marik Commonwealth didn't know?"

"Certainly Thomas didn't."

"But how could he not?" For the first time Lee's calm demeanor abandoned him. "We paid for messengers to travel to Atreus. My own nephew waited outside the palace for two weeks for an appointment with an official."

"The Free Worlds League is made up of hundreds

of worlds. There are many functionaries, many bureaucrats.''

"Ah." The farmer sat down, a weariness passing
over his shoulders and spine. For a moment he reminded Masters of Thomas. "Well, now we have a
war, which is what the leaders of the GFL wanted so
badly. But the people, you know, the people don't want
war. We don't want to fight. We want peace. It was
impossible for the people to go to *war* against their
own government. People won't normally do that. But
then Word of Blake arrived. Then we had a war. We
were invaded.''

"They didn't come to invade.''

"Have you ever spoken to any of them?''

"Point taken. But not all of them are . . .''

"So now we have a war.''

"And people will keep fighting until Word of Blake
leaves?''

"Of course. We will drain them of money, and
sooner or later they'll have to give up. That's the way
a guerrilla war works. Grind your enemy down, wear
them out, make him use up everything he's got.''

"But this is their home now. The Captain-General
has given them permission to live here.''

"He should have dealt with Hsiang before doing
that.''

"He didn't know.''

"There it is.''

"What if the GFL takes power?''

"That would be bad too. So many of them are
thieves and sadists, as cruel as the True Believers.''

"They torture True Believers?''

"They torture everybody. Why do you think I hide
you? Because I'm not allowed to feed who I want to
feed, help who I want to help. The GFL has seized
this village's crop production. I have no voice. They
would kill me if they found out what I was doing. They

paint themselves as peasant saviors. Bah! They've been courting the Principality of Regulus, the very people we broke away from two hundred and fifty years ago. Regulus has one goal—to claim our planet once more. And the GFL will surrender us in return for rulership power of Gibson."

"So you aren't concerned about Word of Blake?"

The farmer laughed. "Concerned. I'm terrified. You really heard nothing about this on Atreus?" He sighed. "Sir Masters, factions of Word of Blake have paid Principal Hsiang a great deal of money to get exactly what they want. They overtax us, they've taken over key offices in the Gibson government, and we are afraid, perhaps without reason, that they want to impose their religion on us. These two issues, taxes and religion, were the very reasons we broke away from Regulus two hundred and fifty years ago. We will not sit still for this."

"But if Word of Blake were here on Gibson, but not a threat. . . ."

"If such a thing were possible. But it seems that the Countess is happy with the way things are."

Masters thought he'd known what was going on when he arrived on Gibson, and now he realized he had been completely in the dark. Was the farmer telling the truth? Or perhaps it was only the truth as far as Lee knew it, and there was something more going on. Ideals meant nothing in the face of ignorance.

"I'm leaving tonight."

"You're not well enough."

"I thank you for your concern, but I can't wait."

"Very well. But you will let me give you food."

The offer moved Masters. "How can you be so generous to me, someone who until recently worked with your oppressors?"

"Well, you have not shot me, have you?"

"Excuse me?"

"You have a machine gun with you, Sir Masters.
You have not used it. During wartime there is a surfeit
of cruelty. I have had enough. I treat you well because
you treat me well. I pray that you will get Word of
Blake and the GFL to agree to behave in a similar
way."

"I don't have the power to do that."

"But I can see that you will try. And for that I help
you and I wish you luck."

19

Masters left late that night. He made his way through the forest under a moonless sky, armed only with food and a compass. He had left the machine gun behind, burying it in a field. Only a few rounds remained and it would only call more attention to him. As a disguise, he wore a cotton tunic and a wide-brimmed straw hat that the farmer had given him.

Masters walked for hours at a brisk pace, but when the sun began to lighten the sky he took shelter in a hole under the roots of a large tree. He slept through the day, then was on his way again at nightfall.

That was how he journeyed, sleeping by day, traveling by night, for seven days. On the third night Masters heard gunfire—artillery and lasers—in the distance. He paid it no heed, but continued steadily on his course toward the city.

On the seventh night he topped a ridge and saw the brightly lit city of Portent. Moonlight reflected off the Old Walls. He made his way across a plain and into the city.

* * *

The sun had already risen, and the citizens of Portent's shantytown were already up and about. For the most part they resembled the farmer who had helped him—shoulders ready for work, hands worn from labor—but their faces, etched with fear and sadness, betrayed the changes in their life. He also noticed swaggering young men, thugs of some kind, wandering the streets, mocking the inhabitants of the shantytown with taunts and condescending laughter.

Hungry and out of food, Masters stopped at a small vegetable stand. After picking out two of the best-looking apples, he paid the vendor with currency the farmer had given him. He was about to continue on his way when he felt the stiff end of a gun touch the small of his back.

"Sir Masters," a woman's voice said softly. He recognized it, but could not place it. "Please be calm. Please do not make any sudden moves. Thirty meters from here is a shack made of riveted sheets of metal. Do you see it?"

He nodded, then realized suddenly who was speaking to him. It was Maid Kris.

"You will walk toward it, slowly. If you move at any speed greater than a casual walk, or if you do not move directly toward the shack, I will shoot you."

Could he take her? Masters couldn't be sure. For now he'd go along.

"All right," he said.

Walking down the street, he eyed the people he passed to see if they were abetting Maid Kris, knew what she was up to. But no one caught his eye.

When they came to the door of the shack, he turned the knob and it opened easily. They stepped inside. For a moment he thought of slamming the door shut behind him, but before he could act, a foot shoved him in the back and knocked him to the dirt floor.

As Masters rolled over on the ground, the door shut, plunging the small shack into darkness. The sun had baked the metal roof and walls, and sweat had immediately begun to bead all over his body. The only light came through the thin gaps between the metal plates. Gradually his eyes adjusted to the darkness.

"You are a most wanted man, Sir Masters."

"Yes?" When he looked up at her, the first thing he noticed was the Sternsacht heavy pistol in her hand. Then he smiled to see that she was also wearing a cloth tunic and straw hat. "Are you disguised too?"

"Better than you."

"Undoubtedly."

"Three weeks ago Word of Blake tried to arrest you, the GFL wants you back again, and, in recent days, the Principality of Regulus has redoubled their diplomatic efforts to seize you for attacking Colonel Roush on Atreus. Rumor in the Old City has it that a delegation is on its way from Regulus to Gibson to deal with the matter directly."

"No," he said with mock horror, and sat up against a wall.

"Yes. And, of course, your liege has been making inquiries about your health."

"It's good to have friends."

"Yes. Yes it is." She smiled and sat down on the floor. The gun, however, stayed trained on him.

"Who are your friends, Maid Kris? Whose possession am I in now?"

"Back with the GFL, I'm afraid."

He blinked. "I thought for sure you were some deep agent set up by Hsiang."

"Well, if it's any consolation, Hsiang does have a very, very nasty secret police." Her face betrayed dark memories, but she quickly shook them off. "But no. I'm GFL."

"Are there many GFL working in the Old City?"

"More than enough, actually."

"And you work for the countess. A ruse?"

"Yes."

"It seems that I'm pretty much in the dark about how politics actually work on Gibson, so can you tell me where the countess' loyalties lie? Who is she tied to?"

"What do you mean?"

"I mean she's supposed to be a vassal of Thomas Marik, but as far as I can tell, she's kept secret from him much of the misery taking place on this world. Is she working with Hsiang? Word of Blake? Or is she really loyal, but simply not very observant?"

"Are you serious?"

"Absolutely. I . . ." He faltered, embarrassed at the memory of how confident he'd been upon first arriving on Gibson. "I came here blind, and I'm trying to learn as much and as quickly as I can."

"You really don't know?"

"No."

"She's running with both Hsiang and Word of Blake. She made all the contacts, set up the deals. She's collecting most of the taxes and the profits from the war effort. Hsiang is a little puppet who could stand on his own feet without someone's help."

"She's a traitor?"

"To Gibson, yes."

"And to Thomas Marik. Her primary loyalty is supposed to be to the Captain-General."

Maid Kris was incredulous. "You're telling me he isn't getting a part of this?"

"I swear to you that he's as innocent as I am of these matters."

"How can that be?"

Masters sat silently for a moment, then said, "I've recently learned that the conflict with Hsiang started even before Word of Blake arrived."

She rolled her eyes and said, "Yes."

"So, I take it that the Countess was working with factions of ComStar here on Gibson even before the ComStar schism occurred."

"Yes."

"Well, we, like everyone, depend on ComStar to provide communications between the stars. Even if some bureaucrat received personal messages, such as those sent to Atreus by representatives of the GFL, perhaps they didn't carry the weight of communications received via HPG. Official messages must certainly have more impact. It's not right, but I'll wager that's what happened. And on top of that, Word of Blake could have been sending lies to Atreus specifically designed to counter the GFL's pleas."

She shook her head. "No, no. They . . . they're performing a religious act when they operate the hyperpulse generator. Every activity they perform . . . It isn't just a matter of money for them. It's a sacred trust. They're zealots. They wouldn't betray that trust."

"True. But what if the schism had actually begun years before Word of Blake actually split off from the ComStar organization, before the dissidents sought refuge in the Free Worlds League. Precentor Blane and I came here together from Atreus, and we spoke of the schism. He told me that there are other, smaller schisms even within the ranks of Word of Blake. The institution is still searching for its identity. Perhaps a group of people working at the hyperpulse generator station, a more militant group, perhaps one connected with ROM, thought that doctoring messages was the price to be paid to further the cause of Blake's vision." Excited, and without thinking about the gun trained on him, he stood.

"What are you doing?" Maid Kris said with surprise.

"I've got to get to Precentor Blane and speak with him. He's an old friend of the Captain-General's and I think I can trust him. Besides, I have no choice. I have to get word to Thomas, and I can only do that if I have a link with a True Believer who is on my side."

With her eyes still on him, Maid Kris ran her tongue along her teeth, as if thinking something through. "You are naive, Sir Masters," she said. "So much so that I might think you dissemble. Yet I believe your naiveté is sincere. I would never have thought that the Knights of the Inner Sphere were made up of such cherubs."

Her words both amused and embarrassed him. "It's one of our more endearing qualities," he said.

"Unfortunately, I have bad news for you, though it supports your theory. Precentor Blane has been arrested by Word of Blake security. His former assistant, Precentor Starling, has seized the reins of the True Believers on Gibson."

Maid Kris and Masters spent the better part of the day walking back to the Old City. "At this point, I don't want to risk a cab driver recognizing you," she said. "You're rather famous, you know." They walked close to each other, their heads bent forward under their hats, speaking softly.

"Where are they keeping him?"

"As if I know. It's ComStar. . . ."

"Word of Blake."

"Either way, they're an odd bunch, and I can't possibly guess their thinking. They might have him locked up in a clock for all I know, one of those ancient ticking things. Doesn't that seem like just the kind of thing Word of Blake might like for a torture device? A rhythmic knocking every second."

He thought of Spinard. "They can do it without clocks."

"What?"

"Nothing. Well, how are we going to find him? Does the GFL have any contacts in Blake?" Maid Kris looked at Masters as if to say of course no one had agents planted in Word of Blake or ComStar. "Sorry," he said. "I don't know what I was thinking."

"We'll find him somehow. You'll contact Thomas. We'll see what happens." She said the last with a kind of sarcasm.

"You still don't believe me."

"No. Of course not."

"Fair enough."

"Do you really want Gibson to go back to Regulus?" he asked after a short pause. He still didn't know how all the players fit together, and wanted more information.

"No," she said softly. Then, her voice cut with an edge, "But we had to do something. Countess Dystar ignored all our pleas after Hsiang came to power. We now know why, of course. It took us months after Hsiang took office to realize what was happening."

Masters shook his head. "I can't believe we didn't know."

They traveled on in silence for a long while, being bustled along by the many people on their way to work. The streets had quickly filled with traffic, and a tremendous cacophony built up as the city came awake.

"How did you get the Regulans to back you?"

"They're not here in any official capacity. Only MechWarriors sponsored by 'private backers' out of the Principality of Regulus."

"After all the bad blood between your people and Regulus, that was your only option?"

She sighed. "Some of us hate the idea. But many of our people at the top were courted by the Regulans. And they've been made promises of power." She bit her lip.

"So there's dissent within the ranks of the GFL, too."

"Why is it that everyone accepts a complicated spectrum of political views in their own government, but are surprised when other people aren't uniform and single-minded?" she said angrily. "Of course there's dissent!"

"I don't know why people do that," he said calmly. "But let me point out that you have based all your assumptions about Thomas Marik and me on Countess Dystar because she swore fealty to him, assuming we were all playing the same game. Now, I take it you want peace. What I want to do is break down the walls and find the compromise we need—"

"No compromises. Word of Blake leaves."

He shook his head. "That's impossible. First, because my liege has promised Word of Blake a home here, and he cannot renege. And that is that. Second, though Blake has provided a focus for the conflict, a flag for the GFL to rally around, your people's real problems are the countess and Hsiang. Correct? So even if Blake goes, nothing has changed. The war will settle down most likely, but you'll still be ruled by greedy, unjust people who manipulate the truth. Right?"

"Yes."

"So we've got to deal with that as well."

"Why do you care about that? It has no effect on you."

"You're wrong, though I can understand why you might think that. This world is owned by Thomas Marik. I am sworn to protect all the property of my liege. I serve Thomas Marik's vision, and his vision does not allow for the kind of duplicity that your people have suffered."

"This sounds too easy."

"The *words* are easy because we know how we

should behave. It's *doing* that is difficult. But I'll give it a try.''

"And how do you propose to make all this happen?''

"You forget—I am a Knight of the Inner Sphere. I have dozens of friends with very big BattleMechs.''

20

Portent, Gibson
Principality of Gibson, Free Worlds League
27 February 3055

By the time Masters and Maid Kris reached the Old Wall that night, his legs ached. "This way," she said, leading him to a rusted door at the base of the Old Wall. A dark passage waited beyond.

"The lights don't work anymore, but it runs straight through." She stepped into the darkness, running her hand lightly against the wall as she began to walk forward. Masters followed. Rust caked the wall, flaking off as he ran his fingertips along the old metal.

After a long time in darkness they stepped out of the tunnel into the Old City, its high walls illuminated by the bright lights of the city. Weeks ago the Old Walls seemed to huddle around the buildings like a mother's protective arms making it a safe place. Now Masters thought those same walls looked cold and heavy and stifling.

"Come," Maid Kris said. "We'll go see a friend of mine. He might have an idea of where they've taken Precentor Blane."

"GFL?"

"Yes."

"I'll just wait here, if you don't mind. Or better, in the park, the north park in front of the palace."

"You don't trust me?"

He smiled, repeating her words. "Of course not." Then he said seriously, "Right now we don't trust each other, but it seems we're both willing to play out the plot to see if the other's going to betray us. I'll wait for you in the park. When you get there, just wander around a bit. I'll find you."

"All right." She looked at him curiously. "You're rather cagey for a noble knight."

"I'm learning."

Masters walked to the park, where he decided to hide in a tree until Maid Kris' return. He wandered through the area, which was lit with glowing white spheres mounted on posts, until he came to a tree that seemed suitable. He jumped up to the lowest branch and swung his legs up around it. Though his arm still ached, it was nothing compared to the pain of nearly three weeks ago. He pulled himself up onto the branch, then stood, reaching for the next one overhead. This maneuver was easier than the last, for there were many branches available at this height. Soon he was ten meters in the air, looking down at the benches and lamps of the park and out across to the towers of the Old City.

He was breathing fast, for the climb had tired him out completely after the day's walk. But Masters was also exhilarated. How long had it been since he'd climbed a tree? The last time had to be at least twenty-five years ago when he was still in his teens. Maybe longer, for the last memory of climbing a tree was when he was no more than eight or nine. Climbing a 'Mech ladder, an activity so common in his life, did not count; the feel of it was simply not the same. Rungs made the whole effort manageable, while a tree was a bit of puzzle. The path up had to be discovered anew for every tree, and perhaps for each climb. As a child got older, as his limbs and strength grew, the same tree would yield different possibilities, as branches once out of reach now became accessible.

It was easy, he realized, to forget about all that when climbing up a 'Mech. The ease, the repetition—one could get lazy. One could become . . . what? A machine?

Like Spinard?

Yes. Both a person and a machine, doing the same thing over and over again without thought.

The bark, rough and irregular, felt wonderful against his hands. It reminded him of diagrams he'd seen of the human brain, a gray mass with folded layers.

The brain. A secret had just revealed itself, but like the knots back at the GFL base, he could only touch it, not see it whole. It had something to do with what he sought for himself and other MechWarriors. It wasn't a matter of simply saying technology was bad. Society now rested upon technology. Starflight, shelter, BattleMechs themselves all depended upon science and machinery, and Masters would give up none of them. Humanity was a tool-user. Nature wanted men and women to build, and build humanity would.

No, there was something else. What was it he and Thomas wanted to hang on to?

The idea of humanity as the tool-user stuck in his mind. It was incomplete, didn't take into account the complexity of people. Chimpanzees used sticks to dig ants out of the ground. He'd also heard of animals, perhaps extinct now, that actually gathered small pieces of wood to damn up streams, altering the environment to their needs. Many animals used tools. So what was it about people . . .?

He thought of *Le Morte d'Arthur*. That was it. People made up words and strung them together to discuss things that sometimes did not exist. He could read a story about an England that had vanished two thousand years ago, an England that had never actually existed, for Malory's tales were not truth. They were ideals.

A chimpanzee could only work with what *existed*, but humans could strive to shape reality itself.

Humanity wasn't a tool-user, but a symbolmonger. King Arthur. Merlin. Lancelot. All of them ideals for people to hold in mind, to help stave off the despair technology *could* bring, but didn't have to. What Thomas wanted to save was nothing less than humanity's humanity.

Movement on a path below caught his attention, and he saw Maid Kris, now changed into a rather chic jumpsuit. He looked around to see if anyone was following her. Seeing that apparently no one had, Masters made his way down the branches of the tree to the ground.

While he was working his way down, Maid Kris spotted him. "Having fun?" she said, as he touched the ground.

"I was thinking."

"Do all your thoughts require such a lofty perch?"

"I was thinking about words and stories." He felt like he'd been handed the key to something, but he had no idea what it unlocked. Stories, stories, stories. Thomas had said, back in his study, something about stories. "I don't think you understand yet," Thomas had told him, "but you will."

"You all right?"

"Yes." He looked at her, used her presence to focus on the moment at hand. She had not only changed, but cleaned up. Her dark, smooth skin made his own flesh become warm. "You look beautiful."

"Often. But I believe there's an imprisoned Precentor at hand."

"Did you find out where he is?"

"He's supposed to be in a cell in the Word of Blake building at the edge of the city. Their offices are apparently as heavily guarded as the hyperpulse generator station."

"So there's no way . . ."

"The two of us? No. Even if we got him out, we'd still have to get to the station, defeat that security nightmare. . . . I don't see how to do it."

"In this case fighting may not be the best means."

"What do you suggest?"

"Guns would be rather repetitious at this point anyway," he said, thinking out loud. "A straight-out fight, at least."

"What?"

He looked back at her. "What would make the better story?"

"Excuse me?" Concern filled her face, and she looked around, as if he were toying with her now, had led her into an ambush about to be sprung.

Masters stepped away from her, a delighted grin spreading across his face. He raised his arms high, and turned about once, a showman about to introduce a lion tamer. "What would make the best story? What would be something for us to tell our children?"

"I don't have children."

"You might someday."

"What in the name of Allah are you talking about?"

Masters laughed. "If we try to shoot our way through the mess, we'll die. Correct?"

"Most likely."

"All right then. Bad story. So we need something better, right?"

"I'm sorry. . . ."

"There are many greedy, selfish people in this city,

Maid Kris, bound together by their hunger for power. But are they a unit? Are Hsiang, Starling, and the countess whole?''

''No.''

''You,'' he said, and pointed at her, a magician picking someone from the audience. ''As a native of this world, who do you think is the strongest of the three?''

''Each one is as worthless as the last.''

''Please try to answer the question. Who is the strongest.''

''What are you talking about?''

''For the children, the children we might all have. Specifics.''

''It's a toss-up,'' she said quickly,''Three factions, none of them complete. They've worked together so far. . . .''

''So their strength comes from cooperation?''

''Of course their strength comes from cooperation. Have you seen nothing since you got here?'' She threw up her hands, about to storm off, when her eyes widened with understanding.

Masters smiled. ''But what if we forced them against one another?''

''Yes,'' she said softly. ''Yes. This has never come up before.''

''The situation was never so volatile. There must be True Believers still loyal to Precentor Blane who did not like sitting and watching his rival seize power. Meanwhile, I, a favorite of Thomas Marik, am being hunted by all three powers, each for their own reasons. And Blane is a friend of Thomas' as well. Meanwhile, Regulus has just shipped BattleMechs, probably at a high cost to the GFL leadership. Most people in the GFL probably don't want to trade one oppressor for another. The cracks in the alliance are getting deeper now. We might be able to use that to our advantage.''

She took a step toward him, her voice warm and pleased. "Do you have a plan?"

"It's forming. Tell me, does the GFL have a plan for an uprising in Portent?"

"Yes, we prepared it—"

He raised his hand. "Don't use it. I will not allow it."

"But . . ."

"No buts. I'm perfectly willing to let the vultures on this planet chew on one another, but I will not allow the city to destroy itself in a guerrilla uprising. It's not only to bring about peace that I came here. I'm also here to bring Thomas's vision to light. Civilians blasting away at each other in the streets is anathema to everything Thomas Marik stands for. We'll come up with something, and it will make a lovely tale."

"Who do we go to first?"

"Whoever is most filled with fear."

"I have an urgent message from Countess Dystar," Maid Kris said to the guard at Principal Hsiang's palace gate.

"Who's this?" asked the guard.

"My escort, to keep me safe at this late hour."

"Well, I can let you in. But he stays here. You'll be safe in the grounds."

"Do you really think so? I'd much prefer to have him with me."

"Have you a pass for him?"

"Well, no."

"Then I'm afraid he cannot enter."

Masters eyed the guards at the gate, and saw more guards beyond. Storming Hsiang's palace was not an option. Maid Kris could deal with Hsiang alone if she had to. It would all work out.

"Very well," she said.

"I will see you later, mistress," he said.

She walked into the palace, escorted by a guard. She would tell Hsiang that she had overheard the countess making plans with Precentor Starling to overthrow his government. As a loyal Gibsonian, she thought it her duty, of course, to tell him.

Masters sat down on the ground and waited to see if the guards would take the bait. They did. He could put his time waiting with them to good use.

"Do you know what is so important that your mistress would travel this late at night?" one of the guards asked him.

"I know very little," Masters said, his head bowed humbly under his straw hat. "But I know my mistress is very afraid."

"Afraid?"

"Have you not heard? Countess Dystar's mercenaries and the Word of Blake MechWarriors have been speaking of late."

"Speaking of what?" asked another guard.

"Enough. I have said enough."

"You've said nothing."

"That is all I should say."

One of the guards slammed Masters in the shoulder with the butt of his gun. "Speak more or you'll leave here on a stretcher."

"Sir, please. Do not force me to talk of matters that are no more than rumors."

"What rumors?"

"Whose rumors?"

"Rumors of the villagers, sir. Out in the farmlands. But we speak nonsense. It is not worthy of your time."

"We'll decide that. Speak."

Masters paused dramatically, letting them see how difficult the decision was for him. Then he said, "We have heard that the Countess' mercenaries and the Word of Blake warriors are planning to join forces."

"They already work together. What's so special about that?"

"They plan, so I have heard, and this is nothing but rumor—"

"Just say it!"

"They want to remove Principal Hsiang, to take over the government."

Both guards fell silent for a moment, then one of them said, "What?"

"That's nonsense," said another.

"Certainly it is," said Masters.

"Word of Blake would never allow such a thing."

"Not while Precentor Blane is in charge," Masters agreed.

The guards looked at him carefully. "What do you mean?" one asked.

"Precentor Blane is a friend of the people of Gibson," Masters said in a light tone. "He has always done well by us. As long as he is charge of the immigrants, nothing can go wrong. Precentor Blane is the keystone of our world's peace." A long silence followed. "What is it, good sirs. Have I said something to disturb you?"

"You haven't heard?"

"Heard what?"

"Precentor Blane has been arrested. His assistant, Starling, has taken his place."

Masters gave out an audible gasp.

"What is it?" The guard didn't wait for Masters to reply, but kicked him in the side.

"I cannot say. It is nothing."

The other guard kicked him, too. "Speak!"

"I had heard this might happen. We had heard rumor of his arrest. It signals the coup. This is the first step. But sirs, this is—"

"Shut up. Is this what Maid Kris is telling the Principal?"

"I would assume so. I don't know."

The guards called more guards over. There were six, then eight, then twelve. They discussed the matter among themselves, ignoring Masters. They added one bit of evidence after another, details Masters could never have known, the conspiracy growing in their minds from a possibility to a concrete force against which they must defend themselves.

They talked for more than twenty minutes, but ceased when Maid Kris reappeared. Only after she had left with Masters did they resume their rumor-mongering once more.

"How did it go?"

"The disgusting worm tried to put his hands all over me."

"Are you all right?"

"Yes."

"So, how did it go?"

"He's frightened out of his mind. He's convinced that if he doesn't get Blane back in office he'll be standing in front of a firing squad within twenty-four hours." She grinned broadly. "You know, this might work."

21

Portent, Gibson
Principality of Gibson, Free Worlds League
27 February 3055

Masters and Maid Kris had little trouble getting to their next stop—Dystar Castle. The chopper pilots and security guards knew Maid Kris well, and she introduced Masters as a new servant hired from outside the Old Walls. He kept his head bowed under his hat, pretending to be embarrassed and uncomfortable. The guards accepted the story, and the two of them passed the checkpoints, flew up to the castle, and got off at the helipad.

Things became a bit trickier once inside the castle, however. The guards around the countess' chamber would not bend rules. Maid Kris took Masters as far as she could, then gave him directions to the countess. They decided Maid Kris would not confront the countess in order to protect her cover. Instead, she would contact another GFL operative in the castle who would arrange for all the GFL sympathizers in Portent to begin spreading rumors of an impending power struggle. Their task was not to fire bullets, but to assault the city with lies.

* * *

Masters made his way through the corridors with Maid Kris' Sternsacht, crept up to a few guards, surprised them, tied them up and gagged them. One, two, three guards. He moved smoothly, lightly, more relaxed than he'd been in years.

He found the door exactly as Maid Kris described it: huge, carved ornately from dark wood, a golden ring for a handle. With a look down either side of the corridor he assured himself the area was clear, took the ring in hand, and pulled it.

As the door opened, he heard a series of moans, then the countess crying out, "What is it! You know I'm not to be disturbed!"

He fumbled along the wall and quickly found the light switch. As the lamps went on, he saw three men and the countess sprawled about the bed in a state of undress.

"You!" she said.

"Um," said Masters, startled. Had Lancelot ever encountered anything like this? "The three of you, the men, out of the bed and against the wall."

They looked to the countess, and she said, "Go on, dears. I'd probably be dead by the time you reached him." She rolled over toward Masters, resting on her right side, her lovely left thigh curving up wonderfully. "Some men are good for some things, but you can't count on them to come through when you need them to for other activities."

"We've got a lot to talk about."

"Talk? Oh, I had hoped you'd charged in here out of some desperate need."

"The matter is desperate."

"Then why are you waving that gun in my face, instead of something much more interesting?"

"Assistant Precentor Starling has seized Precentor Blane. . . ."

"Are we really going to discuss politics?" She pouted like a child.

"From what I understand, you're *quite* political."

"But I never discuss politics with men I want to bed. It makes everything so complicated."

"I don't want to be bedded by you."

"As if I care, young man. I'm the countess." She turned to the three men, who stood quite docile, their faces to the wall. "Right, boys?"

Each one mumbled something or other in awkward reply.

"So I would have been just one more for the group?" Masters asked.

"Well, it depends. I try everyone out, and see how they do. If I like a man, but he doesn't quite have the spark, I might keep him around, but match him with some others of the same nature." She turned back to the three again. "No offense."

"You have a stable?"

"Somewhat. Actually, these three are paid by my people's tax dollars. They're mercenaries hired from off world to fight the GFL."

The image of the corpses hanging from the tree came to mind, and a tight fury began to buzz around in Masters' head.

"You needn't look so upset. At least I'm keeping them safe from the war."

"Precentor Blane must be freed."

"Bosh. That's a Word of Blake internal issue. Come here to bed."

Masters leaned against the wall, realizing that she was probably frightened, but trying to throw him off balance with her brazen attitude. It was working. He had to seize the initiative again.

"Not true, Countess. It is *not* only a matter for Word of Blake. It has a great effect on you as well."

She yawned and rolled onto her back, stretching like

a cat. "Yes, of course it concerns me. Blane is rather a stick in the mud. I think things will work out quite well with Precentor Starling."

"Despite the fact that he plans to push Hsiang out of office?"

Her languid stretch stopped. "What?"

The lie began. "The Captain-General supplied me with a report gathered by ROM—"

"The Captain-General received a report from ROM?"

The bigger the lie, the more it will be believed. "He was once a ComStar adept, Countess. His connections didn't simply die out. The report warned of Precentor Starling's ambitions. Thomas sent me here to keep an eye on Starling, but we never dreamed he'd act so swiftly. It is clear he means to carry out his coup soon."

The countess tried to sound nonchalant, but the look in her eyes was one of deep thought. "What does all this matter to me? Hsiang is an idiot. A puppet."

"But he is your idiot, your puppet." Masters was guessing, but he went on. "Blane helped keep the peace these last two years, correct? You were able to push the buttons hard because Blane worked as a peacemaker."

"Yes."

"With him gone, and Hsiang removed from power, the entire world of Gibson will rise in revolt. It will be all too apparent that Word of Blake is about to take away their rights. Their fear of a Word of Blake inquisition will drive them to a frenzy. They'll turn on you, seeking help from anywhere they can."

"This is nonsense!" she said, sitting up and drawing a sheet up over herself. "You have no proof."

"The GFL has already made strong ties with the Regulan government."

''Fanatic mercenaries from Regulus who think Gibson can be wooed back . . .''

Put as much truth into the lie that you can: ''Not at all, Countess. That is what they would have you think. I was at one of the bases. The Principality of Regulus has given their blessing.''

She turned to him, caught by his deceit. ''We have to stop them.''

''We? Who is we? The people don't trust you.''

''Then who will they follow? The GFL? The GFL is tearing the countryside apart. They don't want to be ruled by those terrorists!''

''Countess Dystar, the simple truth is this: people will always accept oppression from their own government over oppression from invaders. Gibson has a strong history with Regulus. None with Word of Blake. You must act quickly. My operatives tell me Word of Blake will begin their assault on the government offices in six hours.''

''Operatives? Six hours?''

''You don't think Thomas sent me down into this hotbed of intrigue alone, did you?''

''But you didn't know.''

''Oh, we knew. We knew enough to be concerned.''

''We must get word to the Captain-General,'' she said. ''Help won't arrive for days, but we have to prepare.''

''Of course. The only problem is that the one person I would trust to take the message is under Word of Blake lock and key.''

The countess stood up and draped the sheet around herself. ''You three, get out of here now.'' The men turned awkwardly, looked around for their clothes, found them, and rushed out the door half-dressed.

''All right,'' she said, ''I really don't believe you, but I can't afford to ignore you. I'll look into it.''

''We have to get Precentor Blane.''

"They arrested him on a matter of religious heresy. I have no jurisdiction."

"My God, woman, you can think of something."

"All right. I suppose we can find some technicality or other." She stood and gripped the sheet to her body as she walked to a window overlooking the city. "Good God," she said, her shoulders tightening visibly.

Hearing the almost abject terror in her voice he crossed quickly to her side. The sight startled him as well. Hsiang had moved so quickly. In the gray light of dawn, Masters could make out the Principal's Loyalist troops running along the sidewalks while armored personnel carriers rolled down the streets. Martial law had been declared. The conflagration was about to erupt.

Staring down at the streets, he said, "And now, if you'll forgive me Countess," then quickly grabbed her by the waist and brought the sheet up around her wrists. "I'm a wanted man, and I can't have you using me as a bargaining chip." She tried to scream after the first surprise, but it was too late. Masters stuffed a corner of the sheet into her mouth and carried her to the bed. "I must say you are a very attractive woman. Physically."

"Hmmphamph."

"Yes, I'll send someone for you as soon as I'm safe. Goodbye."

He met up with Maid Kris at her chamber, and the two of them rushed to the castle's helipad. "How'd it go," she asked.

"I left her speechless."

Masters and Maid Kris waited in an alley near the Word of Blake building. They waited for hours, and Masters began to wonder if something had gone wrong. With the soldiers all over the streets someone should have started shooting by now.

Every half hour or so Maid Kris put in calls to her contacts. For most of the day she received very little news, but in the early afternoon she came back with a full report.

"Both the Countess and Hsiang are demanding that Precentor Blane be released into their care."

"Are they working together?"

"Not at all. The Countess called Hsiang as soon as a maid came into her room and freed her. Hsiang, of course, thought it was a trick. When he rebuffed her it made the Countess think that your information was somewhat incorrect and that Hsiang was really working with Word of Blake."

"Good. I was hoping her fear and greed would fill in some gaps."

"Meanwhile, Hsiang called his troops back from their rural outposts, though most of them haven't reached the city yet. The same is happening with the countess' mercenaries and the Word of Blake MechWarriors." Maid Kris' eyes revealed great excitement in these last details, for now the field was open for the GFL. Masters had to remind himself that though they currently worked for a common goal, a gulf of policy and goals separated them.

"All well and good, but something better happen fast before they all get a chance to sit down and compare notes. Does it look like Word of Blake is going to give the Precentor to either Hsiang or the Countess?"

"Best guess is no. If they knew what was going on, or if the Countess and Hsiang presented a united front, they might give in. But everyone is too edgy."

At that instant they heard the rapid popping of machine gun fire, followed by reports of shells fired by tanks. Explosions echoed down the streets, followed immediately by the roar of stone walls collapsing.

"This is it," Masters said. "Let's go."

They rushed out of the alley and took up positions behind a large truck. Across the street stood the big Word of Blake building. Around them men and women were cutting each other down with gunfire, as well as hitting innocents on the street and inside buildings. Tanks rolled along the broad avenues, firing one shell after another, sometimes at tanks, sometimes at buildings. Mortars let loose shells that lobbed up, then fell and caused horrible explosions. Craters and rubble began to appear everywhere. Masters had never seen fighting inside a city before, and the sight tore at his heart.

Word of Blake soldiers had taken up positions in the windows and at the large front doors of the building. Tanks from Hsiang's loyalist guard fired into the building, ripping huge holes in it. All around the city, Masters knew, madness was taking hold. But as long as it stayed within the Old Walls he could live with it.

"Come on, let's go."

The two of them rushed across the street, ducking for cover behind parked and ruined cars. They approached the Word of Blake building from the south side. Already huge cracks ran through the base of the building. "I hope he's still alive," Maid Kris said.

They slipped through a crack just wide enough for each of them to pass through, and found themselves in a hall lit only by the sunlight behind them. "Stairway," Masters said, for he saw the glint of a railing through a door. "Come on."

With each step they took, the building shook from the assault of shells. Just as they reached the stairwell, a circle of light passed over them. "Stop!" someone shouted. They did not, but jumped in through the doorway. When a burst of bullets slammed into the door frame, Masters' flesh felt alert and warm, and a perverse thrill bubbled up in his chest. He and Maid Kris ran down the stairs at top speed, but in the darkness Masters didn't see that they'd reached a landing. His knee buckled as he tried to continue stepping down, and he tripped. From behind Maid Kris slammed into him, sending them both sprawling into the wall opposite the stairs.

A beam of light fell on them. Masters grabbed Maid Kris and rolled her over him as bullets crashed down where she had been. Then he rolled himself out of the way, bullets following him across the landing, splintering the concrete floor behind him.

Breathing heavily, frightened, they stood under the stairs from where the Word of Blake soldier had fired. "Go down the stairs and shut the door loudly," Masters whispered. She touched his hand in confirmation and took the stairs, this time more carefully.

Masters waited, watching the beam of the flashlight bounce along the wall as the soldier also descended the stairs. He came down cautiously. He had no reason to rush. He had the light.

Suddenly Maid Kris slammed the door below, and the soldier began to run down the stairs, thinking they had escaped. As the man turned the corner of the landing, Masters swung blindly into the soldier, catching him in the abdomen. The man gave out a cry and doubled over, and Masters pushed him into the concrete wall. The soldier's Rorynex, with the flashlight taped to the barrel, clattered down the stairs, the beam of light flying wildly about the stairwell.

"Give up," Masters said through his teeth, pressing the man to the wall with all his might. He pulled the Sternsacht out of his belt.

"Blake shall prevail."

"To the death, then?"

"Yours!"

Masters pulled his trigger, the blast muffled by the close press of their bodies. The soldier fell against Masters, the body going slack as Masters stepped away and let it drop to the floor. Blood soaked his cotton tunic, but he had not noticed until now. The feeling of being in danger and somehow pulling through—the heat of battle—was like no other. He loved it.

A light fell on him and he turned to see Maid Kris on the stairs holding the soldier's Rorynex toward him. "Why didn't you just kill him?"

"I didn't want to."

She lowered the flashlight beam so he could see the stairs. "Point the light back up here," he said. She did, and he used the beam to find a set of keys on the soldier's belt. "All right, let's go."

= 22 =

Explosions from street level traveled through the foundations of the building. Thick dust floated across the flashlight's beam as they made their way through the basement passages.

They found the cell area quickly, then located Precentor Blane, the only prisoner, in the last cell. Masters shined the flashlight's beam through the door's small window and over the Precentor's face. The man's elaborate, curled mustache seemed to glow white.

"Are you all right, sir?" Masters asked, and moved the light so that it illuminated his own face.

"Blake's ghost," Precentor Blane said. "Sir Masters, what are you doing here? Half the planet is after you."

"I thought I'd save them the trouble," he said, using one of the keys on the soldier's ring to open the lock.

Precentor Blane walked to the door of his cell. "What's going on up there?"

"A war. A short one, I think, but a war."

Seeing Maid Kris as he stepped into the hallway,

Blane greeted her and said, "Good to see you're all right. So what is it, then? Has the GFL invaded the city? I would have thought such a thing impossible."

"Actually, no. The GFL is right here," Masters said with a gesture to Maid Kris. "Hsiang, the countess, and Starling are going at it up top."

Precentor Blane ran his hand through his thinning hair and stared at Maid Kris. "Well, this is a surprise. As for the other three, it's what I expected. But what started it?"

"We did," said Maid Kris. "Come, we'll tell you about it as we go."

They left the building the way they had come. As they neared ground level the sound of the fighting increased in intensity. With a good shove Masters forced Precentor Blane's thick body through the crack in the wall, and then the trio made their way back out into the sunshine.

"Oh," said Precentor Blane, his mouth round with grief, "Oh, my city."

Where once the city had been a model of perfection, it now resembled a still photo of some war in times long gone. Fractures ran down walls. Stone blocks lay scattered about the street.

"Come on," said Masters. "We've got to keep moving." They ran down half a block, with snipers taking pot shots at them as they moved, then ducked into an alley.

"Where?" asked Precentor Blane with heavy breath, "Where are we going?"

"To the hyperpulse generator station. The fighting will probably be heavy there, but we need you to get word to Thomas."

Precentor Blane looked at him in confusion. "What word?"

"We've got to let him know what's going on. Sir,

do you know what the relationship between Hsiang and the countess is?''

He rolled his eyes. ''Oh, has she been carrying on with him as well?''

''No, no. I mean the way they manage the world.''

''Well, no, actually. I've tried not to meddle too much in the local politics. In fact, until the refugees arrived, Word of Blake pretty much stayed out of the affairs of state. But then, we were a small bureaucracy at the time. Now we're trying to assimilate our people onto the planet. We're only starting to work with the government.''

''And doing a terrible job of it,'' put in Maid Kris.

''Be that as it may,'' Masters said, ''both Hsiang and Countess Dystar have been remiss in their responsibilities as leaders.'' Precentor Blane looked perplexed.

''They've been over-taxing us,'' Maid Kris said, ''and now, with Word of Blake's arrival and ties to the government, our religions are threatened.''

''I thought that was just guerrilla propaganda.''

Maid Kris slapped one hand up to her forehead.

''I didn't know, dear! I don't work in your government. As members of ComStar our job was to keep the hyperpulse generator working properly and the flow of messages in order.''

''We let you know what was happening!''

''It wasn't my business. Goodness. If you can't run your own planet, it's not my problem.''

''Well, now it is, Precentor, for it is the planet of your people, too,'' Masters said.

''Yes . . . Well . . . You see, I put Starling in charge of such matters.''

''And so we need help,'' continued Masters. ''Regulus is backing the GFL. They've been supplying weapons, and they have 'Mechs on Gibson as well. And now the situation is even worse than I expected, for the countess is essentially a traitor to my liege. We must get in touch with Thomas.''

''But Sir Masters—''

''No buts. It will be dangerous, but we have to get to the hyperpulse generator.''

Precentor Blane held up his hand. ''I spoke with Thomas the day you fought with your own lance, Sir Masters. Thomas was convinced you were in the right, despite—I'll confess now—my reservations, and decided to come here with the Knights of the Inner Sphere. He's supposed to arrive today.'' The Precentor pulled a watch from his pocket. ''He should be here now, actually.'' He turned his gaze skyward and toward the starport. Masters and Maid Kris did the same. High overhead they saw three DropShips descending toward Gibson.

''It's getting quiet,'' said Masters, and indeed it was. The sound of shelling had stopped completely, and the gunfire came only sporadically.

''The Captain-General's arrival has probably prompted all the villains to reconsider their positions,'' said Precentor Blane.

''The war won't hold. I think they'll be mending their ways soon,'' added Maid Kris.

''But the blood spilt . . . The city . . .'' Precentor Blane gestured around at the damage done to the Old City. ''They can't back down from this tragedy.''

''I don't think they'll invest too much concern in it, Precentor,'' Masters said. ''To the countess the men are money, to Starling the men are machines, and to Hsiang they are living statues for his vanity, the more dead the more glorious. We've got to get out of here. But I don't know how we're going to get past all the soldiers.''

''I do,'' said Maid Kris.

* * *

She led them through little-used alleys and secret tunnels. The Old City was a shambles, but the fighting had stopped. She got them through the Old Wall, and arranged for transportation to the starport. "I trust you now," she said to Masters. "You'll get a ride."

They saw a full regiment of Word of Blake 'Mechs stationed around the city, silent giants waiting for instructions. "This is bad," said Masters. "Very bad."

Meanwhile a host of red and silver 'Mechs—piloted by the Knights of the Inner Sphere—had taken up positions around the starport. The silver reflected the late afternoon light, giving the group a truly majestic appearance. A thrill ran through Masters. Assembled here, the Knights of the Inner Sphere.

Thomas' guards now manned the gate, and Maid Kris' driver came to a stop. The guards, guns drawn, stepped up to the car and looked inside. "Sir Masters!" one of them exclaimed. "Good to see you, sir."

"Good to be seen. We've got to see the Captain-General right away."

One of the cargo holds of one of the DropShips had been transformed into a war room. Functionaries and strategists moved briskly about tables covered with maps and charts. Thomas sat at a large round table in the center of the room. His assistants came to him with questions and proposals, and rushed back to their paperwork. When Thomas saw Masters coming through the door, he got up and quickly crossed the bay to meet him. Masters dropped to one knee, suddenly thankful for all that Thomas had given him by sending him to Gibson. "My liege," he said.

"My loyal and noble vassal. How do you fare?"

"Well, now that you are here."

Maid Kris and Precentor Blane walked up alongside Masters.

"Thomas," said Precentor Blane.

"Bill. And who is this?"

"Maid Kris, formerly in the service of Countess Dystar, and an active member of the GFL."

Thomas raised an eyebrow. "Well, this is an interesting turn." He gestured to the table. "You must tell me all about it."

They did. When they finished, Thomas Marik gave out a long sigh and said, "Well, this is quite a mess." The three waited patiently for the rest. "There's only one thing to do."

"Sir?"

"Get everybody in here. We've got to figure this out."

Masters had been right. When Thomas announced his arrival at the starport, all three corrupt factions in the Old City pulled back their soldiers and opened diplomatic channels to sort the situation out. Their negotiations came to a sudden halt when three hours later Masters invited each one to a conference with Captain-General Thomas Marik. Protocol and curiosity inspired their promises to attend.

Maid Kris went off to wrangle with Deraa, nominal leader of the GFL, so that he would come to the meeting. She had also been asked to bring back Colonel Roush, if he was willing, to represent Regulan interests on Gibson. Both men agreed to attend.

Thomas also asked for a cease-fire until the end of the conference. The GFL resisted, as the government forces had essentially collapsed during the Old City battle. But the Captain-General was actually on Gibson, and he was taking them seriously enough to invite them to the conference, so finally even the GFL agreed. For the time being peace came to the planet Gibson.

The conference was set for the next day, to begin shortly before noon.

* * *

They all gathered in the cargo bay, now decorated with a massive banner displaying the Marik eagle. The banner dominated the chamber, and it made all the guests feel as if Thomas meant to eclipse them. Or rather, that he already had.

Thomas sat in a great chair carried from the palace on Atreus. A seat for each of the participants was set around the table. Watching quietly, the functionaries kept a distance from the meeting.

Masters sat to Thomas' right. After him, going around the table, were the Countess Dystar, who on several occasions rubbed her knee against Thomas' leg; Principal Hsiang; Assistant Precentor Starling, who insisted that he was Precentor on some technical matter that Word of Blake theologians were still debating; Precentor Martial Arian; Deraa, from the GFL; Maid Kris, whose revealed alliances cause the countess to say, "Ah," as if she'd always known; Colonel Roush; and Precentor Blane.

"Well," said Thomas, as servants passed around tea, fruit, bread, and cheese, "let's get started. Countess Dystar, it has come to my attention that you have been remiss in your responsibilities to the land I have granted you, and are, in effect, a traitor to my house."

"Well!" the Countess huffed with annoyance.

"Principal Hsiang, although my jurisdiction does not concern you directly—"

"No, no it does not. And you would do well to remember that."

"—I still feel compelled to take action concerning your policies. I have promised the Word of Blake a home, and your government—"

"Our government has done everything in its power to extend the full cordiality of our world," Hsiang said, smiling an evil, impish, supposedly ingratiating smile.

"Yes, sir. Precisely. You gave it fully, leaving nothing for your own people. Please, little man, don't waste my time. Of everyone here, you have the least to say, because none of us takes you seriously." Except for Starling and Arian, who remained somber, everyone smirked despite themselves. "What you have done to your people, your *own* people, is a disgrace, for you have sold them out for material gain. You have betrayed their trust and earned their wrath."

He turned to Starling. "I have given your people a home, but you would abuse a good man, Precentor Blane, because he stands in the way of your vision—a vision not welcome in the Free Worlds League. I am afraid there was a misunderstanding. Let me make it clear now. Gibson is not yours. I chose it because it is a world that honors religious tolerance. Your people will honor it as well, or the only home you will know is the space you wander among the stars."

"They must leave!" said Deraa.

"No, they must *not*. For I gave my word, you criminal, and my word shall stand. Now as for *you*—you claim to represent the people of Gibson. But this is only partially true. You represent the *fear* of the people of Gibson. Your actions do not make you a leader, but a monster."

"We were given no choice. Our petitions to the countess and then to you—"

Thomas' deep tone silenced Deraa quickly, "I failed you," he said, then let the statement sink in. "Do you understand? I am telling you, openly, that as the ruler of House Marik, I have failed your people. I am not here to prove myself right by punishing the people doing the complaining. I am here to set things right. I am here to listen to your grievances. I am here to act on them."

Deraa smiled.

He turned, finally, to Colonel Roush. "A pleasure

to see you, Colonel. A disappointment to know that the Principality of Gibson would throw in with these criminals.''

Deraa's smile faded.

"We want Gibson back, Captain-General," Roush said simply. "And we offer them protection from Hsiang's corruption." He bowed.

"How bloody noble. Officially, your people have covered their trail, so technically I cannot implicate Regulus. You are hired mercenaries, and your services were paid for."

"True."

"Know this: the days of mercenaries are coming to an end."

"So you think, Captain-General."

"So I know, Colonel. Here, in the Free Worlds League, we will stop the nonsense of hiring men to carry out the whims of the rich."

"You make it sound so evil, Captain-General."

"I see it as such."

"The people of Gibson did not. They saw our presence as a boon. They desperately needed help."

"You aided a war without an end in sight, did so for your own world's profit, at the expense of countless innocent lives."

"There are no innocents on Gibson."

Thomas stared at him, shocked. "What an immoral thing to say."

"He's right, Marik," said Arian, his voice gruff and tired. "The people here are savages."

"And your practices are not?" Thomas snapped back. "Sir Masters has given me a full report on how this war was conducted. If this is the logic of the Word of Blake, I rue the day the schism occurred."

"You miss the point, Captain-General," said Roush. "When someone wants to win, he will do anything he must. I would do it. Word of Blake would do it. You would do it.''

"I would not," Thomas said coldly. "Such thoughts may soothe your conscience—and yours, too, Precentor Martial. But it is not the case. You sorely underestimate me, and yourselves, if you cannot see the trap of your logic. We choose what we will and will not do. And a man who is willing to behave like his enemy is no more than a puppet, controlled by the actions of others.''

Everyone fell silent.

"Sir Masters," Thomas said.

"My liege."

"The Dystar House has ruled Gibson for two hundred years. The Countess, who is—*somehow*—without heir, has proven herself incapable of sustaining my trust. I remove the patent from her, and pass the title of count and all the lands of Gibson to you and your family.''

Masters felt dizzy, but his confusion was cut short as the countess stood up quickly, her chair falling over backward. Her wry humor completely evaporated. "Thomas Marik. How dare you?''

With mock-confusion, he said, "I am the ruler of House Marik. Am I not allowed to do this?''

"No, you spoiled adept. How dare you suddenly leap in with all these pretensions of yours. I have done nothing that my family has not been doing for generations.''

"Then I have arrived on Gibson far too late.''

"And in countless worlds across the Free Worlds League and the Inner Sphere. For goodness sake—'' She gasped for breath, incredulous. "You relieve me of my lands because of monetary corruption?''

Thomas looked at her, his gaze boring into her. "Yes I do this. The time of change has come. I cannot speak for the other houses. I cannot speak for everyone in the Free Worlds League. But I can speak for all those bound to me by an oath of fealty. You have broken that oath. And let me make it clear: failing your trust to me is the least of your crimes. Greater than anything else is the fact that you betrayed your responsibility to this world. By betraying Gibson, you made *me* betray Gibson!''

''I will back you, Countess,'' said Roush.

All eyes turned to him.

''What?'' said the countess.

''If you would war with Captain-General Thomas Marik, I will side with you. *You* can lead your peop back to the Principality of Regulus.''

Masters leaned back as a wave of dizziness washed over him.

23

Countess Dystar turned to Thomas, and Masters thought he heard her purr like a contented kitten. "What do you think of that, Thomas Marik?"

Thomas shrugged his shoulders. "I'd advise you against trying to fight me, but you will do what you will do."

"Oh! you are impossible." She turned to Roush. "I accept."

"Excellent."

Hsiang, who had remained still, with head bent low, now lifted his gaze toward the countess. "Lady?"

"Very well, you little worm. If you wish to throw in your lot with me, I'll take you along."

"Oh, thank you!"

"Wait!" said Deraa. He turned to Roush. "You cannot do this. They are the enemy. We don't want them in charge. The GFL—"

"Of course they can do it, Deraa," said Maid Kris. "They only want the planet back. They don't care about our principles or our freedom." Her eyes settled on Thomas. "But he does."

''But Regulus provided us arms, supplies.''

''No longer,'' she said.

''I will accept all who wish to ally with the Principality of Regulus,'' Roush said.

''No, thank you,'' said Maid Kris. ''Not with the bedfellows you're accumulating.''

''Yes,'' said Deraa, coming out of his funk. ''Captain-General, we will fight alongside you.'' Masters noticed that Deraa gave Roush a smile full of dark mirth and hidden meaning. Roush saw the look, too, and his expression immediately became one of surprised fear as if he had just realized something. Roush glanced at Masters as though wanting to say something, then apparently changed his mind.

Deraa sat back in his chair and smugly folded his arms. Masters and Maid Kris exchanged glances. She'd seen it too, but the shake of her head said she did not know what it meant either.

''Well, if the GFL is siding with House Marik,'' Starling said, ''we have no choice but to cast our lot with the Principality of Regulus.''

Masters slammed his fists down on the table. ''The Captain-General gave you a home.''

''And now he wishes to take it back. We cannot live as equals with these people.''

''That is not true,'' said Precentor Blane. ''We agreed to come here under that stipulation.''

''I never agreed to it.''

''You were outvoted.''

''Well, now I am Precentor.''

''Is this true, Bill?'' Thomas asked.

''For the time being, yes. I'm sure the council now at work will clear me of the heresy I have been charged with, but until that time . . .''

''Very well. For the time being, Starling rules Word of Blake. But these are difficult times, and rulers cannot always depend on their subjects. Precentor Martial Blane, for which side will your MechWarriors fight?''

Blane thought it over for a long while. "There is no choice," he said finally. "Precentor Starling is the Precentor. We command together. I will work with him.''

"It doesn't matter," put in Deraa, again grinning malevolently. "When we fight, it doesn't matter how many BattleMechs you have." And once more Roush looked frightened.

"I'm afraid not, my new ally," Thomas said. "Your people are outlaw warriors. I will not associate with you on the battlefield.''

Deraa and Maid Kris said at the same time, "What?''

"Very simple. You are outlaw warriors. I will fight for you, but I will not let you fight.''

"But . . . ," stuttered Maid Kris. "But we're legitimized now. You're on our side.''

"First, you're on *my* side. Second, no. The precedent began the day I created the Knights of the Inner Sphere. Your tactics have shamed warriors throughout the stars.''

"But you'll meet Arian's MechWarriors?''

"Exactly," said Thomas. "They are the enemy. I'll do what I must to defeat them.''

"You speak like a Clansman, Captain-General," said Arian.

An uncomfortable silence fell over the group. Masters noticed Arian reflexively touch his war-damaged shoulder just as he had the day they'd discussed the Clan invasion at the TOC.

Thomas finally broke the silence. "And what do you mean by that, Precentor Martial?''

"I met them face to face, sir, defending my home-world on the other side of the Inner Sphere. We captured some of them, and I questioned them. We had no idea what we were up against when they invaded the Inner Sphere, for when Kerensky and his followers left human civilization three hundred years ago, we lost all contact with them and their descendants. We did not know what kind of society they had built for themselves.''

"Their society, from what I understand, is built on winning war at any cost."

"No. They have a detailed warrior code, it is true. And their society is built around a warrior class. But they are not indiscriminate. In fact, if a warrior breaks the code, he is discredited, just as you have discredited the GFL."

"But they destroyed Turtle Bay," said Masters. "They used atomics."

"In their opinion, the civilians of Turtle Bay deserved it. The Clans believed they were defending themselves after they had already won. A civilian is never allowed to raise a hand to a warrior in Clan society."

Thomas started to say, "Well, I am not a Clansman—"

Arian cut him off. "Not yet. Not yet. But I see potential in you." He added quickly, "I do not mean that as a fault. Not completely. There is much to admire about the Clans." Everyone at the table looked at him. "It's true that I hate them for destroying so much of what I loved. But they had their laws, their principles, their ideals, and they lived by them. Tell me, Captain-General, is it easy to live by strict laws?"

"Not at all."

"No. Because sometimes we must do what our hearts tell us we must not."

"Yes."

"I do not think the Clans wanted to destroy Turtle Bay. I think they were very confused when the civilians refused to surrender. But they had their laws, and the laws must be followed, or the price paid. Think about this, Captain-General, as you lead your Knights of the Inner Sphere.'' Arian stood. "May we have safe passage back to the Old City?''

"Of course,'' Thomas said with a wave of his hand. He stared down at the wooden table, lost in thought. Then he looked at Arian. "Precentor Martial?''

"Yes?''

"Your 'Mechs already have hold of the city. By remaining in it, you will have an excellent defensive position.''

"And if you come for us, and there is a fight, Portent will be flattened.''

"Exactly.''

Precentor Starling smiled. "Good for us, bad for you. I don't think your ideals will allow you to take such an action, eh, Marik?''

"Precentor Martial, I am told the Clans invaded cities, in complete contrast with our traditions.''

"That is true.''

"Did they want to do it, or was that also a decision foisted on them by the defenders?''

Now it was Arian's turn to look down. "I don't believe they wanted to, actually. I know the press said otherwise, that it was in their blood to attack cities, but . . .'' He paused.

"Yes,'' Thomas prodded softly.

"They had no choice. We chose to defend from the cities. We dug our 'Mechs in. They had to come get us.'' Arian's voice cracked slightly. "I don't think they would have . . . You know, the thing is, I didn't think they'd try it. That was the thing. I didn't think they'd try to dig us out.'' He raised his eyes to Thomas, and the two of them stared intently at each other.

"I may have to study these Clans more closely,'' said Thomas.

"You may,'' answered Arian.

"I can't let you, the countess, Hsiang—simply take over a planet."

"I know."

"I will come for you and your 'Mechs."

Arian touched his shoulder once more. He swayed a bit, and Masters almost thought he was drunk. "You won't have to."

"What?" Starling exclaimed.

Arian turned to him. "You heard him. He'll come for us. We won't dig in. We'll fight on the plains."

"That's absurd," said the countess. "We have him. He can't succeed."

"I won't take that chance. The people of Portent deserve better."

"I insist we hold our position," Starling said.

"Sir, I am in charge of our forces, and I will make military decisions as I see fit. At the moment it's an even battle. When the Regulan 'Mechs show up, we'll outnumber the Knights of the Inner Sphere. We can wait in the city until they arrive, because Sir Masters would rather not fight in the city." He looked at Thomas, and Thomas nodded.

"But once the Regulan 'Mechs arrive he'll be forced into action. He cannot afford to let the Regulan 'Mechs into the city, and he'll charge them as they cross the plain toward Portent. At that time we will also charge and flank the Knights. We will win, but we will not fight in the city."

Before anyone else could speak, he left.

Starling ran after him, then the countess and Hsiang got up and followed more slowly.

"Your people, I believe, have my 'Mech," Masters said to Deraa. "I'd like to have it back."

"Of course, Sir Masters." Deraa got up from the table, and Roush followed him toward the cargo bay door.

"I can't believe he said he'd clear the city," Maid Kris said, almost to herself.

"He is a good man," answered Thomas. "I don't think he's seen his fill of war. Just certain kinds of war."

She stood, her eyes set on a distant thought, and left without a word.

When everyone was out of earshot, Masters said to Thomas, "Sir, the Precentor Martial is correct. When the Word of Blake 'Mechs are combined with the Regulan 'Mechs, they will outnumber us."

"Yes. I know."

"Something is happening between Deraa and Roush," he said to Thomas. From here they could see Deraa and Roush in silhouette, standing together at the doors leading outside. They were arguing—or rather Roush was arguing, and Deraa was letting him. Then Deraa laughed, threw his hands up at Roush and walked off.

"Yes."

"Do you . . . ?"

"I have no idea. I suppose we'll find out soon enough."

"Are you all right?"

"Not really. It's not every day one has one's ideal plan compared to the blueprint of monsters."

"The Clans may not be monsters."

Thomas smiled ruefully. "But it is so good to have monsters around. They let one feel so much better about oneself."

Later, Masters traveled with Deraa in an AT out into the farmlands. The stars shone clearly, and he thought of all the people on all the worlds circling all the stars. Once no one had lived on any world other than Terra. That idea always startled him. Humanity had worked so hard to get where it was, had overcome so many difficulties. But humanity was still its own worst enemy. There seemed to be no easy way around that. After Arian had compared them to the Clans, the ideal plan he and Thomas had concocted seemed dangerous now.

Deraa informed him that Regulan technicians had repaired the 'Mech and it was, from what he understood, ready to go. This information worried Masters. Had it been sabotaged? "No, no," Deraa laughed, "They were planning to use it. It's fine."

The *Phoenix Hawk* stood ready and waiting in a clearing amid a forest of Gibson's great trees.

Masters stripped down to his cooling vest and shorts, climbed the rungs, and slipped into the cockpit. It had been more than two weeks since he'd last sat inside his 'Mech, and the command couch felt good against his flesh. Correct. His. He had his controls and he knew how to use them. But then he remembered Spinard, and knew he had to be careful. True life remained outside the 'Mech. The *Phoenix Hawk* was a tool and not his life. Could that be the difference between him and a Clan warrior? Did they have lives outside of fighting? If he were ever to meet a Clansman one day, his questions might be answered.

He fitted the neurohelmet over his head, pressed the sensors in place, and started the 'Mech's engines. He looked down to wave at Deraa, but the man was already gone. Then he spotted the AT moving deeper into the woods. Masters thought briefly about following to see if he could discover the meaning of the man's mysterious grin at Roush during the meeting, but he knew there was no way to shadow someone in a 'Mech.

He had a long walk ahead of him, and had to beat the Regulans back to Portent. He pushed the throttle forward and began to make his way through the forest.

* * *

Thomas decided it was more important to set the battlefield according to their strengths and weaknesses. The Knights moved out of the starport, despite its value, and took up positions on the plain. Three days had passed since the summit. It was now morning, and Gibson's chill night air had given way to a warm breeze. The Knights' BattleMechs were arrayed around the plain like a manmade mirror of the giant, yellow forests in the distance.

Scouts reported that the Regulan 'Mechs were closing.

At the feet of the 'Mechs walked Techs, MechWarriors, and staff, still continuing the final checks on ammunition and energy supplies.

Masters looked around for Maid Kris, whom he had not seen since the day before. Indeed, it seemed that no one from the GFL was present. They must have taken seriously Thomas' statement that they would not participate.

Soon trumpets began to blare, signaling the approach of the Regulans. All around the massive encampment the Knights ran to their 'Mechs.

An intense energy ran through the Knights, though no one put the feeling into words.

It would not be an easy battle, but as Masters climbed up his 'Mech, it occurred to him that it had been years since he'd experienced the kinship that had sprung up among the Knights in the last three days. For years the MechWarrior had become more and more a well-trained tool, put into a 'Mech to move a weapons platform around. But no more. These men and woman were the *elite*, skilled warriors chosen by Thomas Marik to work together. He treated them with a respect that had been lost in the rush for body counts and statistics.

His own dark concerns about the odds lightened as he settled into his *Phoenix Hawk*. They might be outnumbered 'Mech to 'Mech, but it was still the individual pilot that mattered. And as it stood, they had the Word of Blake and Regulus 'Mechs completely outclassed.

Masters looked over to Thomas, who was making his way slowly and methodically up his *Archer*. He wished his friend didn't feel compelled to enter the combat, but he saw little likelihood of arguing him out of it. Last night Thomas had told him simply, "This is the way it is done."

When Thomas reached the *Archer*'s cockpit, he looked over to Masters and shouted, "Beautiful morning, eh?"

Masters looked around. It *was* a beautiful morning, the sky a perfect, thin blue. In the distance the massive yellow forests. To the north, the sprawling metropolis of Portent, with the Old Walls still tall and impenetrable. He called back,"Yes, a fine morning."

"It would be a shame for you not to see it through to sunset. Don't die on me, Sir Masters."

"Nor you on me, Captain-General."

"Excellent! Now that we've promised to live through the fight, I suppose it's time to start." Thomas stepped into the cockpit and pulled the hatch shut.

Masters reached out to shut the hatch of his own 'Mech, thinking, How can I die today? But even if I do, we'll live on in memory as people tell the story over and over again of the glorious idiocy of our idealistic goals.

Masters punched up his long-range screen, which showed him two Regulan lances making their way toward Portent from the north end of the plain. He opened a frequency that could be picked up by both sides. "Colonel Roush," he said.

"Yes, Masters," Roush sounded annoyed.

"I salute you, sir."

"I wouldn't give you the satisfaction."

Flipping back to the Marik channel, Masters heard Thomas saying,"This is Archer One. God speed, my knights. Masters' Lance, Vern's Lance, Sequord's Lance, take the Regulan approach." From the south the Word of Blake 'Mechs began to pour out of Portent. "All other lances follow me toward the Word of Blake line."

With that the 'Mechs of both sides, dozens of them, charged one another.

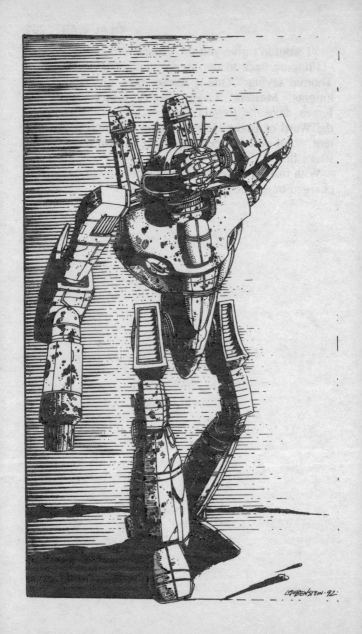

24

Plains of Portent, Gibson
Principality of Gibson, Free Worlds League
3 March 3055

Masters had Knights Gainard, Sullivan, and Osaka in his lance. As their 'Mechs ran across the plain, he said, "Let's keep the shots tight on the targets I pick. We've got to reduce their numbers as quickly as possible, and that means concentrating fire from the start."

"Phoenix Hawk One, this is Vulcan Three. I've got a Word of Blake lance coming in."

"All right, they're going to try to support. Let's go for the biggest 'Mech in the bunch."

On his monitor, Masters saw the 'Mechs charging toward them as miniature machines only about fifteen centimeters tall. But they quickly grew in size as the two fronts rushed toward each other. He gripped his joystick and brought the cross hairs over the distant targets. The lock numbers flashed on and off as he tried to align the cross hairs. Chatter began filling the headset, low voices from other lances. "All right, Masters' Lance, I spy a Word of Blake *Ostroc* that I want gone. It's coded Blue Five on the screen."

"Check."

"Check."

"All, right. Got it."

Masters punched up a computer outline of the Mech's configuration on his display, then said, "It's got almost everything loaded in the torso. Let's keep slamming that until it collapses."

He dropped the cross hairs toward the *Ostroc*, and found the shot blocked momentarily by a Regulan *Firestarter*. The Blake and Regulan 'Mechs seemed to be maneuvering into each other's way. Even though they had the numbers, it didn't look as if they were going to work well together. "They're bunching up. Fine. We'll take the shots. If you hit anything in front of the target, that'll do for now."

His finger hovered around the blue thumb button, which was now configured for his large laser. He held the joystick as steadily as possible, the lock numbers slipping in and out.

And then the cross hairs glowed bright yellow. As Masters squeezed down on the trigger, a bright red flash of energy shot out of the massive pistol in his *Phoenix Hawk*'s right hand. The laser bolt slammed into the *Ostroc*'s chest. It was the first shot of the battle, but it sparked a quick succession of shots from both sides. Large lasers fired orange and red beams between the two forces, cutting so thick through the air that it was soon impossible to determine which beams were going which way.

Then long-range missiles, grouped in packs of five, ten, and fifteen, shot across the distance between the 'Mechs, from Marik to Word of Blake and Regulus, and from Blake and Regulus back. Their smoky trails arced through the air like dark rainbows.

Some missiles crashed into the ground, ripping up huge craters of dirt. Other missiles and lasers slammed into 'Mechs, ripping armor from legs, arms, heads, and torsos.

Masters felt the *Phoenix Hawk*'s heat rise markedly after his large laser shot. Still, even combined with full acceleration, his heat sinks could dissipate all the excess heat as long as he didn't fire. Rather than risk burning his 'Mech out, he decided to wait the few moments it would take for the heat to drop down to safe levels.

Meanwhile, Gainard, Sullivan, and Osaka all took their shots at the *Ostroc*. The shots all hit true, four long-range missiles and two autocannon shells. The *Ostroc*'s front torso turned charcoal black as the blasts ripped off the first layer of armor and dug deep into the 'Mech's core.

A series of blasts rocked Masters' 'Mech and threw him back and forth, his body straining against the straps. Seeing smoke billow out from the *Phoenix Hawk*'s right shoulder, he was about to check his damage display when he saw another five-pack of long-range missiles coming toward him. Their arcs brought them in on dead strikes to the same arm.

Masters pressed the green thumb trigger and his anti-missile system kicked in, sending a spray of small shells out around his 'Mech. The shells smacked into the missiles, sending them off course or detonating them in the air.

He punched another button and the heat gauge popped up on the screen. The situation wasn't great, 20 percent higher than was safe, but he wanted that *Ostroc*. Bringing up the cross hairs, he got a lock almost immediately; very little room remained between the two clashing sides. He squeezed the blue button again, and once more the large laser fired into the *Ostroc*'s chest. The other MechWarriors in his lance immediately followed up his shot with autocannon and laser fire. A fiery red explosion ripped through the *Ostroc*'s chest.

"He's up but useless," shouted Gainard.

"All right. Let's move along to another target!"

A laser blast flashed just outside Masters' cockpit, and warning lights for his right arm blinked on and off. Punching up his status display, he saw that the anti-missile system had been rendered inoperable.

"Down the missile defense," he noted for the group.

Osaka came on. "I've almost—" There came the sound of static, and then he continued, "I've lost my right missile launcher."

"Noted. Let's keep it tight."

The two sides loomed up at each other, now passing within meters. Seeing a chance to get a good hook in at a Word of Blake *Wasp*, Masters sent the *Phoenix Hawk*'s left hand smashing into the small 'Mech's cockpit. As the *Wasp* wobbled slightly, Masters stopped short and spun his 'Mech around. At such exceedingly close range he found an easy shot on the *Wasp*'s back and pulled his red finger trigger. Red bolts from his medium pulse laser and two short-range missiles rushed out of his 'Mech's arms and slammed into the *Wasp*'s back, shredding its back torso armor all the way to the interior. Then he rushed forward to get behind the *Wasp* and finish it off.

Shocks from missile and cannon blasts rocked his 'Mech as he moved, but none of the shots seemed to go deep. The *Wasp*, aware that Masters was coming for him, turned around quickly and brought up its arms to fire.

Past the *Wasp*, Masters saw Gainard battling a *Centurion*.

"Gainard?"

"Masters, great to hear from you."

"There's a *Wasp* at your three, butt-naked on the back."

"Check."

The *Wasp* raised its medium laser and fired nearly

point-blank into the *Phoenix Hawk*'s chest. The beam cut armor, but didn't go internal. On the other side Gainard's *Vulcan* whirled and fired its large pulse laser into the *Wasp*'s back. The *Wasp*'s motions came to a complete stop, it teetered for a moment, then fell over.

"Nicely done," Masters said.

"Wouldn't have happened without your help, sir."

He looked down at the screen and saw Osaka and Sullivan being attacked by two *Wolverines*. "Sullivan? Osaka? Are you clear?"

"Get here as soon as you can, sir," Sullivan said.

The *Centurion* fired into Gainard's *Vulcan*, and sent sparks running up and down the *Vulcan*'s left arm. Masters targeted the *Centurion*, and pushed the blue thumb button. The large laser beam glanced off the *Centurion*'s torso, doing little damage, but grabbing its attention. It immediately turned toward Masters' *Phoenix Hawk*.

"Damn," he said, then slapped the configuration switch to make the blue button trigger the large laser and both pulse lasers. Ignoring the heat buildup he thumbed the trigger again. The pulse beams hit, but the large laser went wide.

The *Centurion* raised the giant that was its right arm—no more and no less than an LB 10-X autocannon—and fired at Masters. The shell slammed into the *Phoenix Hawk*'s right arm and tore off the lower half, sending the large laser to the ground. He checked the status screen. One medium pulse laser had gone off line.

Gainard, meanwhile, took a clean shot at the *Centurion*'s torso with his large and medium pulse lasers. The shots, combined with the damage Masters had done, pierced the right torso and ripped into the ammo housing for the *Centurion*'s autocannon and long-range missiles. The *Centurion*'s center exploded with a fiery bloom, sending the 'Mech wheeling around before it froze in mid-motion, poised on the brink of a terrible fall.

"Leave it, sir?"

"Of course. It isn't doing anyone any harm. Let's deal with the *Wolverine*s on Osaka and Sullivan."

But as Masters turned his 'Mech, something in the distance caught his eye. At the edge of the field he saw a group of six ATs drive up, each mounted with what looked like missile launchers. They kept driving until they found shelter from sight behind bushes and heavy cloth camouflage, apparently planted sometime earlier.

So that's what Deraa and the GFL had been up to for the last three days!

He remembered the devices on these ATs as those he'd seen in the GFL weapons depot. But what were they doing here? What effect could they possibly have on a battle waged by BattleMechs?

And then, in a flash, he remembered the label half-hidden by the cloth and the single word "Davey" that he'd been able to make out.

He jabbed his communication button and set up an open channel to all 'Mechs, both friend and foe. "Atomics on the battlefield!" he said, unable to refrain from shouting. "Tactical nukes on the field!"

Thomas' voice came over the speakers. "Paul, are you sure?" But Masters was already bringing his 'Mech about toward the ATs. Although he had just seen them a moment ago, their camouflage kept them hidden amid the smoke and flames of the battlefield.

"At the eastern edge. GFL ATs. Davey Crocketts! They've got old tac nukes on those ATs."

Deraa's voice now broke into the communications. "Colonel Roush gave them to us for use in our war, and now we gladly give them back to him. We suggest the Marik MechWarriors clear the area immediately."

"Knights of the Inner Sphere, stay true to this order!'' said Thomas Marik, ''We will not desert MechWarriors to those who would use atomics.''

A barrage of chatter filled the background of Masters' headset as everyone around him—Knights of the Inner Sphere, Blake troops, and Regulan warriors—tried to determine what was happening.

Masters spotted one of the ATs now aiming the Davey Crockett toward the battlefield. He jerked his joystick left, and as the cross hairs dropped onto the AT, he fired his remaining pulse laser, desperate to shake the gunners up enough to prevent them from launching the tac nuke. The bolts ripped up a long stretch of grass alongside the AT, sending dirt into the air and spraying over the gunners. Some of the gunners dove for cover, but others kept the missile turning toward the field.

''I've got them, Sir Masters,'' Gainard said, and he fired his large laser. It slammed into the AT and the vehicle exploded hot white. Their clothes on fire, the surviving guerrillas rushed away to roll on the ground.

Masters twisted his 'Mech's torso, looking for the other five ATs. He spotted another one behind a large cluster of bushes. Still disregarding heat concerns, he fired his laser again, this time hitting the AT directly. It too exploded.

''Flash! Flash!'' screamed Deraa, and Masters saw a puff of white smoke near some trees and then a missile arc high into the air. He turned and saw it heading for a lance of Regulan heavy 'Mechs that had been patiently working its way around the field to flank Marik's MechWarriors. His hand instinctively grabbed for the joystick, and then he realized it was too late. He slammed the controls to turn away from the flash, closed his eyes, covered his face with his arms, and doubled over, straining against his seat's straps. Over and over again he screamed into his microphone, "Stay away from the blast. Don't look! Turn away!"

A moment later the air around Masters glowed bright white, and he heard a horrible high-pitched whistle. A deep roar followed. The noise and light overwhelmed his senses so fiercely that in that instant it seemed he had always lived doubled over, tight against the world, a terrible rumble passing around him forever.

Then suddenly a silence fell. Unable to resist, he turned his 'Mech back and saw a crater of glass three hundred meters wide. Three of the 'Mechs had simply vanished. Only half of one of the lance's 'Mechs remained; it had crashed into a red and silver Knight of the Inner Sphere 'Mech some five hundred meters away from ground zero, and the two 'Mechs lay motionless now, sprawled on the ground.

Over his speaker he heard the screams of blinded MechWarriors who hadn't turned away in time or hadn't known what to do with tacs on the battlefield. It had been so long since anyone had used them.

A terrible scream tore at Masters' throat. He rushed toward the area where the Davey Crockett had launched, his gaze darting left and right. Before he spotted the AT, another white plume drifted out of the trees. This time he brought up his cross hairs over the AT and jabbed both thumb triggers, letting loose both the pulse laser and the short-range missiles. The pulse laser fell far short, but the missiles struck home and tore the AT to shreds.

He slammed his head down into his knees and once more saw bright light through his closed eyelids. His 'Mech trembled against the mighty energy unleashed by the bomb. Before the rumbling ended, he lifted his head to find the other ATs.

There—another one in a small group of trees.

He ran toward the it, dropping his cross hairs over it as he closed ground. His hands shook so much from fury and panic and heat that the lock faded in and out. He growled, and fired the pulse laser. Missed. Again. Missed.

He felt warm and feverish as sweat poured down his body. He fired his missiles, the shots exploding ten meters to the right of the AT.

The cockpit got hotter.

He brought the cross hairs right on top of the AT. They glowed bright yellow. A lock . . . and then suddenly his *Phoenix Hawk* froze up.

He hardly needed to glance at his status board to know that the 'Mech had overheated. Sweet and simple. Roaring his anger, he punched the roof of his cockpit.

Looking back at the AT, Masters was close enough now to see Deraa manning the Davey Crockett. The nuclear missile pointed right at him.

Deraa smiled at him.

Masters checked the display again. He could not do anything that would create any heat.

That left only the MGs. Machine guns didn't use heat.

He slapped the weapon configuration toggles, and grabbed the joystick.

Deraa picked up a radio microphone. "I'm sorry you didn't appreciate our help, Sir Masters."

He pulled up the cross hairs.

Deraa leaned down to fire.

Masters squeezed the trigger, and machine gun fire ripped Deraa's body into scarlet scraps, his crew along with him.

The missile was still in place.

"You said there were six, Masters," Osaka said. "That's it. We got them all."

Masters sat for a moment in the command couch, trembling. Then he brought up the open channel and started shouting, "Roush? You gave them tac nukes!

You gave them tac nukes!'' His voice was high-pitched, as frightening as a madman's.

Thomas cut the tirade short. "Sir Masters."

Masters fell silent, and Thomas said coolly, "Colonel Roush, Precentor Martial Arian, I suggest we truce now, to tend to the wounded and dying."

"I . . . Yes, we should do that," said Arian, dazed, drunk with disbelief.

"No," hissed Roush. "Arian, no. We've just lost too many of our 'Mechs. If we take the time to regroup, they *will* win. We've got to get into the city now, take up defense. . . ."

"What?" asked Arian.

"Take up defense in the city. It's the only way to secure a victory."

"You would have us go into a city? After this?"

"There is no choice."

Arian sounded distracted, as if someone else were speaking to him on another channel. Masters heard him say in a tired, faraway voice, "No, Precentor Blane, we cannot do that. No, I know what Colonel Roush just said. . . ." Then his voice became alert and strong, "I don't care, sir. We will not take up a defensive position within the city. We will *not* 'do what we must to win.' We will simply do what we must."

Roush clicked off the channel, and a moment later all the Regulan 'Mechs began to move toward Portent. Arian's voice came back on the open channel. "Colonel Roush, if you attempt to take the city, I will direct my men to work with the Knights of the Inner Sphere to stop you."

The Regulan 'Mechs stopped.

"Do you surrender to me, then, Precentor Martial Arian?"

A long pause followed, and then the man said, "I do. You are the most honorable warrior I have ever met. I swear myself and all the Word of Blake forces to you, Captain-General Thomas Marik.''

''And you, Colonel Roush. Do you surrender to me?''

''If I do not, my men will be slaughtered.''

''True. I take it then that you surrender.''

''Yes.''

''Do you swear loyalty to me?''

''You must be joking.''

''I take that as a no. You and your forces are free to go, though your 'Mechs will remain. The battle is done. But know that someday, perhaps in the not too distant future, the same question will be posed to you. The answer will have more serious implications on that occasion. The city is ours. The war is done.''

''But . . .''

''There are no buts. You swore to defend Countess Dystar and Principal Hsiang. You have failed at this. The attempted coup is finished. They are deposed. The world is still mine. Sir Paul Masters will become Count of Gibson. It is done.''

The ceremony drew a great crowd, for the time of oppression on Gibson had come to an end. Masters would replace the Countess, and for this the people were grateful. Hsiang was removed from office, and Masters declared that his first act would be to arrange legal, secure elections for a new Principal. For this the people were even more grateful. He assured them that Word of Blake would not acquire undue influence in the government of Gibson, but that the group would remain on the planet. Some grumbled about this, but that is the way of it. It would take time. But the war was over, for Captain-General Thomas Marik and Masters had stood by the people against their oppressors, and this impressed everyone most of all.

At the door to the great hall of Castle Masters, formerly Castle Dystar, Sir Paul Masters stood at attention while Kris and some servants busily fussed about him, arranging his scarlet robe so it hung off his shoulders just so. "You don't have to do this, you know," he said to Kris.

"What—and leave the staff on their own on a day like this? No, this will be my last duty, and then I leave the castle." She looked into his eyes, and he saw the same sadness that had been there since the day of the battle. Most of the GFL had not known about the atomics, and a deep shame lived in their hearts.

Precentor Blane came over and looked him up and down. "You still look too much like a soldier. If you want to be a statesmen, you should seem somewhat less sure of yourself, ready to equivocate at a moment's notice."

"Soon the soldiers will be the statesmen and stateswomen."

Blane nodded. "I suppose you're right. Word of the Regulans handing out atomics is putting more and more of the Free Worlds League into Thomas' camp. Even though Roush did it without the authorization of his superiors. With the realization of how far civilians can go if properly armed, the Knights of the Inner Sphere are growing every day."

"There's still a lot of resistance to the idea."

"Oh, Thomas hasn't unified the Free Worlds League under his rule yet. But I can see the day. . . ."

"It will take work."

"No, doubt. The stars may be safer, but only at the expense of freedom, and most people won't give that up easily. The Free Worlds League has always been torn between rule by parliamentary democracy or by a feudal warrior class. Now one side or the other is clearly going to win."

"I think I know how it will work out," said Maid Kris, and brushed a speck of dust off the robe. Although she said the words with pride, he caught something in her eyes, a small, secret threat. He knew that if he failed to fulfill his responsibilities, the people of Gibson would rise up again, and Kris would once more be a leader among their ranks. Good. He could think of no better prod than having Kris' fire at his back. Trumpets sounded and she stepped back. "Sir Masters, your liege awaits you."

The great doors opened, and Sir Paul Masters turned to look into the hall. A thousand people stood on either side of a long red carpet that led up to Captain-General Thomas Marik. All heads turned to look at Masters, with many nobles and warriors from distant stars among the guests. But many more, especially those near the front, were peasants from the farms of Gibson and professionals from Portent. Masters had made a point of sending the invitation far and wide on his own world, the world of Gibson. A feudal system did not cut the people out of society, it gave them a strong place within it. They no longer had the right to bear arms, true, but then they need not fear slaughter from the arms anymore, either. He looked at the people, and saw their eyes alive with the excitement of pageantry and a passion for nobility.

He stepped onto the carpet and felt a kind of vertigo. Red stretched out before him, for a moment seemingly endless, was a path that led both backward to his arrival on Gibson and forward into the future he was forging with Thomas.

Standing along the aisle he saw the farmer who had hidden him and the man's daughter and wife. The farmer held the girl-child in his arms, and she waved her small hand as Masters passed. Further down he saw Chick and a few of the other men who had escaped. They were civilians now, for Thomas had outlawed all mercenaries on the worlds he ruled. He believed they promoted the attitude of war through attrition and of lives as fodder. Chick smiled and bowed his head as Masters passed.

As each step carried him past people he had met on Gibson, Masters saw Thomas, tall and regal, waiting on ahead. His old friend smiled at him, and Masters felt drawn forward. So much hope in the man.

As his thoughts carried him on, he spotted Precentor Martial Arian. Their eyes met, and Arian bowed his head slightly. In that moment Arian once more lightly touched his ruined shoulder, the wound acquired while fighting the Clans on the other side of the Inner Sphere. A chill passed through Masters. He looked back at Thomas, so full of ideals but still piloting by his heart. Would that be enough? Where would this dream lead?

It would be difficult. There would be problems. But if it worked, the stars would finally know peace. . . .

At last Masters reached the steps where Thomas stood waiting. His friend and liege spread his arms wide, and raised his face to the crowd. But before addressing all present, he said softly, without looking down, "Do you think it will work?"

"Yes, my liege," Sir Paul Masters whispered, closing his heart against doubt. "Yes, I think it will." And in that instant his spirit buoyed, rising to float amid all the stars of space and all the souls that had gone before him.

CRUSADER

LOCUST

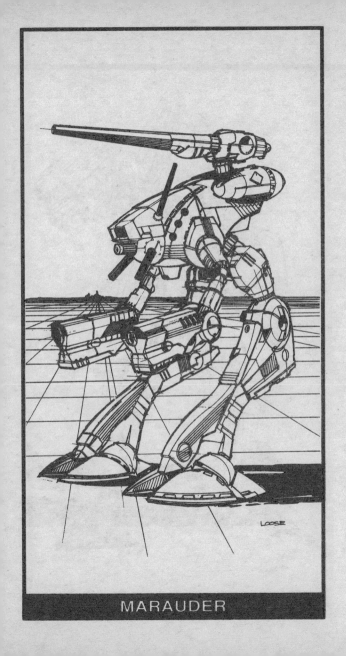

MARAUDER

PHOENIX HAWK

RIFLEMAN

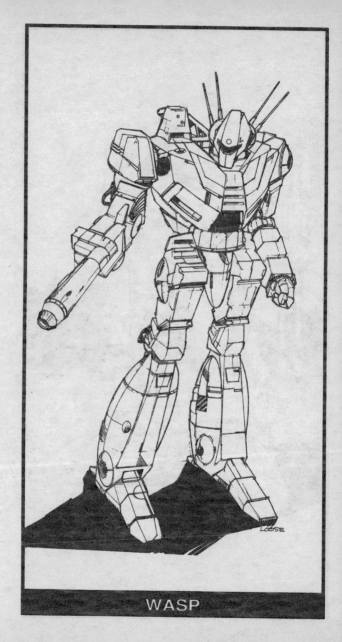

WASP

LOOSE

WOLVERINE